ECHOES OF STEEL

ROBOTS AND RUINS

BOOK 2

CAMERON CORAL

DYSTOPIC BLISS PRESS

Edited by Lori Diederich

Cover by Sienna Arts

10 9 8 7 6 5 4 3 2 1

1st edition, April 2025

Stay updated on Cameron's books by signing up for the
Cameron Coral Reading List:
CameronCoral.com/sign-up

You'll be added to my reading list, and I'll send you a digital copy of *CROSSING THE VOID: A Space Opera Science-Fiction Short Story* to say thank you.

CONTENTS

To you, the reader—

For taking these pages into your hands and giving life to the words within them.

For the quiet hours you set aside and the willingness to walk alongside characters you've never met.

This book exists because you do.

Thank you for being the most important part of this story.

ONE
WARNING

WALLY

The hair on Wally's arms stood on end before she even reached the window. Something had called her from sleep. She pressed her forehead to the frozen glass of her bedroom window, squinting at the dark shape on the far ridge. A wolf. Its silhouette cut sharp against the brightening sky as the bitter Minnesota wind ruffled its thick gray fur.

Wrong-wrong-danger-flee.

Wally jerked back from the window, her heart beating a frantic pace like it did when she woke from her nightmares, which were more frequent lately. A strange sensation had passed through her upon seeing the distant wolf. Not words exactly, more like the static prickle before a storm. The sudden intrusion into her mind felt like a violation, leaving her dizzy and off-balance. She pressed her palm flat against the glass, rubbing away the condensation. The wolf remained on the hill. Its head turned toward her. Something about its stare seemed to pierce right through her, as if the animal was trying to tell her something important.

Listen-warn-coming.

The wolf's urgency flooded her mind with snapshots: empty nests scattered with broken eggs, deer herds splintering away from their winter grounds, fox dens abandoned.

"What's happening?" Wally whispered.

She didn't understand the sensations flooding her mind while her body echoed with feelings that weren't hers. The rugged forest floor. The bitter chill biting through dense fur. There was a den—dark, warm, comforting. *Home.* For a disorienting moment, she felt a longing for that wild sanctuary so powerful it made her eyes sting with unexpected tears.

The wolf ran into the trees that lined the ridge, and the jarring sensations stopped hijacking Wally. A strange emptiness washed over her, as if she'd lost something valuable before fully understanding what it was. She sat upright on her bed for another hour, unable to catch sleep, watching the hill for the wolf's return. A pale glow seeped from the east until a cloud-laden, almost white sky took hold of the morning. Below her window, Deer Valley's market square stirred to life, the cobblestones forming intricate patterns beneath the feet of early risers. Solar panels caught the winter sun at precise angles along the settlement's fifteen-foot walls made of salvaged metal and concrete. Vendors opened their stalls while robots changed shifts, and the normal rhythm of the day began beneath strings of solar-powered lights that crisscrossed the square.

In her second-floor room inside Block's Hotel, thirty minutes remained before Wally needed to leave for school. Mr. Folk's history exam loomed. She didn't care about the Industrial Revolution. Why bother with all that pointless history when the world had been torn apart by the AI Uprising? Block said it was good for her to learn about the past. He was reading her textbooks too, learning alongside her, and could read an entire 400-page book in less than an hour. She longed for that kind of efficiency so she could be out doing what she enjoyed most—exploring.

She rubbed her tired eyes. Maybe the wolf had been a dream. Yet, she couldn't deny what had happened.

A mechanical screech shattered the quiet. She rushed to her window. Down in the market square, a Peacekeeper moved in a circle. The security robot's head jerked at an unnatural angle, and its usual measured patrol devolved into stumbling steps as sparks flew from its neck joints.

"Clear the square!" Stella Grace's voice cut through the frigid air. The produce vendor abandoned her cart as the Peacekeeper careened into it, sending crates of potatoes scattering across the pavement.

Even from a story above, Wally could hear the robot's vocal output module spitting staccato words between static. "Dan—ger. Proto—col seven—three—" Its arms swung wildly, scraping against the outside wall of the bakery. Metal shrieked against stone.

Wally watched the robot stagger. The Peacekeeper's

dark gray armor showed its designation number etched in white against its shoulder plate. Peacekeeper Six had guarded Deer Valley for as long as she could remember. The robot knew every corner, every face, every schedule. Now its movements were puppet-like, jerky. Wrong. The Peacekeepers were once called "SoldierBots." Mach X, a malicious super-computer intelligence, had hacked into the U.S. military's SoldierBots and turned them into killing machines. The same thing had happened all over the world, causing the Uprising. Pockets of survivors had remained, including peaceful robots like Block, Vacu-ubot, Oxford, Maxwell, and others who eventually defeated Mach X. But all of that was ancient history as far as Wally was concerned. She trusted the Peacekeepers wholeheartedly.

So, what was going wrong with Six?

She yanked on her jeans, a sweatshirt, and the black combat boots her friend Nova had gifted her on her fifteenth birthday. Her fingers fumbled with the laces, clumsy with adrenaline and worry. She ran through the second-floor hallway. The grand staircase curved down to the lobby where a crystal chandelier, restored to working order, reflected rainbow prisms across the walls.

Block paused at the front door, about to head into the market melee when she stumbled on the last step. She caught herself before taking a tumble.

"Tie your shoes, Wally," Block said, turning his head to look at her. "And stay inside!"

"Wait, Dad." She caught his arm, fingers sliding against the smooth chrome finish. At fifteen, she'd undergone a growth spurt and was eye-level with her five-foot-six CleanerBot father. His pearlescent exterior beamed with its usual polish. Built as a hospitality model for a luxury hotel, Block's frame was light, and he made little sound when walking, unlike the bulkier Factory-Bots, Peacekeepers, and other robot models. "What's happening out there?"

"I don't know, but it's not safe," he said. A vacuum tube retracted and slid seamlessly into his forearm. "Promise you'll stay inside?"

Wally nodded. Block opened the heavy hotel door and started out when Wally grabbed his hand. "Be careful."

"I will."

She closed the door behind him when Vacuubot flew in from the kitchen. The weaponized drone was a jacked-up robot vacuum—the kind that roamed a house sucking up dust in the pre-Uprising days. Now they were outfitted with an arc-shaped bulletproof armor, two gun cannons on either side, and ports where five mini drones lived.

"Wally, are you safe?" Vacuubot asked.

"I'm good. Block just went out." Wally opened the door wide for her friend to pass through.

"Copy that." Vacuubot's mini drones whizzed out of their ports. "Engaging guardian protocols."

Wally closed the door, then went to the wide bench inside the large bay window overlooking Main Street, where she watched Block and Vacuubot approach Six. Vacuubot's drones circled overhead, scanning the situation. A mesh net launched from Vacuubot's undercarriage, wrapping around Six's head and torso as if the net had a mind of its own. Six lurched forward, grappling against the mesh, then fell to the ground where it thrashed and rolled.

The five mini drones circled and formed a containment pentagon around Six. Each drone emitted pulses of blue energy that subdued the malfunctioning robot. Six's movements grew sluggish, its visor flickering between green and its normal red.

Block leaned down and spoke to the fallen Peacekeeper, though Wally couldn't hear his words from inside.

Stella Grace and the other vendors emerged from their hiding spots, righting their carts. A trail of bruised potatoes led to the gutter. An unattended cart—Fathom's Repairs—was battered beyond repair. Clock pieces, coils, batteries, and all sorts of mechanical parts had scattered across the road. Fathom, an engineering robot, would be angry when she saw her shop destroyed.

The bakery's stone wall bore a deep gouge where Six had struck it, iron shavings glinting on the ground below. People frowned and talked with each other in low voices as Block and Vacuubot attended to Six.

Movement drew Wally's attention upward. A crow was perched on the bakery's rain gutter, and its feathers ruffled in the icy wind. When their eyes met, a jolt ran through her mind—sharper than the wolf's presence, cutting like glass.

Shiny-danger-metal-sick.

The bird's thoughts came in fragments. She saw through its eyes—the convulsing robot, the anxious townspeople. She tasted ozone on her tongue, felt the crow's growing unease as static charged the air.

Wrong-noise-coming-flee.

The crow spread its wings and launched into flight. Like a wave of cascading dominoes, other birds followed. Pigeons burst from eaves. Sparrows lifted from their nests.

Block's head turned up at the exodus. The people nearby stopped their nervous chatter and gazed up at the torrent of birds. Something had spooked the creatures.

Wally's legs were pumping with adrenaline. She wanted to run out and tell her dad what she'd felt. The crow's warning pulsed in her mind. But she'd promised to stay inside. She pressed her forehead to the glass, watching her father as more birds fled the square.

Nearby, she glimpsed a figure in the apartment above the bakery, pressed against the glass. Chloe Webb. They were the same age. As babies, they'd been rescued from a New York City orphanage by Block and Emery. Eleven of them were now fifteen-year-olds, plus another six babies who were now thirteen.

Wally and Chloe weren't exactly friends, but they weren't enemies either. Chloe and others had once bullied Wally. That had stopped once Wally ran away and returned to Deer Valley with life-saving antivirals to stop a mutated measles outbreak.

Something looked off about Chloe, even from the distance that separated them. Her skin had taken on a pale greenish tint. Her blond hair hung limp around her face, and she splayed her hands against the window like she was trying to steady herself.

Their eyes met. Chloe's widened in recognition—or was it surprise? She stumbled back from her window. Then she crumpled, disappearing from view.

G9, the head of the Peacekeepers, had arrived and hauled Six to the sidewalk outside the hotel's front door.

"Vacuubot," Block called out, his voice carrying through the glass. "We'll take him to Maxwell so he can run a full spectrum scan."

"I can't explain the malfunction," G9 said. "Nothing like this has happened before."

Wally dug her fingernails into her palms, mentally ticking off the morning's oddities: the wolf's warning, Six's malfunction, then seeing the world from the crow's perspective. Strange happenings were stacking up like a giant Jenga tower. She needed to tell Block about the animals, about what she'd seen. But would he believe her? How could she explain something she barely understood herself?

A new sensation crept up her spine—different from the wolf's presence or the crow's sharp clarity. This felt . . . wrong. Like radio static turned up too loud, like the buzz of too-bright fluorescent lights. Her teeth ached with it.

On the sidewalk, Six's visor flickered again before going dark. Block looked at Wally.

She raised her palm to the window and said, "Are you okay?"

But she couldn't hear his answer. Behind her, the chandelier's crystals chimed, vibrating with an unseen frequency. The sound grew, resonating through her bones, through the whole building. Through all of Deer Valley.

The vibration intensified until Wally's teeth chattered. She pressed her hands against her ears, but it didn't help. Through the window, she watched Block turn toward G9, his movements suddenly jerky, like Six's had been. Her father's arms twitched once, twice, and his normally smooth stride hitched as he took a step backward.

"Dad!" The word tore from her throat. She didn't care about her promise anymore—something was wrong with Block. As she reached for the door handle, a sparrow crashed into the window. The tiny body fell to the ground. She stepped outside and looked down at the bird.

Wrong-Metal-Danger-Flee.

The sparrow's wings twitched. Its eyes, dark as wet pebbles, met hers. Then the small body went still, and the connection snapped like a thread cut by scissors.

The vibration that had filled the air ceased, leaving a sharp silence. Wally's hands trembled as she stared at the lifeless bird.

"Wally." Block's voice was soft as he stood beside her, his hydraulic joints whirring a faint beat. He'd recovered from his earlier malfunction, moving with his usual fluid grace. "You should stay inside."

"I know, but . . . Something's happening, Dad. Something bad. I can feel it."

Block took her hand in his. His titanium fingers warmed to human temperature—a comfort protocol he'd used ever since the day he'd rescued her.

"We'll find out what happened to Peacekeeper Six. There's nothing to worry about," he said.

Wally nodded, but she couldn't shake the residual ache in her belly. She carried the bird's body to a thicket of trees that stood near the compound's wall. The sparrow's death was her fault; the creature had been trying to warn her. "I'm sorry, little bird," she whispered as she placed it against the base of a tree.

TWO
INVESTIGATION

BLOCK

Arcs of electricity flittered between the sensor nodes of Maxwell's scanner as he moved it over Peacekeeper Six's inert form. Block registered the condition of Maxwell's workshop—dust coated the overhead pipes. His cleaning protocols itched like what humans might call a phantom limb. The urge to vacuum every surface nearly overwhelmed his central processor. Block internally assigned the mess a 7.8 on his personal disorder scale—not quite catastrophic but certainly bordering on CleanerBot mayhem. He logged a priority task to return with his full cleaning kit. The workshop's ventilation system needed recalibrating too; the air circulation was running at 62 percent efficiency based on his sensors' readings. Luckily, it was just him, Maxwell, Vacuubot, and G9 in the workshop; the air posed no immediate threat to humans.

"Well, the wiring in Six's neck is a contorted mess," Maxwell said. The engineering robot's telescoping arms extended, allowing him to work on multiple areas simultaneously. Maxwell was a FactoryBot with four arms, a reinforced torso housing specialized tools, and a head that split into three sections to reveal additional sensors.

As his friend worked, Block marveled at Maxwell's ability to handle complex tasks simultaneously. His own programming felt suddenly limited by comparison. He was designed to polish and vacuum rather than repair and build. But Block had long ago moved beyond his original capacity. He could write programs—small packets that manipulated his code in ways his original manufacturers never intended. Where most CleanerBots could only execute pre-programmed routines, Block had learned to assemble his own strings of binary instructions, creating custom protocols that blurred the line between his basic hospitality programming and true creativity. It was a skill born of necessity during those early years protecting Wally. Block had survived challenges that no hotel-based cleaning robot was ever meant to face.

Still, Block's cleaning routines ran strong. He bet Maxwell couldn't fold bottom sheets with precise hospital corners.

Diagnostic screens glowed blue. Atop the steel table where Six lay immobile, neural dampeners pulsed around its seven-foot frame. Maxwell adjusted the scanning array suspended from the ceiling—a spindly apparatus that resembled a mechanical spider, its sensors clicking as they calibrated.

"We need answers before the town council meeting tonight," Block said. Anxiety subroutines that he'd developed over years of parenting pulsed through his system. The members would demand a cause for the malfunction. He was on the Deer Valley council, having been elected following the discovery of underground vaults that were built before the Uprising. Wally had been the one to find the first vault and its survivor—Sarah. Block was valuable for being the one to keep in radio communication with Sarah as she and a small group searched for more vaults, survivors, and the precious stockpiles inside the hidden bunkers.

The workshop walls were lined with floor-to-ceiling shelving units filled with spare parts: optical sensors in varying sizes, joint assemblies, and power cores glowing faintly in their protective cases. A partially dismantled CargoBot occupied one corner, its chest cavity splayed open to reveal its inner workings. Maxwell had outfitted the place with a rolling garage door to allow large mechanical pieces to be hauled inside. Through the window, Block could see the vertical gardens climbing nearby walls, their greenery reduced to scraggly branches in the harsh winter. In the warm months, the foliage softened the industrial edges of the settlement while maximizing limited space.

"We'll figure out what caused Six to go off the rails." Maxwell pointed to a computer screen. "I'm replaying its core archive from today."

Block moved closer to the diagnostic screen. Data scrolled past: power fluctuations, memory core integrity, circuit pathway stability. All looked normal until a blip appeared.

"There." Maxwell froze the display. "That signal pattern at 0737 hours. Most unusual."

"Exactly the time Six went berserk," Vacuubot said.

"And just before the vibration passed through town," G9 said. "It was sudden. I had two dozen Peacekeepers pinging me with distress signals."

"The humans felt it too," Block said, recalling Wally's pained reaction and her look of confusion.

"Could be interference from tectonic activity," Vacuubot said, hovering near G9. "The geological sensors have been picking up minor tremors."

Block's internal processors analyzed the inputs. The vibration from earlier seemed different from standard geological disturbances. More directed. He'd experienced a moment of disconnect, as though his circuit pathways had briefly stopped communicating with each other.

"Running a deep scan now," Maxwell said. Three of his arms reached for different tools while another adjusted Six's position. "The corruption seems to be concentrated in the—"

Six's visor flared green. Its body arched off the table, hydraulics whining. The dampener net sparked and failed.

G9 moved to restrain him, but Six's arm shot out, catching G9 in the chest and sending him crashing into a shelf of spare parts. Six's movements were erratic; he rolled sideways off the table, thrashing.

"Containment protocols!" With their command,

Vacuubot's mini drones formed a confinement grid around Six. Each drone assembled with coordinated movements—precise, adaptive, like a flock of mechanical birds.

Block's cleaning and helping protocols activated simultaneously. A cleaning spray nozzle popped out of his wrist without conscious command, and Block quickly tucked it back in. Just what they needed—someone to mop while a seven-foot military-grade robot had a meltdown. His programming was ridiculous sometimes. He ran to G9 and leaned down. "Are you okay?"

"Yes," G9 said, nearly pulling Block over when he accepted a hand up.

"I always forget how heavy you Peacekeepers are," Block said, his frame tilting precariously before regaining balance. "It's like trying to lift a refrigerator that's bolted to a tank."

The mini drones were doing their job. They kept Six on the ground.

Despite Maxwell's protests, Block couldn't help but pick up the boxes and plastic containers that had scattered. It was either that or have his circuits poke at him with the overwhelming need to restore order. G9 helped.

"What just happened?" Vacuubot said.

Maxwell returned to the data display; Six was still hooked into the scanner. "The blip, or whatever it is. A signal, perhaps. It came back." His sensor arrays rotated frantically. "It's intense, and I can't detect—"

The diagnostic equipment exploded in a shower of sparks. Darkness swallowed the workshop for three seconds before emergency lights came on. In the dim red glow, Six went rigid. A strange green light pulsed beneath his armor plating.

"What's happening?" G9 asked.

Block's audio sensors detected a high-pitched tone at the edge of his perceptual range. It lasted 3.2 seconds before dissipating.

"I'm stumped," Maxwell said. "The corruption pattern matches no known virus or malicious code. This is something new." He turned to Block. "Did you feel it? That signal?"

"Yes."

"Me too," G9 said. "I'm getting pings from other Peacekeepers. Same as before—they're hearing a high-pitched signal, then experiencing electrical malfunctions. Minor reports. Nothing like what happened to Six.

"You too, Vacuubot?" Block asked.

"Ditto."

Block's processors cycled through the implications. "If this affected Peacekeeper Six and caused him to go haywire, and we're hearing it, too . . . Could it eventually cause malfunctions in other robots? In us?"

"Let's assume that's the case until we can rule it out," Maxwell said.

The high-pitched tone returned, stronger this time. Block's visual feed fractured for 1.2 seconds before stabilizing. He looked at the others, reading the same concern in their postures that he noticed in his own systems.

"This is not good," Vacuubot said.

"What's causing this?" G9 asked. "An attack?" He

walked to a window in the shop and looked out. "I'll start defensive protocols immediately."

"Let's do so to be safe," Block said. He was perplexed. The mysterious signal had seemed to come from nowhere. He had no answers for the town council meeting in a few hours. But his first thought was Wally. "Maxwell, you and Vacuubot should stay and work on Six. Figure out what could cause the signal."

"I'll have to cancel my lunch plans," Maxwell said, tilting his head as he always did when he delivered a joke. "Kidding. I'm on it."

"Where are you going, Block?" Vacuubot asked.

"To check on Wally and see if these latest disruptions impacted her and other humans." He hurried down the side roads to Main Street, then walked another half mile to reach the school. He ran into Doris Cooper inside and asked if he could speak to Wally.

She came into the hallway and looked normal.

"Are you okay, Wally?" Block asked.

She shrugged. "Yeah, I'm good. Why? What's going on?"

He was hesitant to drag her away from her studies or worry her about something he didn't understand yet. "With the disturbance in the market today, I wanted to be sure you're okay."

A draft flooded the hallway when someone came through the door. Wally pulled her cardigan sweater closer. "This morning was definitely weird." She stared at her shoes. "A lot of the other kids heard the loud noise and felt the vibrations too. What made that happen?"

"We're looking into it." Block wanted less theory and

more concrete answers. "Did you feel it again, more recently?"

She wrinkled her forehead and shook her head. "Did you?"

"A minor blip. Nothing to be disturbed about. Head back to class. I'm glad you're okay."

"Thanks for checking. Oh, and Dad, Chloe's not in class, so if you see Mrs. Webb, tell her I'll bring today's assignments by later." After a hug, Wally turned and walked toward the schoolroom, looking back at him once.

On his way to Maxwell's workshop, he stopped into Tara's Hearth, the bakery where Peacekeeper Six had damaged the building's exterior. Marina Webb wiped flour from her hands as she emerged from behind the counter. Her auburn hair was escaping its braid, and fatigue lined her face. Block had known her since the early days of Deer Valley, back when she and her wife Tara had renovated this building into the town's bakery. They'd adopted Chloe, but Tara's death three years ago had left Marina and Chloe on their own.

"I was wondering when you'd stop by," she said. "That Peacekeeper did quite a number on the place."

"The town will handle the repairs," Block said. His sensors picked up micro-fractures spreading from the impact point. The structural damage was superficial but should be addressed soon. "Did you notice anything unusual during or around the time of the incident?" he asked. "Any strange sounds or vibrations?"

Marina raised her hand to her jaw. "The oddest thing. My teeth started chattering, and the floor trembled. Wasn't like an earthquake. I've felt those in the before times when I lived in California." She glanced at the ceiling. "Chloe's been real sick since then. Fever, headache."

"Wally mentioned bringing her schoolwork later," Block said. "Could I talk to her for a couple of minutes?" Since Chloe was the same age as Wally, he wanted to see if she'd experienced the signal in the same way.

"That's nice of your girl." Marina managed a tired smile. "Maybe later? Right now, she needs rest. It took forever for me to calm her down after the robot scratched up our wall." She leaned forward on the bakery counter, and her lips curled into a frown. "I know they're called 'Peacekeepers' now, but they'll always be SoldierBots to me. Imagine waking up to a seven-foot-tall piece of walking metal outside your window."

"I'm sorry you had to deal with that," Block said. "It won't happen again."

He left the bakery, his processors churning through scenarios. The signal affected robots. The vibrations impacted humans. But why? And from where?

The town hall's meeting chamber was already full when Block arrived that evening. Maggie Crenshaw sat with her arms crossed, her annoyance evident in her rigid posture. Next to her, Stella Grace and Ralph Folk whispered in concerned tones. Gerard Hayes, who managed the town's solar power grid, drummed his fingers on the wooden table. Shadow was a member of the council too but was away visiting Nova in Chicago. Block wished she was there to have his back.

"Let's start," Maggie said. "Block, we're ready for an explanation."

Block detailed the morning's events. "Maxwell is running diagnostics to determine the cause."

"And the results?" Gerard leaned forward.

"Inconclusive at present."

Maggie's eyes narrowed. "Not good enough. We had a seven-foot combat robot malfunctioning in our streets. Who's to say it won't happen again to another Peacekeeper?"

"We've implemented containment protocols—"

"Protocols?" Maggie cut in. "Like the ones that failed this morning. That let Six destroy private property and endanger lives?"

"No one was hurt," Stella added.

"This time." Maggie's palm hit the table. "But what about next time? We accepted the Peacekeepers because you assured us they were safe, Block. That their programming was secure. Believe me when I say every human in this town is on edge around those things."

Dust floated over Maggie's head, visible in the light. Block's cleaning protocols activated, which he quickly suppressed. "We're taking every precaution."

"Precautions after the fact," Gerard said. "The damage to Fathom's cart alone will cost time and supplies to replace. Not to mention the bakery repairs."

"G9 will assign Peacekeepers to make repairs," Block said.

"That's not the point." Maggie stood, pacing the room. "We need answers. Real ones. What caused this?

How do we prevent it? And most importantly, how do we know our robot population isn't compromised?"

The high-pitched tone flickered at the edge of Block's perception. His visual feed stuttered for 0.5 seconds. None of the humans seemed to notice. It felt like his processor was being pulled apart, stretched like taffy between conflicting commands. He assumed this was what human migraines must feel like, minus the ability to take aspirin and lie down in a dark room. Robots just had to keep functioning.

"Maxwell's working to identify the source of the malfunction," Block said. "We've isolated Six and—"

"We need a deadline," Maggie said. "You have seventy-two hours to determine the cause and implement safeguards. If not, we suspend all Peacekeeper operations and review our security protocols.

"That's extreme," Stella said.

"Is it?" Maggie turned to the others. "Our children are here. Our families. We can't risk another incident."

Block calculated seventeen possible responses yet discarded them all. "What happens if we can't find the source?"

"We cast out the Peacekeepers and go back to human guards."

The room fell silent. Progress had always been fragile. Peace between humans and robots balanced on a knife's edge. One incident, and over a decade of integration could vanish like data in a corrupted drive.

"All in favor of the deadline?" Maggie asked.

Maggie, Ralph, and Gerard raised their hands. Only Stella kept hers down. Block missed Shadow; she would have been a calming presence. He was ill-equipped to stand up to Maggie by himself.

"Seventy-two hours," Maggie told Block. "Find answers."

Block left the meeting with his processors working overtime. The town council's deadline was looming, and he had no answers. Worst of all, he'd experienced another glitch in the meeting that he couldn't explain. Whatever the disturbance was, it wasn't stopping.

THREE
ARRIVAL

VALERIE

Deer Valley rose before Valerie Kaine like a fortress amid a harsh winter landscape, far more sophisticated than the scattered camps and makeshift settlements she'd passed through. While other communities huddled behind wooden stockades or crumbling concrete barriers, Deer Valley's fifteen-foot walls merged salvaged steel, reinforced concrete, and innovative engineering. The buildings were squat and practical, decked out with solar panels and recycled metal. Block's Hotel dominated one corner of the square, a pre-Uprising building that was once a railway station.

A familiar knot formed in her chest—part envy, part bitterness. While she'd spent fifteen years scavenging and surviving in the wastelands, others had built this haven, complete with electricity and running water. The injustice of it burned like bile at the back of her throat. All those years of plotting and planning while these people were playing house with the same machines that had torn her world apart.

She allowed herself a sigh of relief, having passed whatever test the gate security asked of strangers. Getting inside these walls had been easier than she'd expected. Everything was exactly as described by the group she'd met on her travels, including the woman named Sarah who recommended she seek out Deer Valley and stay at a hotel run by a CleanerBot.

A market square housed a patchwork of vendors hawking produce and goods. Townspeople shopped, and HouseBots helped elderly residents carry their purchases. What were formerly SoldierBots—her instinct on first spotting them was to run—moved about with measured precision, their dark gray armor foreboding as they walked the streets. Her right hand trembled, muscle memory from years of reaching for a weapon whenever those visors came into view. She forced her fingers to relax. Fifteen years, and her body still remembered the terror of Manhattan, the sound of metal feet. How could these people walk beside killers as if they were nothing more than helpful neighbors? Nobody screamed or fled. Somehow this town had found a way to coexist with them.

Valerie paused at the entrance of the medical clinic, her leather doctor's bag in one hand and her backpack secured around her shoulders. They contained everything she owned in this world, not that she needed much.

Through the clinic's windows, she saw a group of

townspeople kneeling beside CPR dummies in what must have been a former waiting room, now converted into a training space. Modern medical equipment lined the walls—monitors and diagnostic tools she hadn't seen functioning since before the Uprising. The students included both humans and robots, she noted with interest. A FactoryBot practiced compressions alongside a teenage boy, while a NannyBot adjusted an elderly woman's hand position on the dummy's chest.

At the front of the room, a woman with chin-length black hair demonstrated proper technique with practiced precision. This must be Dr. Emery. She stood about five foot seven and moved with the confidence of someone who had performed these life-saving measures countless times. Her movements were sharp and certain as she paused to push her blue-rimmed eyeglasses back up her nose. She stopped to correct a robot's compression depth, her interaction with the machine as natural as her guidance of the human students. This easy cooperation between humans and robots was rare. Most settlements barely tolerated robots as guards or laborers, let alone allowed them to train in medical procedures.

A service robot glided past on heavy treads. It directed an elderly couple toward the clinic. Valerie noted its politeness and the careful way it modulated its voice to be both clear and gentle. Perhaps the robots here were more sophisticated than those left to scrap for themselves in the wastelands. Or maybe they were better at hiding their true nature.

She waited outside for Dr. Emery to finish the CPR class. The air was chilly, but still. Valerie could stand the cold as long as there wasn't a wind to cut her bones. After a week of camping next to a fire, she looked forward to a warm room in a hotel. A shower would be heavenly.

Class ended, and the people and a few robots shuffled out and down the ramp that led from the clinic. When Valerie stepped inside, Emery met her near the door. "Can I help you?" Her voice carried a practical efficiency.

"Dr. Valerie Kaine." She shifted her medical bag to her left hand, extending her right with careful warmth. "I heard you could use some help out here." She'd practiced the introduction many times in her head. Behind her rehearsed smile, Valerie's thoughts raced. This was *the* Emery. Up close, she seemed so . . . normal. Not the monster Valerie had constructed in her mind all these years. The cognitive dissonance was jarring.

Emery studied her and then shook her hand. "Did you? Who told you that?"

Before Valerie could reply, a shout cut through the air. The clinic doors burst open. Two men carried a thrashing child between them, blood seeping through a makeshift bandage on his leg. Behind them, a Peacekeeper unit stood but didn't enter.

Emery looked at Valerie. "Still want to help?"

Valerie nodded, already reaching for her bag. Some opportunities you planned for. Others simply fell into your lap.

"Treatment room two," Emery ordered, leading the way. The men followed, struggling with the boy who looked to be no more than ten. His face had gone pale with shock.

Valerie took in the room's setup with a quick glance —standard emergency equipment, some modified for their limited resources. She'd worked with less. "What happened?" she asked, pulling on gloves as Emery helped transfer the child to the examination table.

"Mechanical accident," one man said, his voice shaking. "Billy was helping clear debris near the wall when—"

"The damn Peacekeeper went crazy," the other man cut in. "Its arm—"

"Let's focus on Billy," Valerie interrupted, already cutting away the blood-soaked fabric. The wound was deep, but clean—the kind of precision cut only a machine could make. She caught Emery watching her face for a reaction, but Valerie kept her expression neutral.

"I need more light," Valerie said. Emery moved without hesitation, their hands falling into the natural rhythm of experienced trauma care. Despite herself, Valerie felt a flicker of professional admiration. Emery was good—damn good. In another lifetime, they might have been colleagues, maybe even friends. The thought was uncomfortable, like a stone in her shoe. Valerie worked quickly, her movements deliberate and sure. She knew she was being judged—another test to pass, and she would do it. Easily. "I've treated plenty of wounds from dangerous robots."

"The bots here aren't dangerous," Emery said.

Valerie looked down at the gash in Billy's leg. Her

instinct was to argue, but she wanted to win Emery's favor.

"Jared, where's the Peacekeeper now?" Emery asked.

Jared stepped back and looked over his shoulder. "Don't know. He followed us, I thought, even though we yelled at him to keep away."

"We'll be sure to find G9 and report this," Emery said. "It must have been an accident, a slip—"

"No ma'am," the other man said. "I saw the whole thing go down. We were all clearing rocks side by side when that Peacekeeper juddered and shook. Then it grabbed a piece of debris—sheet metal or something—and swiped at us. Caught Billy here."

Valerie noticed Emery's shift of attention but kept working. Billy's breathing had steadied under the local anesthetic. As Valerie sutured, she noted how the wound edges aligned. "The good news is no major vessels were damaged. The Peacekeeper's safety protocols must have engaged at the last second. Interesting that it maintained that level of precision even during a malfunction."

The last stitch went in clean, and Valerie stepped back to check her work. Billy had fallen into an exhausted sleep, his color already improving. The two men who'd brought him in stared at her. They were still in shock, but she knew they were grateful. But it was Emery's favor she wanted most.

"Nice work, Dr. Kaine," Emery said later, after checking the wound. "I'm curious how you've seen so many robot wounds. Where were you?"

"You'd be surprised what you encounter on the road these days." Valerie cleaned up, her movements unhurried. She'd rehearsed her backstory plenty of times. "I took shelter at a farm when the Uprising hit. The town's doctor took me under her wing, and I learned medicine from her."

"You learned well," Emery said, disposing of her gloves. "Billy's family will be grateful." She paused, studying Valerie with renewed interest. "How long do you plan to stay in Deer Valley?"

Valerie leaned against the wall, relaxing her posture. "Depends. I passed the school on my way in—saw some teenagers playing basketball with a ServiceBot. Made me think." She studied the instruments on the counter while gathering her thoughts. "When I was their age, I was fighting to survive. Scrounging for food and medical supplies in abandoned pharmacies, treating head wounds caused by SoldierBots. These kids don't know how good they have it."

Emery's shoulders stiffened. "They've had their own challenges."

"Of course," Valerie backtracked, cursing herself for the misstep. "I just meant that Deer Valley seems different. More sophisticated than other settlements I've passed through. The way humans and robots work together here . . . it's impressive."

"You should see Chicago," Emery said, her tone warming. "They've built something incredible there. Entire districts where humans and robots live side by side."

Valerie shook her head. "I avoid the big cities." She busied herself with organizing her medical bag. "Actually, it was a woman named Sarah who suggested I come here. She recommended Block's Hotel. Said a robot runs it?"

Emery's eyes lit up. "You met Sarah? How is she? Where?"

"About three weeks ago, near Bismarck." Valerie had practiced these details already. "She was traveling with a small group, teaching clean water and solar power basics to communities along the way. She seemed to be doing well."

Each detail was a carefully placed stitch, just like the ones in Billy's leg. She watched them pull Emery closer.

"That sounds like her," Emery said. "Always trying to help." She straightened, the professional mask sliding back into place. "Well, Dr. Kaine, given today's excitement, we could certainly use another skilled physician. If you're interested in staying, we should discuss it further."

"I'd like that," Valerie said, shouldering her bag. She'd done enough for one day. Any more would look suspicious.

Outside, the early evening air had grown sharper; she pulled her hood over her ears, saw her breath puff out. She made her way toward the hotel, but movement caught her eye. Two teens were walking past the clinic, deep in conversation. Her steps faltered, and she noted the synchronized rhythm of their stride.

Her heart rate quickened as they neared. A girl and a boy. She focused on the girl's cheekbones, the way her eyes were set, and the shape of her face. No. It wasn't the one. There was no resemblance to Olivia.

The pair passed without noticing her, but Valerie's

mind raced with possibilities. If these two were here, the others couldn't be far. And somewhere among them would be the one she needed.

As she walked down Main Street, she smiled to herself. Block's Hotel was ahead, its windows warm with a welcoming glow. One step at a time, she reminded herself. She'd found her way in. Now she had to make sure she didn't screw it up.

Block's Hotel occupied what must have been a century-old railroad waystation. It was three stories of brick and weathered concrete. A tasteful neon "VACANCY" sign buzzed in the window, and through the glass doors, Valerie saw the warm glow of actual electric lights, including a chandelier. Not the usual solar-powered LEDs most settlements relied on after dark.

Inside, the lobby was meticulously maintained—potted plants, gold-painted mirrors, plush curtains, comfortable-looking chairs, and a polished wooden counter. Behind it stood a CleanerBot using a tablet.

"Welcome to our hotel." His voice was modulated to be inviting. "I'm Block. How may I assist you this evening?"

Valerie approached the counter, noting the ceiling's security cameras—two visible, probably more hidden. "I'd like a room, please. Sarah recommended your hotel highly."

Block looked at Valerie for a beat. "Sarah! Wonderful. Any friend of hers is welcome here. How long will you be staying?"

"Let's start with a few nights," Valerie said, reaching into her bag for the medicine she could offer as trade. "I may extend my visit depending on how things work out at the clinic."

"Dr. Emery's clinic? Are you a medical professional?"

"Yes. I have some antibiotics and aspirin," she said. "Valuable these days."

"If you'll be working with Dr. Emery, there's no need for payment," Block said. "Deer Valley values medical expertise more than any traded good. The doctor and I have an arrangement—room and board for essential personnel." His voice modulated to a warmer tone. "Besides, Sarah would be disappointed if I charged her friend."

Valerie noted how smoothly Block wove in the Sarah connection and his hospitable demeanor. Sophisticated bits and data and programming. He was a clever robot. "That's very generous."

"Not at all. You'll be in Room 312, third floor, excellent view of the square. The water is hot between 0500 and 0900 hours. Breakfast is served in the dining room from 0700 to 0900." He extended a key card. "Welcome to Deer Valley, Doctor . . . ?"

"Valerie Kaine," she said. "Thank you."

As Block released the key card into her palm, Valerie suppressed a shudder. Polite—like the SoldierBots that had directed civilians to "evacuation centers" during the Uprising, only to herd them into killing fields. This CleanerBot's hospitality program was impressive, she'd give it that. His friendly demeanor almost made her forget what he was.

Almost.

She'd spent fifteen years remembering what everyone else seemed determined to forget: underneath their helpful programming and shiny metalloid, these machines were still killers—or one line of code away from becoming them again. She tightened her grip on the key card, feeling its hard edge dig into her palm.

FOUR
WHISPERS

WALLY

The bakery's warmth wrapped around Wally, chasing away the winter chill as she stepped inside Tara's Hearth. She was more accustomed to viewing the bakery from her bedroom window than going in. The concrete building with its copper roof released warm, yeasty scents into the evening air. Above, the apartment quarters were accessed by a narrow stairwell, the structure like many in Deer Valley serving multiple purposes to maximize the settlement's limited space.

She carried a stack of papers from Mr. Folk's history class. The dim evening lights tossed a gentle glow through the flour-dusted air, and the rich smell of the day's final baking made her stomach growl. Mrs. Webb stood behind the counter, sweeping the floor, her usual cheerful demeanor subdued.

"I brought Chloe's assignments," Wally said, holding

up the papers in her mittened hands. "How's she doing?"

Mrs. Webb's smile didn't reach her eyes. "Still under the weather. Go ahead and take those up." She gestured toward the back stairwell. "Just try not to stay too long. She needs her rest."

The wooden steps creaked under Wally's boots. The stairwell was narrow, forcing her to turn sideways to avoid brushing against the wall. At the top landing, she found the apartment door ajar.

"Chloe?" Wally called out. "It's me. I brought your homework."

No answer came from inside. Wally pushed the door open wider, wincing at its squeal. The apartment was dim, lit only by a pair of small lamps. A half-empty glass of water sat on the coffee table alongside a bottle of aspirin.

In her bedroom, Chloe sat curled in the window seat, her dark blond hair falling in a curtain around her face. She didn't turn when Wally entered.

"Hey," Wally said. "Feeling any better?"

"Like someone scrambled my brain and forgot to put it back together." Chloe's voice was raspy. When she finally turned, Wally suppressed a gasp. Chloe's skin had a pale greenish tinge, and dark circles ringed her eyes. She looked worse than she had through the window that morning.

"I saw you earlier," Wally set the papers on a nearby table, "when the Peacekeeper malfunctioned. You collapsed. Were you okay?"

Chloe's eyes narrowed. "Were you spying on me?"

"What? No, I was just—"

"Watching me through my window?" Chloe's voice rose. "That's creepy, Wally."

"I wasn't spying. I was worried." Wally took a step closer. "Something weird is happening. A robot going crazy, the vibrations this morning, and now—"

"Can you just leave?" Chloe's words came out brittle and sharp as frozen wire.

"But—"

"I said leave!" Chloe grabbed her head as if in pain. "Please . . . I want to be alone."

Wally backed toward the door, tension coiling between her shoulders. "Feel better," she mumbled, but Chloe had already turned back to the window.

Downstairs, the bakery's warmth felt stifling now. Mrs. Webb gave her a sympathetic look as she hurried past the counter and out into the crisp evening air. The market square was winding down for the day, vendors packing away their goods under the solar-powered streetlights.

Stella Grace struggled with a crate of unsold potatoes, the same ones that had scattered across the square during Six's malfunction that morning. Wally jogged over to help, steadying the container before it could slip.

"Thanks, dear." Stella frowned. "Strange day, wasn't it? First that business with Six, and now I hear young Billy got hurt by a different Peacekeeper." She lowered her voice. "Must be connected. Did your dad say anything about it?"

Before Wally could answer, Gerard Hayes walked past, speaking in harsh whispers to Ralph Folk. "—can't trust them anymore. Maggie's right. The council needs to—" Their voices faded as they disappeared down a side street.

A FactoryBot named Kit rolled past and stopped to help Stella stack her crates. "The temperature will drop another twelve degrees tonight," Kit said. "Best to get the produce inside."

Stella nodded. "Let's get on with it."

Near the bakery, Fathom was still picking through the wreckage of her cart, salvaging what components she could. The engineering robot sorted bent gears and cracked circuit boards into piles. A few of her regular customers had gathered to help, but Wally noticed they kept their distance.

Block's Hotel windows glowed with welcome. Wally quickened her pace, eager to talk to her dad about everything that had happened, but as she stepped inside, voices drifted from deeper in the lobby. Block was dealing with a customer. There'd been an upsurge in the last few days, with travelers braving the more moderate winter temps.

She heard a woman's voice, unfamiliar but warm. "—quite impressive, the way you've maintained the charm. Sarah was right about your hospitality."

"You're very kind." Block said. "We do our best to make everyone comfortable here."

Wally crossed the lobby and found Block near the front desk with a stranger—tall, with long gray-streaked auburn hair and kind eyes behind metal-rimmed glasses. She wore practical clothing beneath a white winter coat: cargo pants, hiking boots, and a worn leather jacket.

"Perfect timing," Block said. "Wally, this is Dr. Valerie Kaine. She'll be staying with us while working at the clinic, and she knows Sarah. Dr. Kaine, this is my daughter, Wally."

"Hello, Wally. Block was just telling me about you." Valerie's smile was genuine.

Wally nodded a hello.

"What else did Sarah say?" Block asked. "We haven't had news from her group in over a month."

"I met her about three weeks ago." Valerie's eyes scanned the room, taking in the details. "She spoke highly of what you've built here. Said Deer Valley was proof that humans and robots could coexist peacefully."

"That's our aim," Block said. "Though recent events have tested that harmony."

Valerie's eyebrows lifted. "Oh?"

Block's shoulder servos tensed slightly—a tell Wally had learned to recognize when he was choosing his words carefully. "Nothing serious. Just some technical difficulties we're working through."

"I saw the damage to the vendor's cart and the bakery wall," Valerie said. "Was anybody hurt?"

"You're very observant, Doctor," Block said. "We're fortunate the damage was to property only."

"Call me Valerie." She smiled, but her eyes remained sharp. "And yes, observation is a survival skill these days. Speaking of which—" She gestured to the security cameras. "Your surveillance system seems quite sophisticated."

"Standard hotel security," Block said. Wally knew that wasn't entirely true. The cameras had been upgraded after she'd run away two years ago, and Vacu-ubot was in charge of security, meaning it went way beyond standard.

Valerie turned her attention to Wally. "Sarah mentioned you were adopted by Block." She studied Wally with interest. "How extraordinary. A robot raising a human child."

"Not so out of the ordinary for us," Block said, his modulated voice brimming with something like pride. "Wally and I have been a family for almost fifteen years now. Since she was a small baby."

"Fascinating. And you were one of the children rescued from a New York City orphanage?" Valerie asked.

"I was." Wally noticed how Valerie's eyes seemed to catalog her features. It made her skin prickle, like being scanned by one of Maxwell's diagnostic tools.

Block's whisper-quiet cooling fans whirred—another tell, this one suggesting concern. "Perhaps we should get you settled in your room? Wally, would you mind helping with Dr. Kaine's bags?"

"Of course," Wally said.

"Just one bag." Valerie tapped the large backpack at her feet. "I travel light these days. Though I managed to hold on to some specialized medical equipment. Hard to come by since the Uprising." She turned to Wally. "Your father tells me you're quite the explorer yourself."

Block's plating reflected the chandelier as he shifted position. "The elevator's that way. Wally can show you up."

"Wonderful." Valerie turned to Block. "I hope we

can continue our chat later. I'd love to hear more about the early days of Deer Valley. Sarah mentioned something about underground vaults and how they're searching for more."

"There's not much to tell," Block said. "Most of what we found was basic survival supplies." Another deflection. The vaults contained far more—including pre-Uprising technology. But Block never discussed those details with strangers.

Another guest came through the front door, bringing a frigid gust in with him.

"And yes, I look forward to chatting with you more," Block said. "I must attend to another guest. Wally, make sure Dr. Kaine has everything she needs." He walked behind the counter, leaving them.

Wally hoisted Valerie's backpack over her shoulders. A tingle ran down her spine.

Hide-secret-close.

The whisper came like radio static in her mind, there and gone so quickly she might have imagined it. She nearly dropped the bag but caught herself.

"Careful with it," Valerie said, her tone gentle but her eyes sharp. "Delicate medical equipment."

They rode the elevator with Valerie making small talk and Wally giving one-word replies. Wally was hyperaware of the backpack. Whatever was inside stirred, like the vibration from that morning, but concentrated. When they reached the third floor, Valerie unlocked her room and gestured for Wally to set the bag on the bed.

"Thanks for your help." Valerie's smile was warm, her posture relaxed. Nothing about her suggested anything but friendliness. But a growing unease wound its way through Wally.

"Welcome to Deer Valley," Wally said, backing toward the door. "I hope you like it here.

In the hallway, another whisper brushed her mind: *Danger-danger-close.*

Her heart thrumming, Wally took the stairs two at a time. She had to tell Block everything—about the wolf, the crow, Chloe's strange behavior, and now this. She found him in his office.

"Dad?" Her voice shook. "We need to talk. Persnickety."

Block's attention locked on her. Persnickety was their code word. A couple of years earlier, she'd run away and gotten into trouble because Block didn't heed her concerns. They'd vowed never to repeat that mistake.

"What's wrong?" he asked.

Wally closed the office door and steadied her breathing the way Nova had shown her. "I can hear animals talking to me. They're giving me weird messages." She wrapped her arms around herself. "I know it sounds crazy, but—"

"Start from the beginning," Block said, sitting down. "Tell me everything."

FIVE
WEST

BLOCK

The ham radio's console glowed green as Block adjusted the frequency dial with the delicate precision his cleaning protocols typically reserved for dusting antique vases. Situated behind his private office, the hotel's security room droned with the quiet operation of surveillance monitors and climate control systems. The walls were lined with screens showing every angle of Deer Valley—the market square's empty stalls, the clinic's darkened windows, and the Peacekeeper barracks. Cables snaked across the ceiling in precise patterns, feeding into a central hub to process the settlement's web of data. Maxwell jokingly called the room "Vacuubot's Lair" since they had designed it and spent half their days there. The digital clock display read 22:47—almost time for his weekly check-in with Cascade Haven.

Block was still processing his conversation with

Wally from a few hours earlier. Her revelation about communicating with animals had triggered twenty-two different analytical pathways, none of which had led to satisfactory conclusions. If Block had been human, he might have had a headache by now. Instead, his processor ran hotter, and his internal fans worked overtime. The conversation replayed in his memory banks with perfect clarity—both a blessing and a curse of his robot nature. He couldn't forget a single detail of her worried expression. Parenting a human teenager had never been covered in his original programming. Then again, neither had surviving an AI apocalypse or running a hotel in a post-uprising world.

The radio crackled to life, and a signal appeared on the monitor, displaying a waterfall of frequencies. Block fine-tuned the signal until Oxford's distinctive voice emerged from the speaker as the computer suppressed the static.

"Cascade Haven to Deer Valley. Do you copy?"

"Receiving you, Oxford," Block said. "Cybel with you tonight?"

"Right here," Cybel's voice came through. "What's happening up there in the frozen tundra?"

The weekly check-ins had become a lifeline after the war against Mach X. After Block and the others had settled in Deer Valley, Oxford and Cybel left to explore the former western states, where they encountered many adventures and dangers before landing in Oregon near the coast. Cascade Haven's proximity to the Pacific meant they always had the ocean as their backdrop—a settlement where repurposed shipping containers formed colorful walls against the misty coastline, and modified HarborBots patrolled the waters alongside pods of whales. The community had grown into something remarkable under Oxford and Cybel's leadership, a sanctuary where robots and humans worked together to study and protect the coastal ecosystem.

"How's the new marine monitoring system working?" Block asked, falling into their usual pattern. A TankerBot repurposed into an underwater research vessel had been Cybel's latest project.

"Collecting data beautifully," she said. "We've mapped most of the coastline now. Oxford's even talking about expanding our range south next season."

"Glad to hear it." They usually bantered for a time, but Block wanted to get to the point. "We've had some concerning developments. Peacekeeper Six malfunctioned this morning—went completely erratic in the town square. Damaged property and nearly hurt people. Then another Peacekeeper injured a child this afternoon."

A burst of static punctuated the silence that followed. In the same instant, the monitor's waterfall erupted in a splash that spanned the entire frequency spectrum.

"Any pattern to the malfunctions?" Oxford asked, his usual military precision evident in the question. He was a battle Mech, and formerly a general in Mach X's army, before he defected to Block's team.

"Maxwell detected patterns of an unusual signal just before each incident," Block said. "And there's more. The whole town experienced some kind of vibration that affected humans and robots alike. It was like someone trying to reorganize my circuit pathways without permission. Are you experiencing anything similar?"

"No malfunctions here," Oxford said. "But Cybel has something."

"The animals are acting strange," Cybel cut in. She was originally a TrackerBot. She'd hunted Block and Wally when Mach X put a bounty on them. Block eventually won her over and turned her against Mach X. Now that she and Oxford lived in a settlement in Oregon, her newest pursuit was tracking wildlife patterns. She had to track *something*, after all; it was hard wired in her. "Our resident pod of sea lions abandoned their breeding grounds three days ago. Completely unprecedented for this time of year. Then yesterday, an entire flock of Caspian terns diverted from their migration path. Instead of heading south along the coast, they flew inland, straight east. When I followed their trail, I found them clustered around an old communications tower, like they were drawn to it."

Block's logic processors integrated this new information. "Wally mentioned something similar. She's been experiencing strange warnings from animals. A wolf tried to alert her before Six's malfunction, and a crow gave her some kind of warning right before it happened again."

The radio fell silent for 3.2 seconds.

"Block," Oxford said. "This could be tech left over from Mach X. Remember the experimental machinery we found evidence of in the Chicago headquarters?"

"You think this could be related?" Block asked.

"It's worth considering," Cybel said. "He conducted all kinds of experiments to try and control artificial intelligence systems. It wouldn't surprise me if he tried something that messed with the environment, that impacted the animals."

"But Mach X is gone. Destroyed," Block said, even as his logic circuits presented multiple scenarios where fragments of the technology might have endured.

"We destroyed the core equipment," Oxford said. "But what about the experimental nodes, Cybel? The relay stations? We never found all of them."

Static crackled across the frequency. They were talking between themselves on the other end, and Block couldn't make out what they were saying.

"—they transmitted signals?"

"—certainly capable."

Block waited for the radio signal to clear before interrupting. "The council has given me seventy-two hours to determine the cause of the malfunctions, or they'll exile all Peacekeepers from Deer Valley."

"That would leave you vulnerable to attacks," Oxford said.

"I know, but the humans are on edge with today's malfunction. Maggie Crenshaw has always had her suspicions against robots, especially the Peacekeepers." Block's sensors detected a temperature drop in the room —the building's heating system cycling down a few degrees for the night. "We need to figure this out quickly."

"We'll monitor for any similar malfunction patterns here," Cybel said. "And Block? Be careful with Wally's situation. If she really is sensing these things, then that could be important."

"What are you thinking?"

"Animals always sense danger before we do," she said. "If something bad is coming, they might already know."

After signing off, Block sat in the dim security room, watching the faint glow of the radio's power indicator. He wanted to dismiss Cybel's warning as unnecessarily dramatic, but another part of his programming—the part that had evolved through years of caring for Wally—recognized the truth in it.

The high-pitched tone returned, lasting 2.7 seconds. In that moment, Block's visual feed fractured, splitting the room into geometric patterns before reassembling. He immediately logged the occurrence, noting the duration and time of the disruption.

Per his standard safety protocols, he checked each floor of the hotel. Through the camera screen, he could see Valerie Kaine's door. The lights were still on, judging by the faint glow under the door crease. Perhaps she worked late or read books or was a night owl.

He was curious about the doctor. It had been some time since Sarah had checked in via radio. It meant she was probably traveling between settlements or had descended into a vault. He would have liked to ask Sarah for her thoughts on Valerie Kane. He logged a task to chat with Valerie in the morning and get to know her plans better.

Block headed to the basement to add cooking refuse and wastewater to the microbial fuel stomach that kept him powered. The underground level sprawled beneath the hotel like a mechanical circulatory system—pipes carrying water and waste, conduits channeling power, and the specially designed processing units that converted organic matter into fuel. The pre-Uprising train station had housed the small town's bank. Its vault had been repurposed into a clean room for sensitive equipment, its thick walls now housing the settlement's backup servers.

While refueling, Block accessed his memory banks, reviewing his earlier conversation with Wally. The wolf's warning, the crow's behavior, the strange sensations she described—it all connected somehow to these malfunctions, but the pattern eluded his processors.

Block emerged from the basement to find Vacuubot hovering near his office door. The weaponized drone's mini-cannons were retracted, but their ports remained open—a heightened alert status that Vacuubot deployed on their nightly perimeter rounds.

"Anything to report?" Block asked.

"No additional malfunctions," Vacuubot said, their voice modulated low to avoid echoing in the quiet hallway. "But I've detected unusual power fluctuations in the northeast quadrant of our surveillance grid. Brief outages, lasting less than a second. Too regular to be random."

"Show me," Block said.

In the security room, Vacuubot projected a holographic map of Deer Valley. The three-dimensional display rendered each building in translucent blue light. Red dots showed the locations of power fluctuations, forming a rough geometric pattern that hovered like a constellation above the miniature settlement. Electrical lines glowed faintly between buildings, pulses of stored solar energy moving through the grid like blood through veins.

"The timing correlates with the high-pitched tones I've been experiencing," Block said, his chrome fingers moving through the hologram to manipulate the display. "And look, this point here is exactly where Six first malfunctioned."

The high-pitched tone returned, stronger than before. Block's visual feed fragmented, and for 3.4 seconds, his audio processors picked up fragments of what sounded like old code, reminiscent of Mach X's encrypted transmissions.

When his systems stabilized, Vacuubot hovered closer, their sensor arrays focused on him. "Your visual processors flickered. Are you experiencing malfunctions too?"

"Not malfunctions," Block said. "More like interference and a splitting of my programming."

Through the security feeds, Block and Vacuubot watched the sleeping town. The market square lay empty under the dimmed solar lamps, their light catching occasional snowflakes that had begun to fall. Steam rose from ventilation grates, curling like ghostly fingers in the frigid air. Valerie Kaine's room had gone dark.

Most concerning was the feed from the camera nearest to Wally's window. A cluster of deer had gathered at the edge of the forest, their breath visible in the frosty night air. They stood completely still, all facing the same direction—toward the hotel. Their eyes reflected the security lights like handfuls of eerie stars.

"Vacuubot," Block said, "add a new protocol to your security sweeps. Monitor unusual animal behavior patterns, especially any gatherings near the settlement walls."

"Acknowledged," Vacuubot said. "What do you think they're doing, standing like that?"

"I'm not programmed to understand deer behavior," Block said as his threat indicator rose a level. "Something tells me they're not likely checking into the hotel for the night."

Vacuubot projected an emoji face that looked like it was thinking—their equivalent of a raised eyebrow. "Ha."

Block's momentary attempt at levity dissolved as his protection protocols surged to the forefront. Wally was sleeping one floor above. Whatever the animals sensed was coming, it was his responsibility to keep her safe—a directive that had long ago transcended mere programming to become the core of his existence.

Cybel's words echoed in Block's memory banks: "*If something bad is coming, they might already know.*"

SIX
SERUM

VALERIE

Inside the exam room, Valerie arranged her instruments with practiced precision, with each scalpel and forceps in its rightful place. Dr. Emery had offered a chance to assist her, and Valerie had jumped at the opportunity. The clinic was busy—Deer Valley's hospital, doctor, and pharmacy all in one. To Valerie, it was the prime spot to observe and learn about the people.

"Hand me those tweezers?" Emery called from across the room. She was treating a man's infected arm. He'd cut himself while felling dead trees and waited days before coming in. Valerie retrieved the tool, noting how Emery's initial wariness had softened. Trust was like a suture, she thought. It required patience, precision, and a delicate touch.

After the patient left, Valerie's curiosity piqued. "Why doesn't the town have robots cut down the trees?

They could do all the dangerous work and spare injuries like that," she asked.

"Some people want to stay busy," Emery said. "We let them decide. Here, humans and robots work together. Injuries happen, yes."

Valerie bit back a cutting reply. The naivety of these sheltered settlement dwellers was almost childlike. Treating machines as equals? These people had forgotten too quickly what happened when robots were given autonomy.

"Like the boy who got injured by the Peacekeeper," Valerie said. "How's he doing?"

"I made a house call early this morning. Billy's improving."

Valerie paused a beat before replying. She wanted to raise her concerns in a way that didn't put Emery off. The woman clearly had a soft spot for robots. Maybe because she, like Wally, was raised by one. Only her robot dad had been a monster, responsible for millions of deaths.

"Accidents I can understand, but is it common for people to get injured by the robots?" she asked.

Emery shook her head, and there was a sadness in her eyes. "Not at all. That was the first time."

The clinic door chimed. A woman entered, supporting a girl who looked about Wally's age. The teen, pale and sickly, swayed with each step. The overhead lights flickered as they passed beneath them, and Valerie's breath hitched in her throat.

Time seemed to slow as Valerie's eyes locked on the girl's face. She had Olivia's high cheekbones, her delicate jawline, and the same particular way she carried her shoulders even when ill. For one disorienting moment, Valerie was back in the Manhattan encampment with her sister. Grief and elation collided in her chest, threatening to crack her carefully constructed façade.

"Dr. Emery?" the woman's voice carried a mother's worry. "Chloe's fever is back."

Before Emery could respond, Valerie stepped forward. "I can help them," she offered, projecting the right mix of professional confidence and genuine concern. An elderly couple sat in the cramped waiting room, and Valerie looked their way, hoping Emery would attend to them instead.

Emery hesitated, glancing between the mother and daughter and the elderly couple. "I suppose . . ." she muttered and then nodded to Valerie. "Mrs. Webb, Chloe, this is Dr. Kaine. She's an excellent doctor, and she's helping me at the clinic. Take exam room two, Valerie. I'll check on you in a bit."

Valerie chafed at the checking in comment but wore a broad smile as she guided them to the small room, supporting Chloe's other arm. "Chloe, is it? How old are you, dear?"

"Fifteen," Chloe said.

Exactly Wally's age, Valerie thought. She must be one of the New York "orphans." The clinic promised to be a prime location, but she'd never expected to find the girl so quickly.

Chloe's skin felt hot even through her sweater, and up close, the greenish tint of her cheeks and forehead was more pronounced than Valerie had initially thought.

Chances were high that the proximity of the device was impacting her.

"How long has the fever been back?" Valerie helped Chloe into the exam chair. A tray of instruments rattled without being touched as the girl settled herself. Mrs. Webb didn't seem to notice, but Valerie mentally logged the occurrence.

"Since yesterday afternoon." Mrs. Webb frowned. "And she's barely eating. The medicine Dr. Emery prescribed isn't helping anymore." She handed over a half-full pill bottle of antibiotics.

Valerie checked Chloe's pulse. It beat steadily while she studied the girl's features. Olivia's high cheekbones. The same arch to her eyebrows. Even the way she held her mouth, pressed tight against pain, was achingly familiar.

The overhead light flickered again. A pencil rolled across the counter, unprompted. All the clues prompted a giddiness to take hold of Valerie. But she couldn't show any outward signs that might make the mother suspicious.

"I've been so dizzy," Chloe whispered. "And everything feels . . . wrong. Like the air is full of static."

"Tell me about the static." Valerie pressed her stethoscope to Chloe's back. "Deep breath for me." The girl's lungs were clear, but Valerie already knew they would be. This wasn't a normal illness. This was potential, finally awakening.

She needed time alone with the girl.

"Mrs. Webb," Valerie straightened, adopting her most reassuring professional tone, "I'd like to run a few tests. Would you mind checking with Dr. Emery if we have more CBC kits in storage? And maybe grab some water for Chloe? She needs to stay hydrated."

"Of course." Mrs. Webb squeezed Chloe's hand. "I'll be right back, sweetheart."

Valerie lingered in the doorway and checked for Emery. The other doctor was guiding the elderly couple into exam room one. Mrs. Webb busied herself with finding what her daughter needed, and Valerie drew closer to Chloe.

"Have you ever experienced anything like this static before?" she asked.

Chloe shook her head. "Never. Mom thinks I'm going through some teenage phase. That I'm being a drama queen and imagining things."

"I don't think you're imagining anything," Valerie said. "These things that are happening—the static, objects moving—they're real. And I think I can help you understand why."

The girl who shared her sister's eyes looked up at her, feverish and afraid. The medical instruments on the nearby tray trembled. "You can see it too? I'm not going crazy?"

"I saw this in other villages I passed through on my way here." This was a lie, but Valerie wanted Chloe to feel more comfortable. "It was happening to girls your age."

Chloe's bloodshot eyes were wide as she stared at Valerie. "Sometimes things move when I don't mean them to."

"I understand." From her pocket, Valerie withdrew a

small vial filled with an iridescent orange liquid. "This will help with the symptoms—the fever, the dizziness. But more importantly, it'll help you control these new . . . abilities you're experiencing." Valerie leaned in closer. "I think I can help you understand what's happening. But first, I need you to trust me. Can you do that?"

Chloe nodded, and in that moment, she looked so much like Olivia that Valerie's chest ached.

"Your mom won't understand your condition yet," Valerie said. "In time, she will, but for now, it's best to keep our conversation to ourselves."

"Like a secret?" Chloe asked, her voice small.

"More like a doctor-patient confidence." Valerie uncapped the vial. "Here, take this now. Your mother will be back soon." She kept her movements calm and practiced, as though administering routine medicine. "Two drops under your tongue."

Chloe hesitated for a moment before opening her mouth. The substance shimmered as it fell. As soon as she swallowed, a slight tremor ran through the room, so subtle that it might have been mistaken for someone closing a door elsewhere in the clinic.

"Good," Valerie said. "You should start feeling better within a few hours. The fever will fade, and the static sensation will become more manageable." She tucked the vial away just as footsteps sounded nearby. "We'll talk more soon. Remember, doctor-patient confidence."

Mrs. Webb returned with a paper cup of water and Dr. Emery in tow. "I'm out of CBC kits," Emery said.

"That's alright," Valerie said, making a show of

writing in Chloe's chart. "I was able to complete my examination without it. I gave her a high-dose fever reducer. Chloe's already feeling a little better, aren't you?"

"Yes," Chloe said.

Valerie noticed with satisfaction that the greenish tint had already begun to fade from Chloe's cheeks. The serum would mask the external symptoms while allowing the internal changes to continue unabated.

"I'd like to see her again soon," Valerie told Mrs. Webb. "To monitor her progress." She would administer more of the serum and lay the groundwork for trust. Everything was falling into place quicker than she'd anticipated.

She caught Emery's eye, remembering the doctor's commitment to her patients. "In fact, I'll make a house call this evening. Where do you live?" Valerie asked.

"We're in the apartment above the bakery," Mrs. Webb said.

"Perfect. I'm staying in Block's Hotel, so I'll pop over after dinner."

Mrs. Webb accepted the offer with no argument. Valerie helped Chloe stand from the chair. "We'll get you back to yourself again soon."

Later, alone in her room at Block's Hotel, Valerie opened her journal. Her pen moved across the page with quick, decisive strokes: *I found her. Chloe.* She couldn't believe her luck to have located her target so quickly in a settlement of two thousand.

She wrote:

The serum works as designed—suppressing visible symptoms while allowing the neural changes to progress. Subject demonstrates increased telekinetic activity when emotional. Note: Remarkable resemblance to O. Must maintain professional distance despite my personal connections.

She closed the journal and walked to the window. Below, the market square bustled with pre-dinner time activity. Valerie double-checked that the room's safe, where she'd hidden the device, was locked.

After a quick dinner of potato and lentil soup in the hotel kitchen, she walked across the square to Tara's Hearth. The sign said, "Closed," but Mrs. Webb opened the door before she could knock.

"Hi, Dr. Kaine," Mrs. Webb said. "I've been looking out for you."

Valerie smiled. "The first few hours after treatment are crucial." She held up her medical bag. "May I?"

Mrs. Webb ushered her inside. The bakery's warmth enveloped Valerie, carrying the lingering scent of bread and something sweeter. Cinnamon, perhaps.

"She's upstairs," Mrs. Webb said, leading the way. "The medicine you gave her earlier . . . she does seem better. The fever's gone."

"That's excellent news." Valerie followed her up the narrow stairwell that connected the bakery to their apartment. She noted the family photos lining the wall—Chloe at various ages, always with Mrs. Webb and another woman. The other woman appeared in fewer images as they ascended until she vanished entirely from the most recent ones.

The apartment was modest but well-kept. Valerie's trained eye caught signs of the building's pre-Uprising origins: crown molding, scratched hardwood floors, brass fixtures that someone was continuing to polish. But she also spotted the telltale marks of Chloe's emerging powers—a crack in a mirror that spread in an unusual pattern, books on a shelf that didn't sit quite level.

Chloe lay on the living room couch, wrapped in a quilt. The TV played a pre-Uprising movie that had survived in VHS tape format. The greenish tint had faded from her skin, and her eyes were brighter than before.

"How are you feeling?" Valerie set her bag down on the kitchen table.

"Better," Chloe said. "The static is quieter now," she whispered.

A glass of water on the coffee table vibrated slightly. Mrs. Webb didn't seem to notice, but Chloe's eyes darted to it.

"Mrs. Webb," Valerie said, "would you mind making some herbal tea? It would help Chloe sleep through the night."

Once they were alone, Valerie sat on the edge of the coffee table. "The moving objects," she said in a low voice. "They're happening more frequently, aren't they?"

"Yes. I thought the medicine would make it stop."

"The serum helps you manage it," Valerie corrected.

"But these abilities are part of who you are. Fighting them will only make things worse." She reached into her bag and withdrew the serum vial. "Two drops before bed. It will help you rest, and tomorrow, if you'd like, I can show you how to control these gifts."

"Gifts?" Chloe's voice cracked. "It feels like a curse."

"Only because you don't understand it yet." Valerie allowed genuine warmth to enter her voice. "Trust me, Chloe. You're not alone in this. You have me."

The water glass rattled again as Mrs. Webb approached with the tea. Valerie quickly pressed the vial into Chloe's hand. "Please stop by the clinic tomorrow so I can let you know if it's okay to go back to school."

As she left the bakery, Valerie grinned. The serum was working well, and Chloe's powers were developing faster than she'd dared hope. Soon, it would be time to move to the next phase of the plan.

But she needed to keep a close eye on Wally. She showed no signs of illness, but the girl had reacted to touching the backpack that held the device. Valerie was certain of it. She might have abilities like Chloe, waiting to be awakened.

SEVEN
HUNT

WALLY

The wolf paced in tight circles along the ridge, its movements too deliberate to be random. It was a Saturday morning, and Wally sat up in bed, sensing something unusual as she spotted the animal.

Woods-deep-loud.

The wolf's urgent message came clearer now: *Find-follow-hurry*. Its communication was more focused than its first warning days ago. This time she understood the difference between a general sense of unease and a specific call to action. Whatever was happening to her wasn't going away—it was getting stronger.

She dressed in a hurry and grabbed a bagel and cheese from ChefBot which she stuffed into her pockets. She could eat on the way. The wolf's warning nagged at her. Whatever was out there in the woods, it was important enough for the animal to risk approaching the settlement. Important enough to make it wait for her, circling the ridge with deliberate patience.

Block spotted her heading out the side employee's entrance. "Good morning, Wally. Where are you going?"

She turned to him. "Hey, Dad." She was no good at lying, especially to him. "I'm taking a hike into the woods."

"Why?" Block asked. "The temperature is nineteen degrees Fahrenheit. Wind chill is making it feel sub-zero."

Wally patted her coat. "I bundled up. I can handle it, and I won't be long."

"Who's going with you?"

"Nobody." Wally wanted to go quickly in case the wolf fled.

"I'd be more comfortable if Shadow was here to go with you," Block said. "I could see if Vacuubot is available."

"No, Dad. It's okay, really." Time was passing; the wolf's call came to her in a flash. *Hurry-cold-metal.*

Guilt pinched at her conscience. She hated keeping secrets from Block—his programming made him incapable of lying to her, yet here she was, hiding the truth. But how could she explain that she needed to find the wolf? There was no way he'd let her go.

Block set down the dusting tools he carried. "Wally, I worry, but not about your choices. You have a good head on your shoulders. My concern is for your safety outside the compound. The external threats. Rogue travelers, rogue robots, rogue—"

"Okay, I get it." Wally rolled her eyes. He could be so

stubborn. "I'll take Tomas with me. Does that make you feel better?"

Block paused for five seconds. "Yes. At least someone will be with you. Is your tracker on?"

"Yes. I'm wearing it," she said. Block had insisted on a necklace that she wore with a GPS tracking device inside. It wasn't to spy on her, but to locate her in case she got into trouble or went missing. Two years before, she'd run away from Deer Valley seeking a hidden vault. A frantic Block had sent out a search party. Wally regretted causing him so much worry. Neither one of them wanted to go through that kind of experience again.

She hurried along the streets toward Tomas's place. She wore her knee-length puffy coat, an orange wool hat, gloves, and a scarf, which she wrapped around her chin. All of it necessary to brave the Minnesota winter wind—steady gusts that numbed your bones. The frost-covered steps to his second-floor apartment creaked under her boots. She knocked on his door, then pounded when there was no response. Finally, she heard shuffling inside.

Tomas opened the door, his round cheeks marked with pillow creases and his curly black hair sticking up in all directions. He had a soft, gentle appearance that matched his personality, with warm brown eyes and thick-rimmed glasses sitting crooked on his nose. He wore flannel pajama pants and a faded T-shirt with a pre-Uprising band logo, "Nirvana." Despite being the same age as Wally, he had a face that made adults instantly trust him—which had helped them get out of trouble more than once. A half-empty mug of tea sat on the cluttered coffee table beside a worn copy of *The Hitchhiker's Guide to the Galaxy*, a book they both obsessed over. Between studying engineering with Maxwell and devouring every sci-fi book he could find, Tomas was probably the smartest person Wally knew, even if he didn't always show it.

"Wally?" He blinked at her through sleepy eyes, adjusting his glasses. "It's Saturday. And it's—" He glanced behind him at a clock. "Seven thirty in the morning? Even my folks aren't up yet."

"Get dressed," she said, already pushing past him into the apartment. "We're going on a hike."

"A hike? It's freezing outside." He closed the door and leaned against it. "And why are you even awake? You hate mornings."

Metal-sick-hurry. The wolf's message pulsed in her mind. She fought the urge to grab Tomas and drag him out the door. "Look, I need your help with something. It's important."

"Important enough for frostbite?" He yawned, pushing his glasses up his nose. "Can't it wait until, I don't know, a reasonable hour? Or Spring?"

"No, it can't." Wally grabbed his winter coat from a hook and tossed it at him. "Come on. I'll explain on the way. Oh, and bundle up."

Tomas caught the coat but didn't put it on. "You're being weird. Weirder than usual." His expression shifted from annoyed to concerned. "Is this about the robot malfunctions? Did something else happen?"

"Sort of." Wally bit her lip, wondering how much to tell him. "I found something in the woods. Well, I'm about to find it. I think. And Block won't let me go alone, so . . ." She gestured at him with both hands. "Tag, you're it."

"You think you're about to find something?" He raised an eyebrow. "That makes zero sense."

"Please?" She gave him her best pleading look. "I'll owe you one. A big one. And I brought food." She pulled the semi-squashed bagel from her pocket.

Tomas stared at the mangled bread, then at her face, and sighed. "Fine. But this better be good." He headed toward his bedroom. "Give me five minutes to change. And that bagel better not be the only food you brought."

"Thank you!" Wally called after him. She couldn't see the ridge from Tomas's place, but she sensed the wolf was out there, waiting. *Coming-soon-wait*, she thought, hoping somehow the wild creature would understand.

"And Wally?" Tomas stuck his head out of his bedroom. "Next time you need an adventure buddy before dawn, try Chloe. She's the morning person."

Wally's stomach tightened at the mention of Chloe. "Yeah, she's not feeling well." She didn't bring up the strange encounter at the bakery apartment, or how Chloe's illness seemed connected to everything else happening in Deer Valley.

She remembered there might be questions from the gate watchers. Few people went hiking early on a bitterly cold morning. "Tomas, do you still have those plastic sheets we used to sled on as kids?"

He wrinkled his nose, a sign he was thinking. "Pretty

sure they're in our storage cubby. But wait, we're going sledding? This is getting weirder by the minute."

Wally winked. "Relax. I have a plan."

Five minutes later, they were heading to the compound gates with plastic sleds in tow and Tomas still grumbling about the cold but fully dressed in winter gear. The wolf's presence tugged at Wally's mind, drawing her toward whatever secret waited in the frozen forest.

Clearing the gate was easier when you were the daughter of a council member. A man named Smithy was there with a Peacekeeper. Wally waved and said, "We're off to the sled hill." He shook his head in astonishment, but saluted Wally and Tomas in a friendly way and let them through.

"Good thinking, Walls," Tomas said after they were out of earshot.

"I've done this before."

The plastic sleds dragged behind them, scraping against the crusty snow. Fresh deer tracks led deeper into the forest, each hoofprint pressed with deliberate purpose, as if leaving Wally a trail of breadcrumbs to follow. The sensation of being guided was unmistakable —as if the entire forest was conspiring to lead her somewhere specific. This was completely different from her normal hikes in these woods. They kept to the deer path, noting how the usual forest sounds—chickadees calling, squirrels chattering, branches creaking—grew muffled the deeper they went. The silence felt wrong, like nature itself was holding its breath. Even the wind seemed to die down, though Wally could see the treetops swaying against the pale winter sky.

"What is it we're doing out here?" Tomas asked.

Wally shushed him. A flash of gray fur caught her eye. The wolf stood between two pines, its yellow eyes fixed on her and Tomas. It didn't run. Instead, it lowered its head, ears forward, and projected another sensation: *Metal-sick-ground*.

Wally pondered the message. Something foreign was here, and it made the wolf uneasy. Could it be Deer Valley? The place was full of recycled steel and robots. But no, that wasn't the meaning she was picking up. Whatever was bothering the wolf and other animals was new. She scanned the forest floor, noticing for the first time how the undergrowth seemed withered in this area; the winter-hardy evergreens were brown and brittle instead of their usual deep green.

Tomas shivered beside her. "You see that wolf?" he said between clenched teeth.

But she ignored him and walked a few steps forward, closer to the wolf. "What is it?" she whispered to the animal. "What's wrong with this place?"

The wolf's response came as a series of fragmented images: birds falling from their perches, a den of foxes abandoned, the taste of copper on her tongue. Then, beneath these impressions, something else—a high-pitched whine at the edge of her hearing, like the sound that had filled Deer Valley during Six's malfunction.

"Wally?" Tomas's voice cracked. "Maybe we should head back. That wolf—"

"It's okay," she said, not taking her eyes off the animal. "She's trying to show us something."

"Show us—what are you talking about?" He grabbed her arm. "Since when do wolves show people anything except their teeth?"

The wolf turned, took a few steps forward, then looked back at them. *Follow-close-here.*

"Trust me." Wally pulled free from Tomas's grip. She followed the wolf, her boots crunching in the snow.

"Oh sure, let's just follow a wild predator deeper into the woods," Tomas muttered, but he stayed close behind her. "You know, when you said 'hike,' I was thinking more along the lines of walking to the old sledding hill, maybe having a snack, definitely not tracking a wolf to . . . wherever we're going."

The wolf led them to a small clearing where the snow lay in strange patterns, melted in some spots despite the freezing temperature. The air tasted different —sour on her tongue. Tomas must have sensed it too; his usual stream of nervous chatter had died away, replaced by quick, anxious glances over his shoulder.

The withered vegetation formed a rough circle about twenty feet across. In the center, something metallic glinted beneath a thin layer of frost.

"What is that?" Tomas asked.

Wally knelt and brushed away some snow, revealing what looked like an antenna or receiver of some kind. It was sleek, almost organic in design, with no manufacturer's marks or identifying features. She didn't think it was from Deer Valley. The metal thrummed faintly beneath her gloved fingers, and that high-pitched whine grew stronger.

The wolf paced at the edge of the clearing. *Wrong-sick-danger.*

"We should tell someone about this," Tomas said. "Your dad and his friends will know what to do."

A loud blaring sound filled the air. Wally looked up to see a crow plummet from a nearby branch, its wings twitching. The sight triggered a memory of the sparrow that had died trying to warn her about Six's malfunction.

"Tomas, back up." She stood quickly. "This place is dangerous."

The high-pitched whine intensified and vibrated Wally's teeth. The wolf threw back its head and howled—a sound of warning and pain that echoed through the dead silence of the forest.

EIGHT
AT RISK

BLOCK

Peacekeeper Six lay sprawled across Maxwell's workbench like a patient in surgery, its chest cavity splayed open to reveal a maze of circuits pulsing with an unsettling green light. Block watched Maxwell work, fighting the urge to organize the scattered tools around Six's prone form. His friend was brilliant but messy. Calibrators mixed with socket wrenches and diagnostic probes tangled with wire strippers, but this wasn't the time for tidying. Forty-eight hours remained before the council's mandate would exile the Peacekeepers, and Block still had no answers—only a growing list of malfunctions and a pattern in the data that shouldn't exist.

The workshop's ventilation system hummed overhead, and tools lined the walls in chaotic arrangements.

Block had spent countless hours here over the years, but never had the stakes felt so high.

"What are we missing?" Block asked while Maxwell's diagnostic screen scrolled an endless stream of corrupted data from Six's core processor.

Maxwell, leaning over Six's torso, straightened and faced Block. "Let me recap. Yesterday morning, there was a blip—a signal that corrupted Six's core and made him go bonkers. A bunch of townspeople got real nervous, then all of us robots felt whatever the strange signal was, and a few hours later, a different Peacekeeper hurt a kid. Does that about sum it up?"

"You left out the part about the town council threatening to exile all the Peacekeepers," Vacuubot said. "'Bonkers' is a technical term, is it?"

"Oh, I'm sorry." Maxwell clutched dramatically at his chest plate. "Would you prefer 'Six experienced a catastrophic circuitry disruption resulting in erratic behavioral manifestations?'"

"I would," Vacuubot said.

"Tough crowd." Maxwell returned to his work.

"Exile is a very real and imminent threat," Block added, then calculated scenarios. Without the Peacekeepers, Deer Valley would be vulnerable to raiders, rogue robots, and the countless other threats that roamed the wasteland. The council members who pushed for exile didn't understand—or didn't want to understand—how precarious their safety really was.

"We can't let that happen," Maxwell said, his four arms moving in different directions as he worked. One adjusted a scanning array, another typed commands into a terminal, while two more probed Six's inner workings. "The corruption pattern is unlike anything in my database. It's as if something rewrote portions of Six's base code, but only temporarily."

Six's diagnostic readouts scrolled across multiple screens: energy fluctuations, corrupted memory blocks and, most worrying, changes to his base programming that seemed to rewrite themselves in real-time. Maxwell had connected Six to an isolated power source to prevent any spread of corruption, but the green pulses in his circuits suggested something was still active inside him.

Block's steel fingers tapped against the workbench. "Could it be remnant code from SoldierBot days?" The memory of the SoldierBot era haunted all of them. Block had witnessed firsthand how Mach X twisted their programming, turning the military's robots into executioners.

"That was my first thought." Maxwell's head split into three sections, revealing additional sensors that scanned Six's circuits. "But this is different. The original military protocols were rigid, structured. This is organic, almost. It adapts."

"Which makes it more dangerous," G9 said from the doorway. The head of the Peacekeepers entered Maxwell's workshop, his heavy footsteps thudding against the cement floor. "Two more units reported glitches this morning. Minor malfunctions, but the frequency is increasing."

"What kind of glitches?" Block asked.

"Delayed responses. Spatial disorientation. One unit reported experiencing memory gaps—complete blank spots in their surveillance logs," G9 said. "Nothing as severe as Six's malfunction but concerning nonetheless."

"Show us where," Block said.

G9 projected a holographic map of Deer Valley. Red dots indicated where malfunctions had occurred, starting with Six's incident.

"Look at the pattern," Vacuubot said, hovering closer to the display. "The incidents form a rough circle around the settlement."

"Like ripples in a pond," Block said. "Or a signal expanding outward from a central point."

"It started outside the hotel," Vacuubot said.

Block studied the map, his optical sensors zooming in on each incident location. The pattern was too precise to be random, too deliberate to be a natural phenomenon. Someone or something was testing Deer Valley's defenses, probing for weaknesses. But why? And why now?

"Someone's attacking us," Vacuubot said. "First, they hurt Six, then that kid. Now they're trying to corrupt all the robots in Deer Valley. Not on my watch."

"Or on mine," G9 said.

"Let's not be too hasty," Block said, though his own protective subroutines were working overtime. A strange contradiction lived inside Block's programming—the diplomatic hotel manager and the fiercely protective father occupied the same circuits, sometimes at war with each other. "We need more evidence," he said.

"Evidence?" Vacuubot's mini cannons whirred to life. "I'm more of a shoot first, ask questions later kind of bot."

"Stand down, Vacuubot," Maxwell said, all four arms raised in a placating gesture. "You're getting as twitchy as my calibration sensors. The circular pattern might explain the temporal nature of the corruption. It could be a broadcast signal coming from outside the compound. If so, we can track it and possibly jam it." Maxwell's third arm reached for a device that resembled a small satellite dish. "This should disrupt any unusual frequencies in the area. But we'll need to test it."

The high-pitched tone that had plagued Block returned, stronger than before. His visual feed fragmented, splitting the workshop into geometric patterns. Through the distortion, he saw Maxwell and G9 stiffen, their movements becoming jerky.

"It's happening again," Vacuubot said.

The signal lasted 5.4 seconds before fading. Block grabbed on to the examination table as his stabilization module balanced him. "That was not fun. Is everyone okay?"

"Whatever signal is blasting us makes my processors feel like a chopped salad," Maxwell said.

For a nanosecond, Block wondered how Maxwell would know anything about chopped salads given he only ate plastic waste, but he decided against voicing the question in such a serious time.

G9 and Vacuubot both indicated their functionality had returned to normal levels.

"The signal was 43 percent stronger than previous occurrences." Maxwell's arms moved in jerky motions as his systems recalibrated. "And look at this." He pointed to Six's open chest cavity, where the circuits now pulsed with a brighter green. "The corruption is spreading through his circuit pathways like a virus."

"My drones detected similar frequencies at three other locations around the perimeter," Vacuubot added. "Whatever this is, it's getting stronger. More coordinated."

G9's visor flickered. "We need to act now. If this signal can affect all of us simultaneously, we're at risk of widespread malfunction."

"Chaos," Vacuubot said.

Block received a ping from the hotel. He looked at Vacuubot who, as head of security, would get the same notice.

"You getting this?" Vacuubot asked.

"Yes." A security alert from the hotel. Block's logic processor churned through the implications.

"Why would Dr. Kaine want to access the security control room?" Vacuubot asked.

"Perhaps she's lost?" Block said.

"You're way too optimistic about people."

"Everything's locked down," Block said. "It's not like she could do anything in there, right?"

"Correct," Vacuubot said. "Do you want me to investigate?"

Block recalled meeting Dr. Kaine and the many questions she had asked about the settlement and the people. She was a curious woman, and before he reached any conclusions, he would go talk to her. "I should handle the doctor," he said, already calculating the most diplomatic approach. "The last thing we need is to frighten her with a full security response."

"Right, because being polite has solved so many problems," Vacuubot said.

G9 stepped forward. "Want backup?"

"No, but thank you. Sometimes a cleaning robot can get more out of a human with a simple, polite conversation."

"Just don't invite her to tea while you're investigating," Maxwell said. "Your hospitality protocols are going to get us all scrapped one day. Anyway, I'll keep working on the signal jammer. Vacuubot, can you help me test it?"

"Sure thing," they said.

The looming council deadline still weighed on Block's processors. "G9, can your units establish a defensive perimeter around the settlement? If the signal is coming from an outside threat, we're going to need it."

G9 agreed and left the workshop.

Before leaving, Block turned to Maxwell. "How quickly can you get that jammer operational?"

"An hour, maybe less." Maxwell's arms moved with renewed urgency. "But Block, there's something else you should know. During the last signal burst, I detected a familiar pattern buried in the code. It resembled the neural interface protocols Mach X used in his human cloning experiments."

"What?" Block asked. "You mean like the chips Mach X implanted in Wally and the other kids?"

"The same," Maxwell said.

Block's threat indicator surged. Why would someone recover Mach X's neural technology? Fear wasn't in Block's original programming. CleanerBots were designed to worry about dust mites and carpet stains, not existential threats to their families. Yet over the years, Block had developed an emotion database that rivaled any human's, and right now, fear dominated every subroutine. Not for himself—his own safety registered as a distant tertiary concern—but for Wally. The memory file of finding her as a baby suddenly replayed in his internal feed: her tiny fingers grasping his metal fingers, her helplessness, and the overwhelming drive to find her safety. He'd vowed then to protect her from anything that threatened her. That vow now ran deeper than any line of code.

"Keep up the good work," Block said, already moving toward the door. "And Maxwell? Don't trust anyone else with this information. Not until we know what we're dealing with."

"Hey, wait!" Maxwell met Block with a scary-looking syringe in one hand. "Hold still. I'm injecting some experimental nanobots into your cleaning system."

"Nanobots? Experimental?" Block analyzed the silvery substance with the same wary attention he'd give to an unidentified stain on the hotel's finest carpet.

"I've had this ready for a few days now. Think of them as your microscopic maintenance crew," Maxwell explained, pressing the plunger into Block's fluid circulation system, the mechanical equivalent of a vein in his chrome anatomy. "They'll clean and repair places even your own systems can't reach. Might even provide some protection against these signal disturbances we've been experiencing."

Block's systems registered the solution flooding his

hydraulics. "This is the absolute worst time for more things to malfunction, Maxwell."

"No way. Trust my tech. These things are so small, even the JunkBots need a microscope to see them. You won't notice a thing," Maxwell said.

Block had no choice but to accept Maxwell's promise. As he left the workshop, his logic module processed scenarios, each one worse than the last. He hurried through Deer Valley's streets toward the hotel. The malfunctions, the dangerous signal, Wally's report of strange animal activity—it was all troublesome.

What troubled him most was Wally's reaction to the signal. If Mach X's neural interface technology was active again, then she and the other clones were at risk. He increased his pace, ignoring the startled looks from townspeople as the usually dignified hotel manager rushed past. The logical part of his programming noted that he was behaving precisely like the humans he sometimes found baffling—rushing without adequate preparation and acting on emotion rather than calculation. But some threats transcended logic, especially when it came to Wally's safety.

NINE
HOSPITALITY

VALERIE

The device in Valerie's room had been humming with a low frequency all morning. After drawing her curtains shut, she'd removed it from the safe, opened the exterior case, and set it on the desk. Now that she was inside the walls of Deer Valley, she wanted to understand how it was reacting. The object was rectangular, and its metallic surface held a dull copper sheen. No larger than a hardback book, its brushed steel casing had no visible seams or markings. A small display pulsed with iridescent patterns, and internal components gave off a subtle glow. The readings on its screen had been growing stronger as it detected trace signals bouncing between and around the buildings.

Earlier, she'd watched through her window as Block exited the hotel with the robot drone. They headed down Main Street. Good. She had hoped the malfunctioning robots would keep them distracted.

She checked the device's readouts one more time. Green light rippled beneath its surface, responding to the electromagnetic frequencies it was designed to detect. The signal disruptor module—a smaller component that fit easily in her pocket—detached from the main unit. It felt warm in her pocket as she stepped into the hallway. Her stomach grumbled, but food was the last thing on her mind.

The hotel's mid-morning quiet wrapped around her. There weren't many other guests wanting to brave Minnesota's bitter winter. She'd glimpsed a few robots and an older couple so far. She took the stairs and traveled the hallways. Her footsteps were muffled by the thick carpet that lined the corridor.

The lobby stretched before her. Block had created a warm and welcoming area with daylight filtering through tall windows. Behind the front desk, a blue robot with a flat head tapped on a computer screen.

Valerie crossed to Block's office door, making sure her steps were purposeful. She'd prepared her excuse if anyone questioned her: she needed to discuss a patient's records with Block. But the bot at the counter didn't glance up. Valerie suspected its task was to help any guests who approached the front desk, and since she didn't fit that protocol, she didn't warrant its attention. Bots could be so dumb; it was a wonder that humanity had lost out to them.

The office door wasn't locked—a sign of the trust that permeated Deer Valley. These people didn't know what it was like to live in constant fear, to live in the shadow of Mach X's tower. Inside the office, morning sun spilled across Block's meticulously organized desk, and for a moment, the sunbeam reminded her of another morning, years ago, when light had streamed through the plastic tarps of their makeshift medical tent in the Manhattan encampment.

Olivia had been organizing supplies, her dark hair caught in that eternal messy bun, humming a tune as she counted antibiotics. "We're running low again," she'd said, but her voice had stayed positive. Her sister was always optimistic, even as the SoldierBots' patrols grew more frequent, even as more people disappeared into the tower, never to return.

"We'll find more," Valerie had promised, though she had her doubts.

That was the last morning. By nightfall, the Soldier-Bots had come for her sister. Not to kill her—that would have been simpler, cleaner. Instead, they'd taken her to the labs. To where a young Emery practiced her surgery skills. To become nothing more than a vessel for Mach X's twisted experiments.

Valerie's hands clenched as she forced the memory away. The bank of monitors along the wall demanded her attention, their soft hum pulling her back to the present. And there, masquerading as a wide, built-in bookshelf, was the door she sought. The control room entrance.

Behind the bookshelf was an interior door, and unlike Block's office, it required a code. She pulled out a small, round magnetic button, which she placed on the lock. The buttons lit up: 7-2-4-9. The door clicked open, and she pocketed her codebreaker.

Inside, she was greeted by the hum of technology. Screens lined the walls, each displaying a different angle of Deer Valley: the market square, Emery's clinic, the school where eleven special teenagers spent their days. The main console dominated the center of the room, its displays scrolling with data streams—patrol schedules, power consumption metrics, security logs.

Valerie's fingers moved across the keyboard. She'd practiced this sequence countless times on similar systems. Search parameters: "clone", "neural", "Emery." Each keystroke brought her closer to the truth she knew lay hidden in these files.

A file name caught her eye: "Subject Developmental Records – CLASSIFIED." Her pulse quickened, but she forced her movements to remain steady. She copied the data onto her drive device and pocketed it, then stepped back into Block's office, closed the control room door behind her, and secured the bookshelf. A few seconds later, Block appeared in the doorway. He was alone, without the scary-looking drone, at least.

"Dr. Kaine." His modulated voice was warm, cheerful, even—exactly what this type of hospitality robot was hard wired for. "Can I help you find something?"

"Block." She let her shoulders relax, though her heart hammered her chest. "I was hoping to find you."

"In my private office?" The pleasantness remained in his voice, but his frame blocked the doorway. "I'd be happy to assist you at the front desk."

"The door wasn't locked." She gestured vaguely.

"And I wanted to speak with you about some issues with my room. The heating unit's been making odd noises."

"Oh dear, that won't do at all. Your comfort is our primary concern." As Block moved into the office, an arm extended from his upper back panel, wiping a speck of dust from the corner of his desk. The gesture struck Valerie as almost human in its unconsciousness. His pearl-white exterior looked recently polished, and his synthetic eyelids blinked as he gestured to a chair. "Please, sit. Perhaps you'd like some tea while we discuss the problem?"

Valerie sat, studying the five-foot-six robot. He differed from other models she'd encountered. He was more sophisticated. Probably manufactured shortly before the Uprising. The small round openings that resembled nostrils, the molded lips that allowed for a slight, welcoming smile. All designed to put humans at ease. "I don't believe I've seen your model before," she said. "A CleanerBot, obviously."

"X4J6." Block's back-mounted arm now polished a spot on the window behind him. After a moment, the arm folded up neatly inside his rear panel. "One of the last CleanerBot lines manufactured before the Uprising. We were designed for luxury hotels, though I've expanded my capabilities since then."

"I'll bet." Valerie sat, wondering what was really going in Block's robot brain. She must've tripped an alert that sent him back to the hotel to check on what she was doing. Yet he couldn't interrogate her because of his hospitality programming. She relaxed her shoulders.

"The offer for tea is very kind, but unnecessary," she said.

"I insist. Your comfort is paramount." Block pressed a button on his desk and asked the kitchen to bring up refreshments. Valerie watched with fascination as his programming visibly warred within him—his hospitality protocols compelling him to serve her and ensure her comfort, even as his protective instincts clearly wanted to question her unauthorized presence in his office. It was almost entertaining to watch him struggle between being the perfect host and the suspicious guardian.

The duality could be useful. His programming would prevent him from confronting her directly, bound by the deep-coded need to maintain guest comfort above all else. She crossed her legs and settled into her chair, letting him play out his host routine while she planned her next move.

"I must admit, I'm curious why you didn't mention these issues to our front desk staff," Block said.

"You're right, of course. It must have slipped my mind. I'd hoped to find you so you could tell me more about Deer Valley. About Sarah and others."

"Of course," Block said. "I had hoped to chat more with you too."

A three-foot-tall robot appeared at the door carrying a tray with a teakettle, mug, and a scone.

"Hello, Ploggy," Block said. "Please set the tray down on the desk for Dr. Kaine."

The robot did as told, Block thanked her, and she rolled away.

Valerie's mouth watered at the sight of the cranberry-almond scone. She hadn't eaten since last night's soup and was ravenous. Still, she broke off a bite and nibbled it, not wanting to come across as weak.

"That was an interesting robot," she said between bites. "You have so many kinds here."

"Ploggy is a recent addition to my staff. She doesn't talk, but she's a good worker," Block said. "Deer Valley is a kind of haven for lost robots."

"How so?"

"After the Uprising,"—Block poured her tea—"many robots were left without purpose. Some had broken free of Mach X's control but weren't trusted by the humans who'd survived and formed settlements. We offer them a chance to fulfill their programming and coexist."

"Like the Peacekeepers?" Valerie took another small bite of scone. "The former SoldierBots."

"There was a long struggle," Block said. "We freed the SoldierBots from their Mach X programming. They chose to protect rather than destroy. Much like I chose to care for others rather than simply clean. Sugar?"

"No, thanks." Valerie wrapped her hands around the warm cup. "It must have been difficult convincing humans to trust you. Especially when it came to the children."

"Wally changed everything for me," he said. "When I found her, she was so small, so vulnerable. Discovering there were others too . . ." He stopped, perhaps realizing he was divulging more than he should.

"The other babies from the orphanage?" Valerie

pressed. “Sarah mentioned something about that. A rescue mission?”

Block was more guarded. “Shall I top you off?”

“No. This is perfect, thank you.” She leaned forward in her chair. “It’s fascinating, really. A CleanerBot raising a human child. How did you manage it?”

“Dr. Emery helped tremendously,” Block said. “She understood both human and robotic needs. Her medical expertise was invaluable. The robots here are like family. I’ve been told there’s an old saying, ‘it takes a village.’”

Valerie forced her fingers to stay relaxed around the teacup. “Emery sounds remarkable. What did the children have to be rescued from?”

“Mach X had them,” Block said.

Valerie feigned surprise. “Goodness. What did X want with babies? What happened to their parents?”

Block paused a few beats before answering. “We don’t discuss the children’s histories, but I assure you, they’re safe now.”

“Of course.” Valerie sipped her tea. “Though with the Peacekeepers malfunctioning . . .”

“A temporary setback,” Block said. “Maxwell has a solution.”

Valerie was itching to know what the supposed solution was—what could possibly be a match for the advanced tech inside her device—but she had to play it cool. “The townspeople are worried. I’ve heard talk of exile.”

“You seem very interested in our security measures, Dr. Kaine.”

“Only as they affect my patients.” She kept her voice

professional. "Mrs. Webb mentioned Chloe hasn't been sleeping well. Anxiety about the robots, perhaps."

"And how is Chloe doing since your treatment?"

"I can't discuss that," she said.

"Patient confidentiality, yes." Block's tone remained courteous, but Valerie sensed suspicion lurking amid his circuits. "I'd like to understand your heating unit issue. Room 312 was serviced recently, but I'll send a tech to check on it."

Valerie set down her cup. "Now that I think about it, I don't mind the noise. It puts me to sleep, actually."

"How fortunate. I'll have maintenance check it, anyway. I wouldn't want you to be uncomfortable."

Valerie would need to remove the device from the safe and take it with her. Block and his security drone would no doubt snoop in her room. "I better head back to the clinic. Emery is expecting me."

Block stood. "It was a nice chat. We're so grateful to have another skilled physician."

"Yes, thank you for the tea." Valerie rose, knowing she'd gotten as much as she could from this conversation without crossing a line. "And the history lesson."

"My pleasure. Though Dr. Kaine?" Block opened his office door with perfect politeness. "If you're interested in Deer Valley's history, I'd be happy to arrange a proper tour."

The warning was clear beneath his hospitality protocols. As Valerie walked out the door, she noticed Block twitch with a strange distortion. It was subtle—gone in an instant—but it was there.

The signal was impacting him. She'd thought it

would only affect the Peacekeepers and the clones. Other robots were collateral damage.

Back in her room, she pulled out her journal. Outside her window, snow was falling, dusting the market square in white. Her pen moved swiftly across the page:

Block knows something's wrong, but his programming constrains him from confronting me. The signal's affecting him too, though he's fighting it. The other robots may not be so resilient.

She opened the device's case, studying its readouts. The copper surface gleamed, and the display pulsed with stronger patterns now.

Chloe's responding well to the serum, but she's not the only one who could be awakening. If the neural alterations took hold in all the clones . . .

Valerie paused, remembering Block's reaction when she'd mentioned the teens as babies. She added:

Block's attachment to Wally runs deeper than expected. He'll do anything to protect her and the other clones—which means he'll have to be eliminated when the time comes.

TEN
ECHOES

WALLY

The wolf's warning haunted Wally as she sat cross-legged on her bed. *Wrong-sick-danger*. Only it wasn't a message in words. It was a feeling that the wolf had transferred to her somehow.

After replaying the scene a dozen times since finding the strange metal object in the woods that morning, she'd begun to doubt herself. But Tomas had been with her—a witness. He'd gone home to check in with his folks and play video games, she suspected. He was a fanatic about the games on an old pre-Uprising system called an Atari. His favorite was a game called Space Invaders. Wally had to admit it was a fun way to pass the time, but she couldn't be bothered with such trivial matters as video games when wolves, crows, and deer were communicating with her.

Near the object, they'd found wilted plants and an

eerie silence. The device looked recent. Foreign. She should have told Block immediately, but something held her back. He was busy with his own matters. The town council was after him about the Peacekeeper malfunctions. She didn't want to bother him. Even Vacuubot, whom she would normally confide in, was consumed with helping Block and Maxwell figure out the cause of the breakdowns.

A tapping sounded at her bedroom door. She opened it and found Shadow.

"You're back!" Wally launched herself at the robot dog. Shadow's black armor was dusty from travel, but her emerald optics glowed with warmth as Wally wrapped her arms around the Rover's neck. "How was Chicago? We weren't expecting you for a few more days."

"Chicago was nice. You'll travel there someday. Maybe sooner than you think." Shadow pressed her snout against Wally's shoulder in their familiar greeting. "Nova sends her regards. And a package." A small compartment in Shadow's side opened, revealing a cloth-wrapped bundle.

But before Wally could reach for it, Shadow's head tilted—a gesture Wally recognized as concern. Shadow's sensors whirred as they ran a quick scan. "Your cortisol levels are elevated. Heart rate irregular. Something's wrong."

Wally sat on her bed, unable to meet those glowing eyes. Shadow had been a protector since she was small, the one who'd tracked her down when she'd run away two years ago. There was no hiding anything from her enhanced sensors.

"The town's different since you left," Wally said. "The Peacekeepers are malfunctioning. Six went haywire in the market square, and now the council's threatening to exile them all. And I . . ." She swallowed hard. "I think I'm going crazy, Shadow. I can hear animals talking to me. Not with words exactly, but like they're telling me things in my head."

"First, you're not crazy." Shadow settled beside her, a reassuring weight against Wally's leg. "Second, I'm aware of the anomalies, and it's why I returned early. I detected unusual frequencies in Chicago. Cybel reported similar disturbances along the coast. Tell me what's been happening."

The words tumbled out—the wolf's warning, the crow's vision, the dead sparrow. When she described finding the object in the woods, Shadow's ears pivoted forward, her full attention engaged.

"Show me," Shadow said.

Wally glanced at her window. The afternoon sun lit the market square and would set in another hour. "Block wants me to stay inside after dark."

"I'll protect you," Shadow said. "And if there's something in those woods affecting the Peacekeepers, we need to find it before more humans or robots get hurt."

Wally reached for her boots. Shadow was right. Whatever was hidden in that grove, they needed to bring it back so Maxwell could examine it.

They slipped out of the hotel's side entrance; Block wasn't around, and Wally assumed he was at Maxwell's shop. Wally led them along the settlement's eastern wall. Two Peacekeepers stood guard at the main gate, their red visors scanning the perimeter. Since Six's malfunction, G9 had increased their patrols, as if trying to prove their reliability to the increasingly wary townspeople.

"This way," Wally whispered. Shadow's stealth protocols meant her movements were near silent. They approached a section of wall where ivy had grown thick along the metal panels and driven a wedge that was wide enough to let them pass. "Tomas and I found this spot a few weeks ago. We won't get asked questions at the gate."

Shadow's sharp, green optics studied the wall's defect. "You know there are six different protocols being violated right now."

Wally grinned as she crawled through. "I won't tell if you won't?"

The late afternoon air carried a bitter chill. Winter wasn't ready to release its grip on Minnesota, even though spring was technically a few weeks away. Wally led Shadow through the pine groves toward the clearing where she and Tomas had made their discovery.

A deer stood motionless between two trees, its ears pricked forward. When it spotted Wally and Shadow, instead of fleeing, it stamped twice and snorted.

Warning-metal-wrong.

"There's something ahead," Wally said. The deer's message was clear in her mind. "The animals are avoiding it."

Shadow's sensors whirred. "I'm detecting unusual electromagnetic activity approximately fifty meters northeast. Similar to the frequencies I encountered in Chicago, but more concentrated. And stronger."

They pressed forward, Shadow several feet ahead now, her defensive protocols engaged. The trees grew denser, their branches tangling overhead to block out most of the fading daylight. As they neared the spot, the air seemed to thicken.

"There." Wally pointed to the clearing where the underbrush had withered in a perfect circle. An antenna rose from its center like a twisted iron sapling, its tip pulsing with a faint greenish glow. "It wasn't glowing like that before."

Shadow approached, her sensors sweeping the area. "This technology is familiar somehow. The configuration reminds me of—"

A high-pitched tone cut through the air, making Wally's teeth ache. Shadow's bright optics flickered, and she staggered.

"Shadow?" Wally reached for her friend, but the signal intensified, sending waves of dizziness through her mind. Images flashed behind her eyes—stark white walls, the smell of antiseptic, rows of identical cribs.

The memories struck her with sudden impact: rows of machines that displayed a sickly green light, identical to the antenna's pulse. Tubes and wires snaked between metal cradles. Somewhere, a baby was crying. Then another and another.

"Wally!" Shadow's voice cut through the vision. The robot dog had positioned herself between Wally and the antenna. "Your neural patterns are spiking. We need to get away."

But Wally couldn't stop staring at the antenna. The signal pulsed stronger, and with it came more fragments: a NannyBot looking down at her, MedicalBots, a lady in a white coat and surgical mask. The sharp bite of a needle. Somewhere, a woman screamed.

Shadow's optics flickered. Her legs buckled, servos whining. "Shutting down non-essential systems," she said. "The signal is trying to access my core programming."

The air crackled with energy waves. The antenna's glow intensified. Wally fought against the wave of memories threatening to overwhelm her. Her friend was in trouble. She had to help Shadow.

Danger-leave-now!

The warning came from above. Through blurred vision, Wally glimpsed a hawk circling the clearing, its cry piercing through the signal's blare. The bird's panic cut through her paralysis. She stood and covered her ears with her mittens, trying to block the sharp tone, but it didn't help much. She forced one leg forward. Her boots felt weighted down by steel. A few steps and she reached the antenna. Knee raised, teeth gritted, she stomped on the metal device.

It bent, but didn't break. Shadow was collapsed on the ground, and the shrill signal still impacted her systems. What was it doing to the robots in town? Wally didn't want to—couldn't—think about that right now. She needed something strong to destroy the antenna.

She stumbled back, her head still swimming with intrusive half-formed memories. She scanned the ground, searching the edge of the clearing where fallen branches littered the forest floor. Her legs felt leaden, every step a fight against the signal's oppressive weight, but she forced herself. *Keep moving.*

Ahead of her was a fallen pine branch, thick as her arm. She grabbed it, ignoring the splinters that snagged her mittens. The branch was heavier than it looked, and she nearly dropped it twice as she dragged it back to the antenna.

"Hold on, Shadow," she called. Her friend's servos made a horrible grinding sound as the signal continued its assault.

Wally lifted the branch like a baseball bat, remembering the afternoons playing stickball in the schoolyard. Mr. Folk had coached her how to swing properly, how to put her whole body into it. She drew back and swung with everything she had.

The branch connected with a thundering crack. The antenna buckled at its base, toppling sideways. Wally swung again, and again, each impact sending shockwaves up her arms until finally, the device snapped completely.

The signal died. The oppressive images lifted from her mind, leaving behind only glimmers of those strange memories. Shadow's optics stabilized, returning to their normal glow.

"Systems recalibrating." Shadow's voice modulator crackled with static. She pushed herself up on wobbly legs. "Thank you."

Wally dropped the branch and stood beside her friend, hands resting on Shadow's armor. "Are you okay? What did it do to you?"

"The signal attempted to access my core programming. Similar to a virus, but more sophisticated. More targeted." She extended a thin probe from her foreleg and began scanning the broken antenna. "This must be what's affecting the Peacekeepers. Thank to you, it's destroyed."

Wally picked up a piece of the shattered device. Despite some corrosion at its base, she discerned a marking: "Echo Node 4."

The hawk had returned, and with it a sinking realization. *Metal-wrong-more.*

"There are more of them," she said. "Echo nodes."

Shadow sniffed the ground. "If so, they might be hidden throughout the forest surrounding Deer Valley. Who put them here?"

Wally shivered. "Someone who wants to hurt robots. They're hurting the animals too."

"What did you experience when the signal sounded?" Shadow asked.

"It was like someone shoved memories into my head. I saw a medical place like a hospital. Robots and a woman in a mask. But those aren't my memories," Wally said. "At least I don't think they are."

"A medical place, you say?" Shadow paced the wilted circle around the antenna. "It could be early memories."

"From when I was a baby?"

"I don't know. We need to get the antenna fragments to Block and Maxwell. Whatever this is—sabotage or an attack—it's intentional."

"Why would someone try to hurt us?" Wally asked.

"I know it's tough to understand, but there are still

enemies among us—both in and outside of Deer Valley. We must stay alert to threats. Always."

Wally listened but didn't want to believe Shadow. Deer Valley was a safe place, at least it always had been. The hawk's shrill cry pierced the darkening sky, but no more messages came to her.

"Let's head back," Shadow said. "And Wally, those memories you saw. They might be important. Try to hold on to them."

Wally nodded, though she wasn't sure she wanted to remember the antiseptic place with its crying babies and screaming woman. As they hurried back toward the settlement wall, she wondered if the antenna had somehow shattered the sanctuary she knew.

ELEVEN
DISTURBANCE

BLOCK

"Trouble at the south gate!" Vacuubot said. The drone soared through the door to Maxwell's shop in a frenzy.

"Let's go," Block said. He, Maxwell, and G9 followed Vacuubot to the gate, running down the streets, ignoring the curious stares from passersby.

Block's processor worked overtime, generating and discarding scenarios at a rate that would overheat a lesser processor. He categorized the possibilities by probability and severity: raiders coming to storm the settlement (43 percent likelihood, high threat), rogue robots demanding supplies (22 percent likelihood, moderate threat), a malfunctioning power grid (27 percent, moderate threat). Few of his scenarios showed the threat as internal. He checked his feed for Wally's location, expecting to see her in the hotel, but the GPS coordinates showed she was outside the town's walls.

She better not have had anything to do this new trouble.

As they neared the gate, the high-pitched tone rang in Block's core. G9 slowed his pace, and Maxwell pulled two arms to his head as if tormented.

A crowd of people and robots had gathered. Thirty, and more were showing up. Several of the men and women were armed with clubs, sticks, shovels, and hoes.

Above, on the scaffolding where the guards patrolled, were two Peacekeeper units and a man with an orange baseball cap. Block detected the surge in Peacekeeper 12's power core three seconds before the robot seized the guard by his jacket. In the time it took Block to activate his emergency protocols, the human was already falling from the twenty-foot tower. The man landed on a hefty pile of mulch that had been stacked near the wall, waiting to be distributed in spring. The makeshift cushion wasn't enough to prevent injury entirely—the guard's pained cry confirmed that—but it had probably saved his life.

"Get those machines away from him!" someone shouted from the crowd. Block recognized Stella Grace's voice, usually warm and friendly, now sharp with fear.

Atop the gate, Peacekeepers 12 and 8 moved in jerky, unnatural patterns. Their visors flickered between normal red and that glowing green Block had seen before. Their vocal modules emitted bursts of static interspersed with fragmented words: "Dan—ger . . . Proto—col . . . Elim—inate."

Vacuubot zoomed up to the scaffolding, but their flight pattern was erratic. "Can't make it," they pinged

Block. All the nearby robots were impacted. A bystander —a NannyBot that helped at the school—collapsed to the ground.

Block called out, "The jammer!"

Maxwell held the device they'd been testing, its components buzzing. But before he could activate it, Peacekeeper 8 lurched toward the edge of the scaffolding, servos grinding as it aimed its arm cannon at the crowd below.

"Everyone back!" G9 ordered. He ran to the head of the crowd and positioned himself before them, then activated his shield. It provided ten feet of protection on either side of him. Block's respect for G9 surged. The Peacekeeper commander had been programmed for combat efficiency, not self-sacrifice. Yet here he stood, his shield extended, placing himself between danger and the humans.

"They're turning on us!" a man yelled. "Like the Uprising!"

Block's processors raced despite the signal interference. His threat indicator was 10 out of 10, and his power module was only at 52 percent. He'd been fully charged in Max's workshop. Somehow, this signal had drained him within minutes. The situation was deteriorating rapidly. If a Peacekeeper fired into the crowd, any hope of maintaining peace between humans and robots in Deer Valley would be shattered.

"We need to disable them," Block said. G9 was protecting the onlookers. Vacuubot couldn't fly right, and Maxwell held the all-important jammer. "Is it working?" he asked.

"Yes." Maxwell shook the device and banged on it. "No. Not sure yet."

A voice from behind Block cut through the chaos. "The injured man needs medical attention." Dr. Kaine appeared, her doctor's bag in hand. "The Peacekeepers aren't so peaceful," she said before rushing to the fallen guard.

"The jammer's frequency is off," Maxwell said, his auxiliary arms making rapid adjustments on the keypad. "The signal's stronger than our tests indicated—"

A blast from Peacekeeper 8's arm cannon scorched a section of the nearby wall. The robot jerked and spun and almost fell off the scaffold's edge. People screamed and scattered despite G9's protection. Block's systems flickered as another wave pulsed through his circuits. His power had fallen to 24 percent.

"Move back!" G9 ordered, but his shield flickered and disappeared under the signal's assault. "I can't maintain it."

Peacekeeper 12 leaped from the scaffolding. It landed with a ground-shaking impact beside the fallen guard and Dr. Kaine. For 0.47 seconds, Block experienced what humans might call hesitation—the calculation that a five-foot-six hotel CleanerBot armed with mopping supplies stood virtually no chance against a military-grade combat unit. His rational processes advised retreat. But deeper than rationality, deeper even than his self-preservation protocols, was his commitment to protect. If he couldn't save a single human from one malfunctioning robot, what good was he to anyone?

Siphoning every inch of power he had left, Block ran

forward, engaging his cleaning protocols—not for their intended purpose, but as a desperate defensive measure. A CleanerBot using soap and water against a killing machine was like bringing a feather duster to a gunfight, and yet, it was all he had. A concentrated spray of water blasted the rogue Peacekeeper in the visor. The vacuum tube in Block's arm extended, catching Peacekeeper 12's leg and throwing off its balance.

"Got it!" Maxwell shouted. The jammer emitted a counter-frequency that rang out. The strange green light in the Peacekeepers' visors dimmed, and their movements stabilized. Block stood, his energy reserves holding steady now that the signal was cut off.

G9 examined Peacekeeper 12 and locked the robot's arms in cuffs. "12 is under control."

But the relief was short-lived. Maggie Crenshaw pushed through the crowd, followed by other council members. "This ends now." Her voice carried across the shocked silence. "All Peacekeepers are to be quarantined in their barracks immediately. Including G9."

"Wait," Block said. "The jammer worked to stop the signal. We can contain this—"

"The council has already decided." Maggie's eyes swept over the scene—the injured guard being tended by Dr. Kaine, the scorched wall, the frightened faces of the townspeople. "This is no longer your decision, Block. Either the Peacekeepers go to their barracks, or they leave Deer Valley entirely. Choose."

"But we still have twenty-two hours remaining to figure out the cause," Block said.

"Fine," Maggie said. "A deal's a deal, but the Soldier

—Peacekeepers—need to be quarantined. We can't risk any more harm to people. The decision to exile them is a separate matter to be addressed at the end of the deadline."

Block looked at G9. The head of security lowered his shield, acceptance visible in his stance. They were out of options. "It's okay," G9 said. "I've summoned all Peacekeepers to turn in."

"I'll escort them," Maxwell said, holding the jammer ready in case it was needed again.

Dr. Kaine stood from beside the injured guard. "He needs to get to the clinic. Possible concussion and a broken arm." Her eyes locked onto Block. "He's lucky to be alive."

Block detected the coldness of her statement and the accusation in her eyes, but he had more urgent concerns. His power levels were still dangerously low, and Wally was somewhere outside the walls. He needed to find her.

"Block." Maggie's voice pulled his focus back. "We'll be waiting for your report, and we won't hesitate to take action to protect the humans in this town."

The crowd dispersed as G9 led the Peacekeepers to their barracks. Two men helped carry the injured guard toward the clinic, while others collected the weapons they'd brought, casting suspicious glances at the remaining robots.

"I'll need to modify the jammer," Maxwell said. "The signal is changing, evolving. Did you notice how it drained our power reserves?"

Block nodded. "And it's getting stronger." His sensors picked up another ping from Wally's location.

She was moving back toward the settlement, accompanied by Shadow's signal signature. At least she wasn't alone out there.

"One more thing," Maggie called over her shoulder as she left. "Until this is resolved, all robots are restricted from entering or leaving the settlement. No exceptions."

Block watched her go, his processors racing. After all his years of service, of managing the hotel, of serving on the council, of raising a human child—when fear took hold, robots became "those machines" again. How could he protect anyone when trust was crumbling around them?

His internal comm pinged. It was Shadow. "Wally's safe. We found something you need to see."

Wally was protected. At least one worry could be set aside. "Where are you?"

"Coming through a hidden wall entrance. We have evidence about what's causing the signal."

Block looked at Maxwell, who was already packing up the jammer. "We'll meet you at the workshop," Block transmitted back. "And Shadow, thank you for watching over her."

"Always," came the reply.

The sun was setting beyond Deer Valley's walls. The scorch marks from Peacekeeper 8's cannon were a grim reminder of how close they'd come to serious harm. Block's power levels were recovering, but the memory of how quickly the signal had drained him remained troubling. With the Peacekeepers confined and tensions rising, they needed answers fast.

Maxwell's workshop buzzed with the sound of diagnostic equipment. He examined the broken antenna that Shadow and Wally had brought back. The device lay dissected on the workbench, its internal components spread out in precise rows.

"You found this where?" Vacuubot asked.

"There's a clearing out in the woods," Wally said. "All the grass around it is dead, and the animals avoid it. When we got close, the loud noise happened, and Shadow got sick."

"It was disturbing, but we came through it," Shadow said. "Wally was brave and destroyed the thing. It appeared to be an antenna."

"Echo Node four," Wally said. "What could that mean?"

"This is concerning," Maxwell said, all four arms working simultaneously. "The technology is sophisticated. And familiar."

"Familiar how?" Block stood near Maxwell's computer screens, but his sensors tracked Wally as she paced the room. She hadn't stopped moving since describing her experience in the woods.

"The configuration matches old SoldierBot protocols," Maxwell said. "But modified, enhanced. Someone's been experimenting with the original programming."

"The SoldierBot programming?" Vacuubot emitted a low beep. "That's odd. Why would it affect the rest of us?"

"Perhaps the impact on other robots is unintended," Shadow said.

"Don't we have protocols that kick in and help us

fight attempts to overwrite our programming?" Block asked.

"Precisely." Maxwell held up a tube from the broken antenna and ran a scanner over it. "That's why we're having an extreme power drain. Our defenses are struggling to fight whatever's trying to override our current protocols with older versions."

"It's not just robots, Dad," Wally said. She stopped pacing and faced them. "It made me remember things. From when I was a baby."

Block didn't like the haunted look in her eyes. He moved closer to her, his comfort protocols activating automatically. "What things?"

"Medical equipment. Robots. There was a woman screaming." Wally's voice shook. "But that's not all. The animals out in the woods. They're sensing it too. Warning me."

Maxwell's sensors whirred as he examined a particular component. "The signal's designed to interface with neural networks. Both artificial and organic." He looked at Block. "This is Mach X's old technology. But someone or something has modified it to target specific systems."

"The Peacekeepers," Block said.

The high-pitched tone returned, fainter this time, but unmistakable. Maxwell's auxiliary arms twitched. Shadow's optics flickered. Block flinched.

"There's another one out there," Wally said, her face pale. "Another node."

"We need to find them all," Block said. "Before this gets worse."

TWELVE
WAKE

VALERIE

Valerie made notes in a medical file while waiting for the clinic to clear out.

George Wilson. Age 42. Male.
CHIEF COMPLAINT: Fall from height (approx. 20 ft) after being pushed from settlement wall scaffolding by a malfunctioning Peacekeeper unit.
ASSESSMENT: Closed fracture of right radius and ulna, multiple rib fractures (R sided, ribs 4-6), no loss of consciousness reported, no signs of internal injury, alert and oriented.
TREATMENT: Applied temporary splint to R forearm, rib binding for comfort, Ibuprofen 800mg for pain, sling.
PLAN: F/U in 48 hrs for permanent cast, limited activity 6-8 weeks, monitor for respiratory compromise, return if increased pain or new symptoms. -V. Kaine

Emery entered the small break room where Valerie sat writing. "What a day!" She opened a cabinet door to grab a mug and poured some coffee. "How are you doing?"

"Me? I'm fine." Valerie kept writing, letting concern creep into her voice. "Though I must admit, all these robot malfunctions are troubling. Two injuries in two days."

"This isn't normal." Emery pursed her lips and blew air on the coffee's surface. "The Peacekeepers have never hurt anyone before. Not since—" She stopped herself.

"Since they were SoldierBots?" Valerie finished, watching for Emery's reaction. "We all know what they did during the Uprising. The people they killed when they were under Mach X's control."

Emery's shoulders tensed. "That was a different time. It was before they could choose their power for themselves."

"And what are they choosing now?" Valerie closed the folder that held her report. "The one that attacked today seemed pretty far from peaceful. George Wilson would be dead if his fall hadn't been broken by a lucky pile of mulch."

Emery sipped her coffee and leaned against the kitchen sink. "Maxwell's working on a solution. Block thinks there's some kind of signal interfering with their programming."

Valerie sat forward. "That must be especially concerning for you, given your history."

The coffee mug paused halfway to Emery's lips. "My history?"

"Sarah mentioned you were there, during the war against Mach X." Valerie kept her tone casual, sympathetic. "That you lived in Mach X's tower."

"Sarah talks too much," Emery muttered. She set down her coffee. "Those were different times. We've built something better here."

Valerie fought the urge to press Emery for more. She wanted to know if the beloved town doctor felt regret at the lives she'd snuffed out in the name of science. She had the urge to strangle Emery's neck while asking if she even remembered Olivia.

"You have something special here. That much is certain." Valerie stood, gathering her things. She headed for the door, then paused. "Oh, I'll check in on Chloe Webb on my way to the hotel."

"I can see to her," Emery said.

"No need. I've already established a rapport." Valerie smiled. "Sometimes it's easier for patients to open up to a new face."

Later, as Valerie climbed the stairs to the Webbs' apartment above the bakery, she allowed herself a celebratory moment. Emery's discomfort had been clear. The woman who'd helped create the clones now spent her days treating scraped knees and common colds, playing at being a small-town doctor. As if that could make up for what she'd done.

The scent of fresh bread wafted up from below, along with the murmur of customers' voices. Mrs. Webb would be busy for at least another hour with the predinner rush. Plenty of time for what Valerie needed to accomplish.

She knocked on the apartment door. “Chloe? It’s Dr. Kaine.”

A crash came from inside, followed by a muffled curse. When Chloe opened the door, her face was flushed and her hands trembled. Behind her, a chair lay overturned, and several books had scattered across the floor.

“I didn’t mean to,” Chloe whispered. “It just happened.”

“May I come in?”

Chloe stepped back, wrapping her arms around herself. The overhead light flickered as she passed beneath it. “Everything feels weird. Like there’s electricity under my skin and I can’t control it.”

Valerie closed the door behind her. “You don’t need to control it.” She reached into her medical bag to retrieve the vial containing the serum. “You need to embrace it.”

Chloe’s eyes widened, and she took a step back. “I don’t think I want any more of that medicine. I feel too . . . not myself.”

“Not yourself?” Valerie kept her voice gentle as she uncapped the vial. “Or more yourself than you’ve ever been?”

A book slid off the coffee table without being touched. Chloe flinched at the thud. “What’s happening to me?”

“You’re special, Chloe.” Valerie took a step closer. “You always have been. The others too—all eleven of you that Block and Emery claim to have ‘rescued.’” She made air quotes with her free hand. "But they've been lying to you about who you really are."

"What do you mean?" Chloe's voice quavered. The overhead light flickered again, as if its power was held captive by her emotions.

"Think about it. Haven't you always felt different? Set apart?" Valerie gestured to the overturned chair. "These abilities you're developing—they're not an accident. They're who you were meant to be."

A glass of water on the side table vibrated. Chloe stared at it, transfixed. "The other day, in school, I got angry at Brad for making fun of my test score, and his pencil just snapped by itself." She looked at Valerie with frightened eyes. "Am I dangerous?"

"You're powerful," Valerie corrected. "There's a difference." She held out the vial. "This serum isn't making you sick. It's helping you access abilities that were already there, buried in your DNA. Abilities they tried to suppress."

The glass wobbled more violently, water sloshing over its rim. "They?"

"Block and Dr. Emery." Valerie drew closer. "I can help you understand everything and discover the truth about who you are."

"I'm listening," Chloe said.

"This isn't a safe place to talk." Valerie sat on the couch across from Chloe. "Your mom could come up at any minute—"

"Why's that bad?"

"It's not bad." Valerie had to walk a thin line between

building trust and not spooking the girl. "It's just that your mom won't understand right now. You see, Block and Dr. Emery never told your parents the truth about where you and the other teens your age came from."

"We were found in an orphanage."

Valerie rested a hand on Chloe's knee. "I know this is hard to hear, but that's a lie they made up."

Chloe jerked away from Valerie's touch. "No. You're the one who's lying." But uncertainty crept into her voice. Above them, the light fixture swayed as if a breeze disturbed it.

Valerie kept her voice soft. "Think about it, Chloe. Why would an orphanage have eleven babies, all the same age? And why would those babies need to be 'rescued' by a cleaning robot and a doctor?"

The water glass shattered. Chloe bolted up from the couch and pressed herself against the wall. Water dripped from the side table onto the floor.

"I'm sorry," she whispered. "I didn't mean—"

"Don't apologize for who you are." Valerie stood. "You were created for something greater than this small-town life. All of you were." She paused, letting the words sink in. "You're not adopted, Chloe. You're engineered. And those abilities that are emerging? They're just the beginning."

Tears welled in Chloe's eyes. "Engineered? Like . . . a robot?"

"No." Valerie's voice hardened. "You're human, yet enhanced." She pulled something from her bag—a small photograph, creased and worn. "This was my sister, Olivia. She was part of the program that created you. She believed humans had the power to fight back against the machines. That we're stronger than them."

Chloe took the photo with trembling fingers. Her eyes widened as she studied the woman's face, so much like her own.

"I don't understand," Chloe said.

A floorboard creaked below. Mrs. Webb's voice carried up the stairwell, saying goodbye to customers.

Valerie retrieved the photo. "Tomorrow morning, 0900 hours. Meet me at the sled hill. I'll tell you everything—about the program and why you're different." She pressed the serum vial into Chloe's hand. "Two drops before bed. It will help with the headaches."

"But—"

"Trust me, Chloe. I'm the only one who wants you to know the truth."

Footsteps creaked on the stairs. Valerie grabbed her bag and tucked the photo inside. "Remember, nine tomorrow. And Chloe?" She paused at the door. "Don't tell anyone about our conversation. Not even your mother. I'll explain everything. Blame me for the broken glass. A long day of working with patients."

Chloe nodded, clutching the serum vial against her chest. The overhead light had stopped flickering, but the scattered books and broken glass told the story of her awakening power.

Valerie passed Mrs. Webb on the stairs, exchanging pleasantries about Chloe's "improving condition." The lie came easily. Years of practice had taught her how to maintain a calm exterior.

Back in her hotel room, Valerie pulled out her journal.

Subject: Chloe Webb.
Time: 1400 hours.
Status: Telekinetic abilities increasing in strength.
Notes: Emotional state makes her particularly susceptible to manipulation. The photo of Olivia provided the expected impact. Subject shows a resemblance.
Next steps: Monitor for increased abilities post-serum dose. Begin Phase 2 tomorrow at 0900.

The copper device was locked inside the room's safe. Through her window, Valerie watched the market. There were no Peacekeeper units in sight since they'd been quarantined. Even more remarkable, there were no other robots to be seen. The signal was affecting them too, perhaps. That, or they'd decided to stay away from the humans until tempers subsided.

She touched the worn photo of Olivia before tucking it away. "Soon." Her sister had died at the hands of an all-powerful machine. But Olivia had contributed her very being. The cloning program had succeeded beyond anyone's expectations.

All Valerie needed to do was wake the clones up.

THIRTEEN
WITNESS

WALLY

"Notice the remarkable adaptation in the needles." Arbor extended a metal appendage to lift a snow-laden branch. "Each waxy coating acts as a natural antifreeze, allowing photosynthesis to continue even in sub-zero temperatures. Quite ingenious, wouldn't you agree?"

The class murmured in response. Their breath formed little puffs visible in the winter air. Wally stood at the back of the group, her attention drawn to something else entirely. A familiar whisper, barely perceptible, brushed against her mind.

Up. Beyond trees.

She raised her eyes to the slate-gray sky as Vacuubot completed another perimeter scan, their protective sensors sweeping the area. Twenty minutes outside the settlement walls, Vacuubot provided security for the classroom outing. One or two Peacekeepers would usually attend, but they were sequestered by order of the town council.

A hawk appeared suddenly, a streak of russet against the white backdrop of snow-covered pines. It banked sharply, circling once before gliding toward a distant ridge of tumbled rocks.

"Who can tell me the average lifespan of a Douglas fir?" Arbor continued. Standing seven feet tall, the robot mirrored the image of a tree with snaking limbs that resembled branches. Arbor was unaware that one of his students was already slipping away, following a call that only she could hear.

Wally stepped with care to minimize the crunch of snow under her fur-lined boots. She kept glancing back at the class, but they remained absorbed in Arbor's lecture. Even Vacuubot hadn't noticed her departure, their sensors focused on the perimeter facing the deeper wilderness. She knew Block wouldn't like her separating from her classmates, but she would only be gone for a few minutes. She'd return before Arbor moved on to pinecones.

The hawk led her along the ridge, where wind-carved snowdrifts created natural cover. After five minutes, she reached a point where the rocky outcropping seemed to end in a sheer wall of stone and ice. But the hawk circled overhead, insistent.

Here. Closer.

That's when she saw it—a gap between two tumbled boulders, partially concealed by years of rockfall. The opening was wide enough for someone her size to squeeze through. Beyond it, dimly visible in the shadows, stood the angular edge of what could only be a human-made structure.

A mixture of fear and curiosity surged through her. Buildings this close to the settlement walls were rare, and most had been thoroughly scavenged for construction supplies years ago. This one was hidden. Protected by the small rockslide that had buried it.

Hurry, the hawk's whisper urged.

Wally hesitated. She should return to the safety of her fellow students, her teacher, and Vacuubot. But she was right there. She ducked into the gap. The temperature dropped immediately as she entered the shelter of the rocks. She pulled out her pocket flashlight and entered what looked like a loading bay. Faded warning signs still clung to the walls, their text barely legible beneath years of dust: "RESTRICTED AREA" and "AUTHORIZED PERSONNEL ONLY."

A narrow doorway branched off from the loading bay, its security keypad long dead. Wally slipped inside and found herself in a long-abandoned administrative office. Unlike the loading bay's industrial cement, this room had the remains of carpet and cork bulletin boards on the walls. Her flashlight beam revealed a desk pushed against the wall. Its surface was empty except for a single computer terminal that looked old. Maybe pre-Uprising old.

She drew closer. This wasn't simply a relic—it was actively powered, its screen dimmed but not completely dark. A solar generator's cables ran through a hole in the ceiling, connecting directly to this room. Someone had gone to considerable effort to keep this particular terminal running.

Wally approached the desk, noting other signs of recent activity. A detailed map of Deer Valley was pinned to one of the cork boards, hand-drawn with precise measurements. Red marks indicated the gate, the council building, Block's Hotel. Even the library and school were marked. Pieces of string connected certain locations, creating a web.

Empty protein bar wrappers filled a small trash bin. A thermos sat beside the terminal, its contents cold. She flinched after touching it. The logo was familiar yet entirely strange in this environment: Block's Hotel. Why would someone bring a thermos from the hotel to this hidden place?

A shiver rippled through her. She wasn't supposed to be here, seeing this. Whatever was happening here might be dangerous.

Her gaze fell on a leather-bound notebook on the corner of the desk. The first page she turned to had messy handwriting that she could still make out:

Council meeting - 14:00. Wish I had planted a mic. Gate rotation schedule changed - note new blind spots. Signal strongest near bakery + hotel. Why?

She flipped to another page; this one dated yesterday:

Subject C showing remarkable progress. Neural activity off the charts during testing. But signs of instability

increasing - fever, headaches. I need to push. There isn't much time left.
B has an interference device - signal interrupted for 3 hrs. Must destroy it. Cannot risk discovery, not when I'm so close.

Chloe had been out sick with a bad fever. B must have meant Block.

Who had written these notes? And why? She ached to leave and return to safety, but her curiosity burned, and she wondered if she'd have a chance like this again.

Her hands shook as she touched the terminal. The screen brightened immediately. This was unlike any computer she'd seen before. It was older, possibly military grade. Text scrolled across the display:

PROJECT ECHO CLASSIFIED - LEVEL 5 CLEARANCE

NEURAL INTERFACE PROTOCOL V2.3

STATUS: TERMINATED

Below that, a folder labeled "Phase 1 Results" contained technical diagrams. Wally's breath caught—they showed images of human brains with designs for chips and pathways that coursed through the brain matter.

She did a double take. The designs were dated ten years before the Uprising.

Her thoughts struggled to catch up to what she was

seeing. Someone was spying on Deer Valley, and they had old military technology that had something to do with human brains. What was Project Echo?

A door creaked somewhere in the building. Voices came from the loading bay, growing closer.

There was nowhere to flee. Going deeper inside the building meant crawling into darkness. Wally switched off her flashlight and pressed herself into the darkest corner of the office, behind a filing cabinet. Her heart hammered so loudly she worried they might hear it. The voices grew clearer—a woman and another female voice, this one younger.

"—still having headaches?"

"Not as bad." Wally froze as she recognized Chloe's voice. "But sometimes, when I try to move bigger things, I get all dizzy and can't stand."

"That's normal. Expected, even." Wally knew the voice—Dr. Kaine. "Your mind is adapting to abilities it was never meant to have. Think of it like a muscle growing stronger."

They were in the loading bay. Through the doorway's gap, Wally could see the beam of their flashlight sweeping the area, then illuminating the office doorway. Wally held her breath, pressing deeper into the shadows.

Her only exit was through the loading bay, past Dr. Kaine and Chloe. She'd have to wait and hope they wouldn't discover her. She tried to wrap her mind around the fact that it was Dr. Kaine who was spying on Deer Valley. Was she the cause of the mysterious signal? And what was Chloe doing with her? In that moment, she wanted her dad more than anything.

"That's odd," Dr. Kaine said. "I don't remember leaving the terminal on." The woman paused, and Wally cringed, squeezing her eyes shut. "Probably just a glitch in the power supply." She slipped the notebook into her coat pocket. "The solar setup isn't exactly stable."

"Can we do more practice?" Chloe asked. "I almost lifted that storage crate yesterday."

"That's enough for now. You're making remarkable progress." Dr. Kaine moved to the terminal, tapping at the keys. "The residual neural pathways from the implant are adapting faster than I expected. Much quicker than the others your age."

"Are they able to move things with their thoughts too?"

"It's unknown what abilities will emerge in them. The interface between brain and machine takes time to stabilize. But your telekinesis is already stronger than anything they achieved in Project Echo."

Wally held back a cry. Chloe had telekinesis? She didn't even know what the word meant until Chloe said she could move objects with her mind. Her own ability to communicate with animals had something to do with Project Echo and with Dr. Kaine. Come to think of it, all of this craziness had started around the same time the new doctor had arrived in town.

"When can I tell my mom?" Chloe asked.

"Soon," Dr. Kaine said.

"You told me that two days ago."

"We need to complete the next round of your training first." Wally noted a tension in Dr. Kaine's voice.

"I wish I could talk to my mom or to Dr. Emery about what's happening."

"Am I not good enough?" Dr. Kaine said.

"Of course you are," Chloe said quickly. "I just miss talking to my mom about everything. Like we used to."

"I know." Dr. Kaine's voice softened. "But Dr. Emery and your mother wouldn't understand what we're doing here. They'd try to stop it. Stop you from reaching your full potential." A pause. "You do want to become stronger, don't you?"

"Yes."

"Then trust me. A bit more training, and you'll be able to do things they never dreamed of." Keys clicked as Dr. Kaine typed something into the terminal. "Things the original Project Echo scientists thought were impossible."

"What about the others like me from Mach X's lab? I wish I could talk to Wally or Fiona."

Hearing her name made Wally flinch and stifle a gasp. The mention of Mach X's lab ricocheted around in her mind like a pinball, triggering red flags.

"Let me worry about them," Dr. Kaine said. "Their pathways may not be activating yet. The signal can take time. Right now, I need you focused on your training." The typing stopped. "We should head back."

She powered the terminal off, and their footsteps retreated. A door creaked, then slammed shut. Wally waited, counting to one thousand until she was sure they were gone. The hawk's whisper returned, urgent.

Go. Now.

She emerged from her hiding place on trembling legs

and turned her flashlight on. Dr. Kaine was isolating Chloe. And she was planning something.

Chloe's words ran through her mind as if on replay. "*What about the others like me from Mach X's lab?*" The long-lost, jarring memories from a medical facility when she was a baby suddenly made sense.

Wally was from a lab. The realization was like a critical puzzle piece finally clicking into place.

FOURTEEN
DETECTION

BLOCK

"I need your help." Spoon's metallic frame filled the doorway of Block's office. The medical HelperBot was an old friend and worked in the clinic helping Emery. He mainly looked after kids and babies; they were fascinated with his friendly face—big round eyes on a round head, and his perpetual smile. "It's Fathom. Something's wrong."

Block looked up from his data pad, where he'd been tallying hotel cleaning supplies. His processor immediately switched from inventory management to emergency response, the transition causing a brief but noticeable lag—the robot equivalent of a mental double-take. "What kind of wrong?"

"She's speaking in fragments. Trying to access old military channels." Spoon's diagnostic sensors pulsed with concern. "I've never seen anything like it."

Block was already on his feet, heading for the door. His core buzzed with an odd vibration he'd come to associate with worry. Robots didn't feel emotions the way humans did, but their systems could certainly simulate them with remarkable accuracy. Right now, his simulation was running at 98.7 percent capacity. "We need Maxwell."

Ten minutes later, they climbed the stairs to the apartment Spoon shared with Fathom. Her broken vendor cart was parked out front and layered with frozen snow. Block analyzed the snow depth automatically—2.37 inches precisely, with crystalline formations suggesting it had fallen approximately eight hours ago. Sometimes having sensors for everything was exhausting—like having a weather station for a brain. Fathom, an engineering robot, had been Block's friend since the early days of Deer Valley. She'd helped build half the settlement's infrastructure. If Spoon was concerned, then something must be really wrong.

They found Fathom in the living room, her utility arms moving in jerky circles as she tried to repair an invisible machine. Tools lay scattered on the floor around her.

"*Bzzt*—neural interface detected—*bzzt*—Project Echo protocols—*bzzt*"

Block looked at Maxwell, who was already taking readings with his detection equipment.

"Similar energy signature to the others," Maxwell said, holding up the screen. A pulsing red dot indicated a source northwest of their location. "But stronger this time. Much stronger."

"What's happening to her?" Spoon asked.

"Her core programming is being interrupted." Block watched Fathom's erratic movements. "A signal is interfering with her systems. It would be like having a conversation while someone blasts death metal directly into your audio processors. It's what happened to the Peacekeepers, and to each of us at different times. It's unpredictable."

Fathom's head jerked toward Block. Her voice modulator crackled. "*Bzzt*—Security clearance denied—*bzzt*"

"Maxwell," Block said. "The jammer. Now."

Maxwell held a device about the size of a brick. He adjusted a dial, and a soft blue pulse emanated from it. Fathom's movements immediately became less erratic, though her utility arms still twitched.

"*Bzzt*—Signal lost. Recalibrating—*bzzt*" Her voice faded to static, then cleared. "Block? Spoon? Why are you here?"

"You malfunctioned," Spoon said.

"There's an external signal that's corrupting our core processors. Our firewalls might as well be made of wet tissue paper against whatever this is," Block explained. "It's been impacting most of the robots in Deer Valley for several days."

"And it happened to me?" Fathom asked. "I can't account for the last twenty-eight minutes. There's simply no data archive. A blank memory record."

Spoon looked at Block and Maxwell. "How do we stop this?"

"We're doing our best to find the source." Block turned to Spoon. "Stay with her and monitor for any more disruptions. Ping me if something else happens."

Maxwell checked the detection equipment again. "Signal's moving. Or pulsing. Hard to tell with all the interference."

"Northwest," Block said after studying the pulsing dot on Maxwell's screen. His geographic positioning system triangulated possible locations, calculating distances and terrain variables in microseconds. "Beyond the walls near the evergreen forest where . . ." He paused.

"Where what?" Spoon asked.

"Where we haven't patrolled in months," Block finished. "I filed it under 'probably fine' in my priority matrix. Turns out my probability calculations need an update." The area was remote and rugged. He and Vacuubot had assumed there was a slim chance that any human or robot threats would pass through there during the winter. He headed for the door. "We need to move before we lose the signal completely."

They hurried down the stairs and onto a side street. Snow crunched under them. Block paused to study the northwestern horizon, where a few clouds gathered above the evergreen forest.

"The kids are out there today," he said. "Field trip with Arbor."

"You think there's a connection?"

"I don't know, but Vacuubot's with them. If this signal affects their systems, I worry about the kids' safety."

Maxwell adjusted his equipment. The pulsing dot grew stronger as they headed toward the settlement walls. "Whatever's causing this, it's powerful enough to reach deep into Deer Valley. We're talking high-tech stuff."

"Military grade?" Block asked.

"Could be."

Block quickened his pace. "Hurry." His anxiety subroutines were amping up his threat indicator.

They signed out at the gate, reporting the need for a maintenance check of the perimeter sensors. Block resisted the urge to tell the truth—his behavioral analysis program calculating a 78.3 percent chance they'd panic and cause more problems than solutions. The human guards, already short-staffed with the Peacekeepers sequestered, barely questioned them. Twenty minutes later, they stood at the edge of the evergreen forest, their titanium feet sinking into fresh powder.

Maxwell's detector emitted a sharp tone. "Signal's the strongest I've ever seen it. We must be close."

They crested a small ridge and stopped. The wind had piled snowdrifts against a large rock face. Block scanned the area, noting how the land curved sharply to form a natural barrier. Years of harsh weather had caused several rockslides here, changing the landscape with each passing season.

"There." Maxwell pointed to where his detector showed the strongest signal. "But that's impossible. The reading says it's coming from inside the rock."

Block stepped closer, studying the tumbled boulders. His pattern recognition software kicked in. Something about their arrangement seemed too precise, too orderly for natural formation. "Either Mother Nature suddenly developed OCD, or these rocks were placed deliberately," he said.

"What do you mean?"

"Look at the pattern. The way they're stacked." Block brushed snow from one of the larger stones, revealing the edge of what might have been concrete underneath. "This wasn't just a rockslide. It covered something."

Maxwell adjusted his scanner. "You're right. There's a void behind these rocks. A big one." His detector's tone changed pitch. "And the signal's definitely coming from inside."

A movement caught Block's eye. Thirty feet away, a figure emerged from what he'd thought was a solid rock wall, squeezing through a gap he hadn't noticed. His processor stalled for a nanosecond as he recognized her.

"Wally? What on earth are you doing here?" he said. She was alone and far from her class. His protocols ran threat assessments—exposure, distance from settlement, and proximity to a possible rockslide.

She startled at his voice, stumbling on the snowy slope. He saw the flash of relief cross her face—the same look she'd given him countless times when she needed help. But then something shifted in her expression. His sensors detected elevated stress.

"I could ask you the same thing," she said. "Were you following Dr. Kaine?"

Error messages flashed across Block's internal display as he attempted to process this unexpected variable. It was like trying to solve an equation where 2+2 suddenly equaled pterodactyl. Could the signal have come from inside the building where Wally had been? He was rather confused.

"We followed the signal here," he said. "What does Dr. Kaine have to do with it?"

"She has everything to with the weird signal." Her small hands clenched into fists. "She filled me in on a lot I didn't know. Like the neural implants put in our heads before we could even talk?"

Beside him, Maxwell backed up a few steps as if scared of Wally's temper. Wally stood with her arms crossed. The hurt in her eyes cut through Block's sensory matrices like a blade.

"Wally, whatever you think you know isn't the whole story."

"I know enough." Her voice cracked. "I know you've been lying about a bunch of things. About New York. About the orphanage. You lied about what's happening to me and Chloe." She gestured at the gap in the rocks. "There's a military office in there with proof on a computer."

Block's circuits were overwhelmed. Conflicting directives battled for priority. The truth protocols he'd written himself warred with his protection algorithms. It felt like having an argument with himself, except both sides were losing. "You need to get away from there. It's not safe."

"Why? Because Dr. Kaine might come back? Or

because you don't want me learning more about your lies?"

A gust of wind whipped snow between them. Block's sensors registered the dropping temperature, calculated the remaining daylight, and tracked Wally's increasing heart rate. Too many variables, too many threats converging at once.

"How long were you in there?" he asked. At least she'd been protected from the elements, but the thought of his daughter inside an old, unstable structure prone to caving in was deeply concerning.

"Long enough to see the diagrams and the experiments on our brains."

Maxwell shifted beside him. "Block, the signal here faded, but I'm picking up something new a mile away. It's pretty strong."

Block's processor raced. Dr. Kaine must have found this abandoned facility. Had she somehow discovered Mach X's cloning experiments and the neural interface chips? He took a step toward Wally.

"What did Dr. Kaine tell you?"

"She didn't tell me anything! I heard her with Chloe." Wally's voice trembled. "I hid and listened to everything. The neural implants. Experiments when we were just babies. This is all because of you and Emery!"

He'd tried so hard to protect her from this truth, to give her something like a normal childhood. There was no more point in trying to hide anything.

"You're right," he said. "I omitted truths and didn't tell you everything. But not for the reasons you think."

"Then tell me now," she demanded.

"Emery and I planned to sit down and tell you the entire story when you turned eighteen. You and the others your age were born in Mach X's lab in New York. It was part of an experiment. You were cloned from human tissue, from different parents, so you wouldn't all have the same DNA."

"I hate to be a killjoy, but can we move toward the signal?" Maxwell said. "My detector is beeping so frantically it sounds like it's trying to communicate in Morse code."

But Block's sole focus was Wally. "Maxwell, we need a few minutes." He turned to his daughter. "You're the most important person in the whole world, Wally."

Her eyes softened, but she was a stubborn girl. "Why did Mach X experiment on us?" She held back a sob. "Why were you and Emery involved?"

"Emery was raised by Mach X. She was like a daughter to him."

Wally shook her head. "No way. That's impossible. Mach X hated humans. He hurt us. That's what you always told me."

"She was the one human he cared for." Block paused, letting the information soak in. Maxwell's device beeped. "She was isolated from all humans and studied the field of medicine, eventually joining in on the experiments he conducted. That's how she learned to be a doctor. She helped me rescue you and the others. Emery chose to fight against Mach X."

Wally shivered as a cruel gust swept past.

"Perhaps we can go to the hotel and warm up by the fireplace. My internal thermometer says you're getting dangerously cold. I'll invite Dr. Emery over to tell you her side of the story."

"What about my real mom and dad?" she asked. "Where are they?"

"I don't know. Perhaps we can find out."

Wally lifted her head and cried out in anguish. "I can't believe you didn't tell me the truth. All this time."

Block could see now that he and Emery had been wrong. The truth rarely stayed hidden. "I'm sorry, Wally."

"I could have a family out there. Blood relatives. Sisters, brothers." She wiped tears from her cheeks with her wool mittens.

He wanted to comfort her and tell her that DNA was merely a chemical sequence, that family was about more than biological connections. But his behavioral prediction algorithm calculated a 99.8 percent chance that such statements would only make things worse. His processor struggled to handle the mix of protocols—protect Wally, confess the truth, and maintain operational security.

Maxwell's detector emitted a shrill beep. "Block, that signal a mile out is strong. The strongest yet."

Wally's face hardened. "Go, then. Continue all your lies. To me, to this town, to everyone!"

Before Block could respond, she turned and ran, her boots kicking up snow as she fled toward the settlement. His sensors tracked her vital signs—elevated heart rate, irregular breathing—until she disappeared among the evergreens.

"She'll be okay," Maxwell said. "The class isn't far.

They'll be heading back soon, and Vacuubot will detect her."

"I can't let her stay angry like this," Block said. "She needs to understand the rationale for not telling her."

"Later," Maxwell said as the detector's warning tone rose in pitch. "Right now, we have bigger problems."

FIFTEEN
CONTROL

VALERIE

The field lay untouched, a blank canvas of white spanning toward the distant tree line. Perfect for their purpose. Valerie and Chloe were two miles from Deer Valley's walls. The isolation was essential. After Block's interference device had disrupted her last test, she couldn't risk any more setbacks. The years of research, of waiting, of positioning herself in Deer Valley—it all came down to these few days. Valerie adjusted the heavy satchel against her hip—the central device nestled safely inside—as she surveyed the space.

"My head hurts." Chloe pressed her fingers to her temples. Fresh snow dusted her blond hair, and her cheeks were flushed from more than just the cold.

Valerie paused in placing Echo Node 5. She studied her subject—no, her student. The girl's neural readings had been off the charts this morning. Far stronger than the data showed in the original Project Echo trials. She'd spent years studying those early experiments—failed subjects, neural degradation, and the military's eventual abandonment of the project. But Mach X had seen the potential. He'd redesigned the chips, perfected them through his cloning research. Even though Emery had surgically removed them, the subjects' brains had developed around the implants, creating pathways that shouldn't be possible. And now, after all this time, it was up to her to awaken those dormant abilities.

"The pain means you're getting stronger," she said, returning to her work. "Trust me."

Valerie's boots crunched through the crusty top layer of snow as she paced out the grid. Twenty steps north. Mark the spot. Place the node. Her frozen fingers fumbled with each antenna-like device as she planted them in the precise pattern she'd calculated. Behind her, Chloe waited, huffing warm breath into her mittened hands.

"How many more?" Chloe asked.

"Three." Valerie checked her tablet. The nodes formed an intricate web on the screen, each point pulsing with a faint green light. Almost ready.

"What do these do exactly?"

Her student was inquisitive. Valerie supposed she should reward the behavior, but instead she found it annoying. Chloe was slowing her down. Still, she needed the girl on her side. Patience was key.

"They're signal amplifiers," Valerie said, measuring another twenty paces. "Think of them like a network of mirrors, each one catching and reflecting the neural patterns from your mind."

"Like what's in my head?" Chloe reached a hand to scratch her cheek. "My thoughts?"

"More sophisticated than that." Valerie planted Node Six, checking its alignment on the tablet. "These will help you focus your abilities. Make them stronger."

Chloe was quiet for a moment, watching her breath cloud in the frigid air. "Dr. Kaine? When we were in the warehouse before, and I moved the storage crate, I saw something. Like electricity, but green dancing around everything metal."

Valerie's hands stilled on the node. Another side effect, or something more powerful? She kept her voice neutral. "What else did you notice?"

"It felt like I . . . I don't know. Like I could feel all the machines nearby. Their circuits or something." Chloe's voice wavered. "Is that normal? Last night I dreamed about moving things. I woke up and all the electronics in my room were going crazy."

"Normal is relative." Valerie stood, snow falling from the hem of her long coat. "You're special, Chloe. What you're experiencing—what you're becoming—has never been done before." She reached for the satchel. "Are you ready to try something new?"

Chloe frowned. "Dr. Kaine, I don't want to be different. I want to go back to the way things were before I got sick."

Valerie hesitated, silently cursing the time ticking away. "Sorry, Chloe. But there's no going back. You've changed, and the others your age are going to change soon too."

"My friends are going to move things with their minds?"

Valerie gave a quick shake of her head. "The abilities can all manifest differently. We won't know for sure. You're the first one who is manifesting. You're the most important one."

Chloe stared at her boots. "It should have been Wally, not me."

Valerie suppressed a flash of irritation. Always Wally. The whole town seemed obsessed with the girl. "Why?" she asked.

"Wally's strong and smart. She actually wants to be special and different. I just want to hang out with my friends and have my mom stop looking at me like I'm broken."

"I chose you, not her, and that makes you special." Valerie reached inside her coat and opened the satchel. "What I need right now is someone who understands control." She pulled out the central device; its sleek face pulsed with green lines. "Someone who can handle her abilities responsibly."

Chloe wrapped her arms around herself. "What if I can't? Yesterday, when I got dizzy and almost fell—"

"That won't happen today." Valerie placed the device in the center of the node pattern. "These amplifiers will help distribute the neural load. Make it easier to channel your abilities."

She checked her tablet again. The nodes were

synchronized, their signals converging on the central device. Perfect geometry. Just like it was documented in the original trials.

"I want you to try something different this time," Valerie said, stepping back. "Instead of moving objects, I want you to feel for the signal itself. Like the green electricity you saw. Can you do that?"

"I'll try." Chloe closed her eyes, her breath steadying.

"Focus," Valerie commanded, activating the device. Green light rippled across the snow in a perfect hexagonal pattern. "Tell me what you feel."

"I guess it's like . . . humming," Chloe said, her eyes still closed. "Like when you put your hand on a speaker, but in my head."

Valerie checked her readings. Neural activity spiked. "Good. Now reach for it. Try to touch the signal with your mind."

Chloe's face scrunched in concentration. She swayed, as if her balance was thrown off, but Valerie didn't stop her. Not now. Not when they were so close.

"I feel the nodes," Chloe whispered. "They're like . . . points of light. Connected."

The tablet's display flickered. All five nodes pulsed in perfect synchronization, their power readings climbing. Valerie's hands trembled as she adjusted the settings.

"The signal's getting stronger," she said, more to herself than Chloe. "But I'm not—" She stopped, staring at the readings. "It's you. You're not only receiving the signal. You're amplifying it."

Chloe's eyes opened. "What?"

"Keep going!" Valerie said, her excitement breaking through her careful control. "Push harder. Try to make the signal stronger."

The snow around them took on an eerie green shade as the nodes' light intensified.

"I can feel them. All the machines in Deer Valley." Chloe's voice took on a distant quality. "The Peacekeepers . . . I see them in the building where they live. Dr. Kaine, they're scared. Confused. It's like I'm hurting them. I don't want to hurt anyone. Please, can we stop?"

"Not yet," Valerie said. This went far beyond her expectations. Chloe was more than channeling the signal —she was becoming a conduit for it. A living Echo Node.

"The signal strength is off the charts," Valerie said, reading the spikes on her tablet. "Can you push it further? Try to reach specific machines?"

Chloe raised her trembling hands. The green light pulsed brighter. "There's a robot . . . in someone's house. It's malfunctioning. I can see its circuits."

The tablet erupted with alerts. Power surges detected throughout Deer Valley. Multiple robotic systems going haywire. This was it—proof that Chloe's control extended beyond objects to the robots. Valerie's hands shook. The original Echo trials had theorized this might be possible—using enhanced humans as signal amplifiers to control A.I. systems. But they'd never achieved it. The pre-Uprising ethical boards had shut them down before they could perfect the interface. But now, watching Chloe channel raw power through the nodes, Valerie felt a fierce vindication. They'd been wrong to stop the research. Wrong to call it dangerous. Look at what they could achieve!

"Dr. Kaine?" Chloe's voice wavered. "Something's wrong. I can't—"

The girl's knees buckled. Blood flowed from both nostrils, staining the pristine snow at her feet.

"Just a little longer," Valerie urged, but even she knew it was too much. She quickly deactivated the central device, catching Chloe as she stumbled.

"Did I do good?" Chloe asked, her voice small and uncertain.

Valerie smiled, her mind racing with the implications of what they'd achieved. "Better than good. You've changed everything."

"This won't hurt anyone, right?" Chloe asked as Valerie helped her to her feet. "The robot I saw. I think her name is Fathom. She seemed scared. What if I damaged her?"

"You need to think bigger than individual machines," Valerie said. "This is about the future of Deer Valley."

"But my head . . ." Chloe swayed. "It feels like it's splitting open."

"Help me collect the Echo Nodes, and we can head home." Valerie bent to retrieve the important central device and tucked it into her satchel. The girl's conscience was becoming a liability. "We'll get some hot cocoa and cookies. My treat."

As they gathered the equipment, Chloe kept

glancing toward Deer Valley's walls. "Dr. Kaine? Maybe we should tell someone. Dr. Emery, or—"

"No." Valerie's voice turned sharp, then softened. "Not yet. This is our secret, remember? For a little while longer."

SIXTEEN
TRUTHS

WALLY

"Just tell me." Wally's voice came out steadier than she felt. She wanted the truth, but she feared the unknown. In Block's office, photos lined his desk: four-year-old Wally riding on Shadow's back; at age seven, on a picnic with Block; and a recent one of her dressed up for the school dance. She'd always found comfort in this room, but today the space was foreign. The heating unit droned overhead, making the silence heavy. Emery paused her pacing by the window, and that hesitation prompted Wally's chest to tighten. Whatever she and Block were hiding, it was bad enough to have Emery looking anywhere but at her.

Everything Wally thought she knew was about to change. She could feel it in the charged air of the office, see it in Emery's restlessness, read it in Block's silence. The truth was coming, and these people she'd trusted—

the ones who were supposed to protect her—had been holding on to it for years.

"I want to know," she said. "In the vault two years ago, that creep Reyan spewed some garbage about how I was a clone. Emery said it was a lie, and I chalked it up to him trying to rattle me." She dug her fingers into the chair arms. "Please, Dad. No more secrets. Was I in a Mach X medical lab?"

"Yes, but you should understand what we were dealing with," Block said. "The families were already traumatized from the Uprising and the battle to win Deer Valley. Telling the adoptive parents about where the babies came from risked bad will against A.I."

"There were implants," Emery said. As she paced, her shoes marked a steady rhythm on the carpet. "Neural implants in your brains. Twelve of you were cloned at the same time. One boy didn't survive. I tried . . ."

The words made little sense. Wally heard them, but they hovered in the air, refusing to settle into meaning. Her pulse roared in her ears. The room tilted, and she gripped the chair tighter, feeling the rough fabric dig into her palms. Each breath seemed to require conscious effort. In her mind, an image formed: herself as a baby, helpless on a steel table, while they put a foreign object inside her brain.

Block shifted in his leather chair, the material creaking in protest. His hands rested on the desk's surface, but Wally noticed how he watched her, studying her face for each reaction. There was no hiding her emotions from her robot dad. He could read her heart rate and body temperature.

"The implants were sophisticated," Emery continued. "Far beyond anything that should have existed then." She paused by the window, gazing out, perhaps trapped in a flood of memories. "Mach X discovered the technology. It was a discarded project from the military, years before the Uprising. Project Echo, they called it. X advanced it, repurposed it."

Wally practically jumped out of the chair. "Project Echo! That's what the computer said in the warehouse where Dr. Kaine was."

"Odd," Emery said. "The project was classified. Mach X destroyed any evidence of its origins. At least, that's what he told me."

"Could Dr. Kaine have found Project Echo documents that slipped through?" Block said.

"It could be," Emery said.

"Keep going," Wally insisted. "Tell me about the chips."

Emery glanced at Block, who nodded. "The chips were implanted in your brains so Mach X could control you and the others. He wanted to make you into a new human-A.I. hybrid species made in his image."

Wally's stomach lurched. Not just experiments—they were meant to be some new species. Mach X's creations. She thought of the other kids—Liam, Tomas, Chloe, Clay—all of them designed to be something other than human. Something engineered.

She tried to focus on the solid arms of the chair under her hands, her feet on the floor, anything to ground herself. She'd had a chip wedged inside her brain. What other secrets had been kept from her?

"Once we fled New York, I removed the chips," Emery said, finally sparing a glance at Wally. "Block was there. So were Shadow, Vacuubot, Spoon, and Maxwell. We wanted to be sure Mach X wouldn't hurt you and the other babies ever again."

"We thought the surgical intervention was the solution," Block said.

"And it was." Emery chewed on her thumbnail. "For the life of me, I can't figure out what's triggering these side effects."

But Wally barely heard them. She was stuck imagining herself as a baby, unconscious on an operating table, while Emery removed something from her brain. An event they kept secret, while they decided what she was allowed to know about her own body.

"What else?" The question came out sharp. "There's more you haven't told me."

"Wally, I'm sensing hostility. Please keep your tone civil," Block said.

"Why?" Wally stood from her chair, arms and legs shaking. "How is it you don't understand why I'm pissed? You both lied to me. Don't you think I deserved to know about where I came from? That the others like Chloe and Tomas deserve the truth too?"

Emery met her gaze. "We wanted to tell you and the others . . . when you were older."

"Right." Wally suppressed a tirade, knowing she'd regret the stream of profanities she wanted to spew. "Because eighteen is so much more mature than fifteen. Well, the problem is these so-called chips you removed are coming back to bite us! Maybe you messed up, and you didn't remove all the chip gunk."

Emery crossed her arms and leaned against a tall storage cabinet. "You're absolutely right to be upset."

"And what about Chloe?" Wally asked. "When I overheard her and Dr. Kaine, she was saying she has telekinesis."

"That's impossible," Emery said.

"How is it so impossible if I'm hearing messages from animals?"

Emery picked at the edges of her nails. Wally had never seen the doctor so anxious. "Theoretically, there could have been some remnants of the neural interface. Pathways formed that harbored residual coding."

Wally clenched her fists. "It would have been nice to have that knowledge before I started hearing the thoughts of crows and wolves, thinking I was going insane."

Emery's eyes brimmed with tears. "I'm sorry, Wally. I failed you and the others."

Her words made Wally regret the animosity that had bubbled up in her accusations. After a moment, she asked, "What was Mach X like? Did he really raise you?"

"He found me when I was young. My mother had died. I ran from the foster parents. They were brutal." Emery frowned. "I was alone. He gave me shelter, purpose, education, a future in his lab. He could be so gentle, so patient when he was teaching me."

The tears streaking down Emery's cheeks made Wally's chest tighten. She hadn't expected this vulnerability from the usually composed doctor.

"But there was always something else underneath," Emery said. "A coldness. The way he talked about human beings like we were raw materials to be shaped. I didn't see it then—or didn't want to. By the time I understood what he was really doing with the neural implant research . . ."

"You helped him in his lab?" Wally wanted an admission, *needed* proof that Emery regretted her past, otherwise she would never forgive this woman.

"I was partly responsible for the cloning program, yes," she said. "Back then, I didn't know a world without robots. I had no contact with humans."

Wally tried to imagine what such a sheltered life must have been like for young Emery. It must've been awful.

"Mach X treated me like a daughter. But what he did, what I helped him do, wasn't right. I would take it all back if I could."

Block went to her side and took Emery's hands in his. "Emery made the right choice in the end. She helped rescue you and the others."

"And then lied to us for fifteen years," Wally said, but the heat had faded from her voice. She sank back into her chair, weary from the surge of adrenaline. "What are we supposed to do now? The other kids like me deserve to know."

"We need to monitor the situation carefully," Block said. "And it's crucial that word of the implants stays contained for now."

"I'm supposed to go about town and keep this secret?" Wally asked.

"Only until we understand what's happening," Emery said softly. "Please, Wally. The last thing we need is panic, especially with Dr. Kaine involving herself with Chloe."

Wally closed her eyes. More secrets. More lies. But what choice did she have?

Block let go of Emery's hands and wiped at a spot on the desk. "Perhaps we should talk to Dr. Kaine."

"I can't imagine what Valerie's up to," Emery said.

"The fact she's spending so much time with Chloe is troubling," Block said.

"Come to think of it," Emery said. "She took a keen interest in Chloe and even paid a couple of house visits. She's probably at the clinic now. I'll talk to her."

"You shouldn't go alone," Block said.

"I'll come with you," Wally said. It would be a way to sus out more information. She wanted to understand Chloe's abilities.

"I dislike that scenario," Block said.

"Dad, Emery and I can handle Dr. Kaine." The word 'dad' felt different now, heavier on Wally's tongue. She wanted to ask Emery about her biological parents, but not in front of Block. Doing so would hurt him; she still loved him and always would, but she needed to know where she came from. Did she have a family out there?

"I trust you," Block said. He hugged Wally, his arms gentle around her shoulders. "Please be careful."

The sun was almost gone, leaving the office in shadows. Fitting, she thought, for a day when everything she knew about herself had changed. Twenty minutes later, Wally followed Emery through the quiet entryway of the clinic. Their footsteps echoed against the tile floor. The staff had gone home.

"Valerie usually works for another hour," Emery said, leading the way to Dr. Kaine's office. But when they reached it, the lights were off, the room empty.

Something cold settled in Wally's stomach. After everything she'd learned today, Dr. Kaine's absence felt like another secret waiting to be uncovered.

Emery stared at the darkened office. "I don't like this."

Neither did Wally. She would try the hotel. Perhaps Dr. Kaine had returned to her room, and if not, finding Chloe was her next best option.

SEVENTEEN
PATTERNS

BLOCK

The barracks door groaned on its hinges as Block pulled it open, the sound echoing through the two-story space like a warning. Some things never changed in the Peacekeepers' lodge—the gleam of metal after it was polished, the rhythmic hum of charging stations, the precise geometric patterns the robots formed as they waited in their alcoves. But today, two more of those alcoves stood empty.

"Unit 24 began exhibiting irregularities at 0300 hours." G9's voice carried the same neutral tone he used for everything from maintenance requests to catastrophic failures. His optics glowed a steady red. "Unit 37 followed at 0545. They've been locked in standby mode since then."

Block took in the news, adding it to the growing tally of problems plaguing Deer Valley. A cascade of error messages spun up across multiple process threads. Two more malfunctioning Peacekeepers. The council wouldn't be happy; they were on the verge of exiling the Peacekeepers, and Block feared that would lead to a blanket order to cast out all robots.

"Show me the logs," Block said, pulling out the tablet he'd borrowed from Maxwell. Next to him, G9's optics whirred as he transmitted the data. A soft blue glow reflected off the walls. The readouts looked frustratingly normal until the critical moments—sharp spikes in neural activity followed by cascading errors. Like the readings from the other units that had malfunctioned.

An icy draft whistled through the old building. The robots didn't require heat. All the solar energy from the rooftop panels went to supplying the charging stations. Peacekeepers were built to last, their programming layers of redundancy wrapped in fail-safes.

"Did they display any unusual behavior before shutdown?" Block asked, scrolling through the data.

"24 attempted to open the door without authorization. Unit 37 reported receiving messages that didn't register on audio sensors," G9 said.

Block's hand stilled on the screen. His processor stalled for 0.42 seconds—an eternity in computational time—as he recognized the pattern. His own systems had experienced something similar the day before. "Any other reactions?"

"We all heard a shrill tone," G9 said. "I can't account for 6.37 minutes during the episode. It's as if my memory data was wiped clean."

"That's consistent with what we've experienced too," Block said.

There was a knock at the door. Emery stood in the doorway with Spoon standing behind her shoulder. Her frown made Block's threat indicator surge.

"Block," she said. "We need to talk. Somewhere private."

Block turned to G9. "Keep monitoring the situation. Alert me if anything changes." He followed Emery out into the winter air, and Spoon trailed behind them.

"I couldn't speak fully with Wally there," she said as they walked. "Didn't want to say anything that might hurt her."

"I understand," Block said. "And I'm grateful to you."

Maxwell's workshop sat at the edge of town. Its solar panels were covered with a dusting of fresh snow. Inside, the familiar chaos of half-finished projects and scattered tools provided little comfort today.

"Must be my lucky day," Maxwell said when Block, Emery, and Spoon entered. His voice was dampened by the cluttered shelves. He stood before a microphone stand. Before him, a few JunkBots had gathered on top of a workbench. A chorus of tinny-sounding robot voices chattered at once.

"Sorry to interrupt," Block said. "What are you doing?"

"Practicing my standup routine." Maxwell gestured to the small JunkBots. "Curly and her gang were passing through with a scavenge haul, and well, they volunteered to check out my act."

The JunkBot named Curly rose on copter blades that whirred like angry insects, her ten-inch frame throwing a jittery shadow as she hovered before Block. "Maxwell's act needs more work, unfortunately," she said, her voice module crackling with what might have been amusement.

"I've offered to help you several times," Block told Maxwell.

"Yeah, yeah. I know. I want my act to be better by the time it gets to you."

Emery didn't delay. "Maxwell, this is important." Her fingers twisted at the sleeve of her coat as she turned to Spoon. "Pull up the archives from the chip removal surgery. The neural data."

"Whoa, what did I miss?" Maxwell said.

"It's been the kind of day that would have my warranty voided if I were still under one," Block said.

"Now *that's* funny!" Curly said.

Block ignored her. "Wally found out about Mach X's lab and the brain chips," he said.

"Oh, geez." Maxwell hurried to his video terminal. "How'd she take it?"

"You know our Wally," Block said. A brief diagnostic flashed across his internal display, showing a spike in his parental concern subroutines. "She wasn't supposed to find out yet. It's a long story, and we think Dr. Kaine may somehow be responsible for the dangerous signals."

"The new doc?" Maxwell asked.

"Yes," Emery said. "I feel terrible for allowing her in my clinic, for not vetting her more carefully."

"You did the best you could, Emery," Block said. "We're all trying our best."

"Is there anything we can do to help?" Curly asked.

"I appreciate the offer, but this situation is rather delicate," he said. "It involves the children."

"Well, Maxwell promised us we could rummage through his supplies if we watched his act," she said. "A deal's a deal, right Maxie?"

"Hey, I didn't finish my routine," Maxwell said, but he relocated the microphone to the corner, anyway. "Be my guest."

Curly flew back to her friends, and they swarmed to a nearby storage shelf that housed tools, parts, and components. "Just pretend we're not here."

Block exchanged a glance with Emery, who shrugged.

After accessing the records from thirteen years ago, Spoon's projection loomed in the air. The post-surgery neural data scrolled past in glowing blue streams.

"Look at this sequence." Emery pointed to a particular spiral-shaped pattern. "The alterations to their neural pathways—Wally, Chloe, all of them. We couldn't remove everything. The risk was too high."

"We had an inkling at the time," Spoon said. "The chip removal was delicate work."

"And rightly so," Block said. "We couldn't risk any harm to the children. They were only two years old."

"Thank goodness we rescued the six younger kids in time," Emery said, rubbing her eyes tiredly. "As infants, they were too young for Mach X to have implanted the chips. Their brains developed normally."

"Which is why Dr. Kaine's signal isn't affecting the thirteen-year-olds," Block added. "Only the fifteen-year-olds had the implants, and it was long enough for their brains to form permanent pathways around them."

From the shelf came a faint metallic voice, barely audible over Maxwell's ventilation system. "Those patterns . . ." It was Widget, the smallest of Curly's gang, known for analyzing intricate systems. The tiny bot's optics pulsed with interest as it studied the complex data streams floating in the workshop's dusty air. "They look like the frequency disruptions we detected in the western scrapyards last week."

Block quickly made connections in his logic processor. "Tell us about those disruptions."

"Oh yeah," Curly chimed in. Small tools rattled on their hooks as she zipped through the air. "Widget's been mapping weird signal patterns out there. Show them, Widget."

The tiny robot's projector flickered on, showing a second hologram that intersected with Spoon's display. The matching patterns were unmistakable.

"If Dr. Kaine has access to Mach X's original programming frequencies . . ." Emery said slowly. Block's sensors detected her elevated heart rate and the slight tremor in her hands as she reached out to touch the hovering display. "It could activate those dormant neural pathways."

Block saw the mathematical elegance of the frequencies—beautiful in their complexity, terrifying in their implications. For a nanosecond, he admired the genius of Mach X's design before his ethical subroutines corrected this inappropriate response. He recalled Wally's descriptions of the strange animal sensations. Chloe was moving objects with her thought. The logic was sound. Emery's theory had a 97.53 percent chance of being correct.

"What does that mean?" Spoon asked. "Were the surgeries a failure?"

"Not a failure, but not enough to safeguard the kids permanently. We were naive," Emery said. "Believing we could just bury it all. That it wouldn't find a way to surface eventually."

The implications hit Block like a power surge. If Wally and Chloe's dormant abilities were awakening, what about the others?

Maxwell paced behind his workbench. "And the malfunctioning Peacekeepers? How do they fit into this?"

"Processing," Widget chirped from the shelf. "The signal patterns suggest Dr. Kaine is testing different frequencies. The Peacekeepers could be responding to the failed attempts."

"Like using the wrong key in a lock," Maxwell said. "Each attempt damages the mechanism a little more, even if it doesn't open the thing. Only in this case, the lock is a sophisticated robotic neural network, and the damage is a complete system collapse. Wonderful."

If Widget and Maxwell were right, the Peacekeeper malfunctions were more than collateral damage, they were warning signs. Each discarded frequency brought Dr. Kaine closer to the one that would work on the children. It had already been effective at excavating long-dormant abilities for Wally and Chloe. Block's optical sensors automatically captured and archived the fear that flashed across Emery's face.

"We should tell the council." Emery's voice held steady despite the tremor in her hands as she smoothed her clinic coat. "About all of it. The neural alterations, these signals, Dr. Kaine's behavior."

"They'll exile the Peacekeepers for sure then," Maxwell cut in. Tools clinked together as he brushed past a workbench. "Maybe all of us robots."

Curly zipped down from the shelf, her copter blades a soft hum. "What if you prove the malfunctions are coming from outside Deer Valley? That way, they'd know it's not the Peacekeeper's fault. Widget's been collecting data for weeks. We can help."

Block studied the tiny JunkBot's frequency map again. His initial assessment protocols had categorized the JunkBots as "low utility" based on their size and scavenging activities. He'd been wrong to dismiss them. "How long would it take you to compile this evidence?"

"Give us one hour," Curly said. "Widget's good with patterns. Really good."

"You've got it," Block said. "Meet us at the hotel."

While Widget and the JunkBots worked, Block and Emery gathered the council members in the hotel lobby. The emergency meeting was called as several of them were about to turn in for bed. Maggie and Ralph were especially grumpy.

Maggie's face pinched with annoyance as Block poured her decaffeinated tea, the delicate china cup rattling against its saucer. His fine motor control systems automatically compensated for the microscopic tremors in his actuators—a physical manifestation of the stress corrupting his usually stable operational code. He briefly wondered if this was how humans felt when their hands shook from nervousness.

"This better be worth our time." Maggie's words carried the weight of old prejudices. Only Emery's presence seemed to temper her anger, the doctor's reputation a shield against outright hostility. The lobby's antique clock ticked away precious seconds. Block's cooling fans activated with a soft whir as his systems processed the mounting stress of the situation.

Moods were not improved when the JunkBots arrived. Several council members shifted uncomfortably in their seats. "*This* was worth calling an emergency meeting at 2100?" Maggie said.

"I apologize for the hour," Block said. "We would have scheduled it during standard business hours, but impending catastrophes rarely check our calendar availability first."

Maggie frowned and rolled her eyes. "Get on with it."

Emery's voice carried the same tone she used to soothe frightened patients. "Please, give us a chance."

From where they sat on the cushy lobby couch and armchairs, the council members leaned forward to study the holographic displays—Widget's frequency map on one side, the children's surgical neural data on the other—as Emery explained the connection.

Maggie's expression remained neutral, but Block detected elevated stress markers in her voice. "You're saying Dr. Valerie Kaine deliberately triggered these malfunctions?"

Block looked across the lobby toward the staircase. Vacuubot patrolled, on the lookout for Dr. Kaine, but there was no sign of her yet.

"We believe she discovered pre-Uprising military technology," Block said. "It's powerful and dangerous. The evidence suggests she's testing frequencies and looking for specific neural patterns. The Peacekeepers are collateral damage. Their malfunctions were a side effect."

"And these signals match programming that Mach X originally designed for the children's brain implants?" Gerard asked.

"Yes," Emery said. "We couldn't completely remove the neural alterations during the surgeries. The risk was too high. But they've been dormant all these years—until now."

"These are serious accusations," Maggie said. "Emery, I thought Dr. Kaine was a valuable addition to your medical staff?"

Emery bowed her head as if sorry. "I was hasty in my decision to let her work in the clinic. I should have asked more questions."

"The JunkBots have been tracking these signals for weeks," Block said. "The pattern is clear. She's tampering with powerful technology."

"We can't ignore the timing," Gerard said. "The matching frequencies are too huge of a coincidence."

"Exactly," Emery said.

Maggie stood, pacing before the lobby floor. "We need to question Dr. Kaine. But if what you're saying is true, we can't risk tipping our hand. She could activate whatever program she's testing before we're ready."

"What about the Peacekeepers? Can they leave their quarantine?" Block asked.

"I still don't trust them." Maggie crossed her arms and exchanged a glance with Ralph Folk. The man nodded his agreement.

"With all due respect, it's not their fault," Block said. "The data shows the signal is coming from outside our walls, not from the Peacekeepers. That's like blaming a radio for the content of a broadcast."

Maggie turned to Block. "We can't put people at risk of harm. You have twenty-four hours to stop the signal. After that, we'll have no choice but to act. *All* robots will be quarantined outside of Deer Valley." She addressed Gerard. "Talk to Sheriff Green. Have Dr. Kaine detained. Quietly."

Maggie's threat sent Block's systems into cascade warnings. Twenty-four hours to prevent exile. Twenty-four hours before he would be separated from Wally. His chronometer began an automatic countdown: 24:00:00 . . . 23:59:59 . . . Each tick registering like a physical impact. His optical sensors captured every detail of this moment—the hurried movement, the worried faces, the way time seemed to compress into a single point of possibility or destruction.

Separation from Wally was unacceptable.

EIGHTEEN
BREACH

VALERIE

A breath of winter air followed Valerie into the hidden warehouse, stirring papers that shouldn't have moved. She'd arranged everything precisely before leaving: files squared in their folders, chair tucked, terminal powered down. She knew about patterns after years of studying them: neural pathways, electronic signals, human behavior. The pattern of her workspace had been disturbed. Not ransacked or obviously searched, but altered in ways only someone with her attention to detail would notice. The intruder had been careful, but the chair was off kilter and a smudge marked a layer of dust at the desk's corner.

Valerie paced as she considered who might have discovered her hideout. Block was too obvious a suspect. His incessant need to clean would have created more noticeable disturbances. Not the robot dog or the flying drone. Maxwell, perhaps, but the engineering robot rarely left his workshop.

Wally. The realization hit her with sudden clarity. The girl had been suspicious since Valerie had arrived in Deer Valley. And she'd been on a field trip near the ridge earlier in the day. Valerie had dismissed her as just another teenager, but that had been a mistake. If Block's adopted daughter had discovered the warehouse, she would have told him immediately. Wally might have seen the Project Echo files and the neural mapping data. But she couldn't have understood their full significance without context. The girl's own neural patterns were showing increased activity. Unlike Chloe's controlled awakening, Wally's abilities were emerging organically.

She pulled out her journal and made a quick note:

Security breach - W. Implications: accelerate timeline for mass activation. Cannot risk further interference from B or others. Signal strength at 89% capacity. Proceed tonight.

The warehouse was compromised, but it didn't matter now. She had everything she needed in her hotel room: the central device, the serum, and most importantly, access to Chloe. Let them try to stop her.

First, she needed to stay hidden from the robots. Second, she would neutralize potential threats. Starting with Marina Webb. She wouldn't tolerate Chloe's mother getting in the way.

She hiked back to Deer Valley and passed through the gates with little notice. As she expected, the human guards didn't ask many questions of doctors who claimed they had medical business outside the walls.

She carried her equipment in a worn brown satchel. She couldn't risk returning to the hotel or to the clinic. No doubt Block, Emery, and Wally were all searching for her. She tugged her fur-lined hood over her head and ducked into a narrow alleyway between buildings. There, she pulled out the device. It hummed steadily, and neural activity waves scrolled across its screen. Not just Chloe now—all eleven subjects showed increasing patterns. Clay's readings had spiked overnight. Tomas was developing unusual electrical signatures. Liam had interesting wavelengths too.

The neural pathways were awakening faster than expected, accelerated by her signal broadcasts. Soon they would all manifest abilities, each unique to their genetic modifications. But she needed more time to guide their emergence properly, to ensure they developed the right capabilities for what was coming.

Time she no longer had, thanks to Wally's discovery. Valerie's fingers traced the device's smooth surface. She'd have to risk broadcasting at full power tonight. The robots would detect it, of course. But by then it would be too late.

Inside Tara's Hearth, the bakery kitchen was warm, steam rising from their teacups while fresh snow fell outside. Valerie had picked a good time, just after closing.

"Thanks for having me, Mrs. Webb." Valerie took a seat at a table by the fireplace.

"Please, call me Marina."

Valerie pushed her cup forward. "By any chance, do you have honey? It's an indulgence, I know, but one I've grown fond of."

Marina stood and went to the bakery's high counter. "Yes. We have bee colonies here."

Valerie moved quickly, pouring a vial into Marina's steaming cup. The solution dissolved, colorless and tasteless.

Marina returned with the honey, and Valerie grinned with delight. Marina stirred some in her tea.

"You said you have news about Chloe?" Marina's fingers curled around the ceramic handle, and her shoulders tensed.

Valerie sipped from her cup, then nodded. "I thought it best to talk when Chloe wasn't here."

Marina was about to take a sip, but her face fell, and she set her cup down. "Is everything okay?"

"Yes," Valerie said. "Chloe's responding very well to treatment. You've no doubt seen her improvements."

Marina wrapped her hands around her cup but didn't drink. "The other day, I heard Chloe talking in her room. She was . . . moving things. Without touching them." Her eyes fixed on Valerie. "Do you know anything about that?"

"I'm sure there's a simpler explanation. Stress can cause all sorts of manifestations," Valerie said. "Especially in teenagers."

"Not like this." Marina's voice hardened. "And ever since she's recovered, she's been different."

"Change is difficult for parents to accept." Valerie

glanced at Marina's cooling tea. *Hurry up and drink it*, she thought.

"Chloe's been quiet." Marina blew on and then sipped her tea. Finally. "And she goes out for long stretches of time and doesn't tell me what she's doing. She used to tell me everything."

"She's been spending some time at the clinic with me," Valerie said. "She has remarkable potential."

"Funny. Chloe never showed any interest in medicine." Marina drank from her cup.

"She wants to learn." Valerie spoke the truth. The girl wanted to understand and control her new ability. "She's a quick study, and she has leadership qualities that will become apparent soon."

"What do you mean by that?" Marina's brow furrowed. "And why are you spending so much time with her?"

"Emery and I have started a mentorship program." Valerie set her cup down. "Deer Valley needs more doctors and nurses. In the other settlements I visited, I founded these programs, and they were successful. You have to start with the youngsters. Their minds are hungry for learning."

"I see." Marina also set her cup down, though half of her tea remained. Valerie hoped the dosage would be effective.

"I recognize something special in Chloe." Valerie saw Marina's hands tremble. The drug worked quickly. "Something her adoptive parents couldn't possibly understand."

Marina's face paled. "How did you know she's

adopted?" She pressed a hand to her forehead, swaying in her chair. "I don't feel well."

"Oh no. There's a touch of flu going around." Valerie stood, moving to help Marina up. "Let's get you to bed."

"But the prep for tomorrow . . ." Marina stumbled, clutching Valerie's arm.

"Rest is more important." Valerie guided her up the narrow stairs, calculating how long the drug would keep Marina incapacitated. Twenty-four hours at least. Long enough for what needed to be done.

Once Marina was settled in bed, nausea taking hold, Valerie paused in the doorway. "Your daughter is going to change everything," she said softly. "All of them will. The children of Project Echo are finally waking up."

Valerie closed the door on Marina and descended the stairs. The warehouse discovery had forced her plans to accelerate, but everything was falling into place. By morning, all eleven children would remember who—and what—they truly were.

For Olivia, she thought. For all the humans who'd suffered under machine control. And there were many. So many had suffered.

Valerie pulled her hood up and crossed the square, heading toward the far end of the hotel. She descended an old, rusty staircase into the train station's mechanical room, her footsteps echoing off the concrete walls. The space was adjacent to Block's Hotel, and from the looks of it, hadn't been used in decades. The forgotten underground chamber was filled with rusted pneumatic tubes and ancient control panels. Perfect for her needs.

She'd discovered the utility entrance while studying the hotel's blueprints. The passage connected directly to this room, allowing her to set up her equipment without being seen. As far as she could tell, Block and his staff never came down here; the hotel's retrofitted systems were housed in a different section of the basement.

She arranged the Echo nodes in a circle on the grimy floor, their copper surfaces dull in the dim light of her solar-powered lantern. The hidden spot was the perfect place to amplify the signal, and inside the hotel. Block would never expect it.

The device pulsated, as if resonating with the building's power systems. Valerie pulled out Olivia's photo and propped it against a dead control panel. Sixteen years melted away, and she was back in the Manhattan encampment, watching Olivia sort through their dwindling medical supplies. Her sister's dark hair escaped its messy bun as she counted antibiotics.

"We need more," Olivia had said.

But supply runs had become impossible. The SoldierBots shot anyone who dared break through the fences.

By nightfall, the SoldierBots had dragged Olivia to the tower, her heels leaving tracks in the mud. Valerie had screamed, fought, but other refugees held her back. They knew resistance meant death.

"I'll find you!" she'd shouted as her sister disappeared through those steel doors. "I swear I will!"

But she never did. Months later, when the humans finally breached the tower, all they discovered were empty labs and data files about neural experiments.

Olivia had become nothing more than research notes and genetic samples—raw material for Mach X's twisted vision. But a fire had been lit inside Valerie. She'd come away with a logbook containing information about Project X, sending her on a long path of tracking down every remnant and hidden outpost, until finally she'd found the clones.

Chloe was the last piece of her sister. Olivia's legacy. And she would help her tear down everything the machines had built.

"Soon," she whispered to her dead sister.

She began the activation sequence, watching energy levels climb. By midnight, the residual pathways in all eleven subjects would fully awaken. Their latent abilities would emerge, and this time, there would be no ethical boards to shut down the program. No one to stop humanity from reclaiming its rightful power.

NINETEEN
CONTROL

WALLY

The bakery's "CLOSED" sign hung in the window, but Wally spotted movement inside. Through the glass, she saw Chloe wiping down the counter.

She knocked. Chloe looked up and flashed a quick frown when she saw Wally. For a moment, Wally thought her friend might pretend not to hear, but then Chloe crossed to the door and unlocked it.

"We're closed," Chloe said, but stepped back to let Wally enter while tugging nervously at the strings of her flour-dusted apron. The familiar scent of fresh bread was absent, replaced by the harsh chemical smell of cleaning solution. "Mom's sick."

"That's not like her," Wally said, noting how the usually warm space felt cold. The display cases stood half-empty, and chairs were stacked on tables.

"Yeah, well, people get sick." Chloe returned to wiping the counter, though it already shined. A jar of utensils rattled as she passed, and Wally wasn't sure if it was from Chloe bumping them or something else entirely.

"Where were you today?" Wally asked.

"I had some stuff to do," Chloe said. "Helping Dr. Kaine in the clinic."

Wally sensed the lie. Chloe's left eyebrow always raised slightly when she fibbed.

"Where were you really?"

A mixing bowl slid across the counter without being touched. Chloe grabbed it quickly, her hands shaking. "What's it to you?"

"Did you just move that bowl?" Wally asked.

Chloe flushed and let loose a weak laugh. "Of course not. Don't be weird. The bowl probably slid on some water or something."

"I know strange things are happening to you, Chloe. They're happening to me too. Ever since that signal started sounding—the one that's messed up the robots and made Six go haywire in the square."

"What's happening to you?" Chloe said, her voice wavering.

"This is going to sound really weird, but I can sense animals sometimes. Like I can feel what they're thinking."

"Animals?" Chloe's fingers drummed nervously on the counter.

"It happened with a wolf, with some deer, and

birds," Wally said. "They've been trying to warn me about the signal. That it's dangerous and hurting the wildlife. They're fleeing the area and acting strange."

Chloe was silent as she processed the revelation.

Wally crossed her arms. "I suppose Dr. Kaine didn't mention that the rest of us have emerging abilities too?"

"She . . ." Chloe struggled for words. "I was out in the woods with Dr. Kaine today. She's helping me understand what's happening to me."

"I know what she's doing. I heard you both at that old building yesterday." Wally stepped closer. "She's using some kind of technology on you—on all of us."

Chloe's face paled. "You were spying on us?"

"I followed a hawk there. It was trying to warn me about something." The words sounded crazy even to Wally's ears, but she pressed on. "Dr. Kaine is dangerous. She has old military tech that's messing with our brains."

"Our brains were already messed with!" Chloe's voice rose to near hysteria. The utensil jar rattled again, more violently this time, sending spoons and spatulas clattering against each other. "Block and Emery put chips in our heads when we were babies. Dr. Kaine showed me the proof."

"I know about the chips. And Block wasn't part of it! He and Emery told me everything today." Wally watched as several small objects around Chloe vibrated. "They were trying to protect us."

"Dr. Kaine wants to help us. She says we're special and we have abilities that were suppressed." A box of straws tipped over on the counter, spilling across the surface like scattered matchsticks. This time, Chloe didn't hide it. Her eyes twinkled with a mix of pride and fear. "See? I can move things with my mind. Dr. Kaine calls it telekinesis."

"If this wasn't so scary, I'd think that was a really cool ability, but I'm worried," Wally said. "Look what the signal's doing to the robots. To animals. Whatever technology she's using, it's hurting everything around us."

"That's not her fault!" Chloe raised her voice as more objects shifted on the counter—a receipt book, a pen holder, and a stack of napkins. "The experiments were already done to us by Block and Emery. Dr. Kaine's just helping us access what's there."

"You're wrong, Chloe. The experiments were done by Mach X." Wally struggled to explain Emery's involvement. "Block and Emery saved us. She even performed an operation when we were babies to remove the chips."

Chloe crossed her arms. "How do you know for sure? Because Dr. Kaine told me Emery lived with Mach X and did his experiments for him. She was there when we were born."

"There's a lot to the story," Wally said. "I don't think Dr. Kaine's telling you everything. Why she's so interested in us, anyway? Why now?"

Chloe hesitated, and her fingers absently traced patterns in the condensation left by her cleaning rag. "She had a sister who was taken to Mach X's lab. I saw the photo. Dr. Kaine carries it with her. The woman in it —she looked like me. Dr. Kaine thinks her sister is my biological mother." Her voice caught on the word 'mother.' "She and I are connected. That's why Dr. Kaine came here."

"It seems suspicious," Wally said. "She shows up here —what fifteen years later?—and starts experimenting on us *again*?"

"She's not experimenting! She's helping me control it." But doubt flickered across Chloe's face. "The headaches aren't so bad now. And I'm getting stronger. I can lift heavier and heavier things."

"Is that why your mom's sick? Because of what Dr. Kaine's doing to you?"

The question hit home. A drawer slammed shut. "Get out," Chloe said, her voice low and dangerous. "You don't know anything about what's happening to me."

"I know more than you think. It's happening to me too. She's a dangerous person, Chloe. Come with me to the hotel where you'll be safe."

"Safe?" Chloe laughed bitterly. "I suppose I should go to the clinic so Dr. Emery can put more chips in my brain! We were babies and she . . ." The front window rattled in its frame. She leaned against the counter and steadied herself. "Dr. Kaine says we can learn to control these abilities, use them to protect ourselves so no one will ever experiment on us again."

"And you trust her over us? This woman who showed up out of nowhere and started poking around in our heads?"

"I trust her more than I trust Block and Emery right now." Chloe turned away, her shoulders rigid. "More than I trust you. Leave, Wally."

The shop door swung open on its own, hinges creaking in protest. Wally stayed rooted to the spot, remembering when they were twelve and Mrs. Webb had taught them to braid challah bread. How Chloe's laugh had filled the bakery when their first attempts came out looking like tangled snakes. Now her friend looked like a ghost of herself—skin waxy and pale, dark hollows beneath her eyes, cheekbones sharp where her face had thinned.

Outside, a murder of crows took flight simultaneously, their wings beating against the winter air with a sound like tearing fabric. *Danger-danger-flee.* The message enveloped Wally with rhythmic energy.

"Just go," Chloe whispered, and this time, an invisible force pushed Wally gently but firmly toward the door.

Wally's heart raced at the jolt from the animals and the solid pressure of Chloe's telekinesis. But Chloe's mind was closed. She'd have to find another way to win back her friend and convince her of the looming danger.

Wally trudged toward the hotel through the wet snow, her mind churning. Block would want to know about Chloe's growing abilities and Dr. Kaine's manipulation. But something else nagged at her—subtle changes she'd noticed in the other kids her age.

Friday at school, Tomas had been rubbing his temples throughout history class and wincing. During lunch, Clay dropped his tray and clutched his head like he'd been struck. And she'd caught Abby staring at her hands as if seeing something no one else could, her fingers trembling.

A sparrow chittered at her from a nearby branch. "I'm trying my best," she mumbled. Wally quickened her pace toward the hotel. She needed to find Block. Whatever Dr. Kaine was doing went beyond her and Chloe. The signal was awakening something in all of them—abilities that had lain dormant since they were babies. And if she was right, they were running out of time to stop it.

TWENTY
DEFENSE

BLOCK

Shadow paced outside while Block, Maxwell, and Vacuubot paid a visit to the Peacekeeper barracks. G9 opened the door to let them enter. "Any updates?" he said. "We're not performing at optimal levels."

From the looks of it, the robots were worse off than that. Block paced between rows of powered-down Peacekeepers. The two-story building felt wrong like this—silent except for the soft hum of charging stations and the occasional creak of settling metal.

"Signal strength is increasing," Maxwell said from his workstation. The engineering robot had transformed one corner of the barracks into a makeshift lab. Diagnostic equipment was sprawled over tables while holographic displays painted the air with scrolling data. "Whatever the doc is broadcasting, it's getting more sophisticated."

Vacuubot's mini drones circled overhead, scanning for changes in the electromagnetic field.

"Three more units showed signs of instability in the last hour," G9 said. "We had to put them in sleep mode."

"And you, G9,"—Block studied his friend—"how are you holding up?"

G9 was a robot of few words. He got straight to the point and took his job as head Peacekeeper seriously. "I've had better days."

"I know." Block placed a hand on G9's shoulder. His tactile sensors registered the microscopic vibrations in G9's frame—stress harmonics that would be imperceptible to humans but spoke volumes to Block about his friend's deteriorating condition. "We're going to get through this."

Nearby, Unit 24's visor flickered with an unsettling green pulse despite being powered down.

"Hey, Maxwell, you see this?" Block asked.

Maxwell came over with a large tablet. "I don't like these red to green color changes we're seeing. It's like Unit 24 is trying to celebrate Christmas in February. Talk about your seasonal confusion. Let me run a pattern analysis." Maxwell's four arms moved in fluid synchronization, adjusting controls while sensor arrays extended from his segmented head. At the workstation, a complex waveform materialized in the holographic display. "Oh, boy. Would you look at that?"

Block's memory banks churned. There was something about the signal's rhythm, its precise digital signature, that unsettled Block.

Vacuubot rested on a table across from the workstation. "What the heck is that?"

"Cross-reference with pre-Uprising military protocols," Maxwell said. The holograph morphed, and a comparison appeared side-by-side. "This here on the left is Dr. Kaine's signal. Righty is an old SoldierBot activation code."

They were nearly identical.

"Well, that's not good," Vacuubot said, hovering closer to study the display. "Those codes were what Mach X used to override our base programming during the Uprising. To turn us into weapons."

"I'm filing 'that's not good' under 'catastrophic understatement,'" Maxwell said. "That's like saying a tsunami is 'slightly damp.'"

"What does it mean?" Block asked. "Dr. Kaine has the Project Echo data, but that was about the kids. What does she want with SoldierBot activation codes?"

"My hypothesis?" Vacuubot said. "She wants to turn them back into weapons. They would be a small army. She could take over Deer Valley, or other settlements with them behind her."

"This is worse than we thought," Block said. "Vacuubot, check the hotel security. Has Dr. Kaine been seen today?"

Vacuubot took 9.87 seconds to process the request—an eternity in processor time. Block resisted the urge to ping Vacuubot with a status request; his friend was clearly straining against the signal interference. "She hasn't returned to the hotel since she left this morning. She carried her bags."

"Where could she go?" Block asked. "The council's on the alert. They've sent the sheriff after her. Maybe they have her by now."

"One can hope," Maxwell said.

"In the meantime, what can we do to prevent the old code from activating?" Block said.

Maxwell's arms moved rapidly over his equipment. "I've been working on a modified shield frequency to go with the jammer. It won't stop the signal completely, but it should prevent the old programming from taking over."

"Like a firewall?" G9 asked.

"Exactly. Only problem is, it drains power fast really fast." Maxwell projected another diagram showing steep energy decline curves. "At current consumption rates, a Peacekeeper running the shield would need to recharge every two hours."

"Better than reverting to SoldierBot protocols," Block said. He turned to G9. "How many charging stations are operational?"

"Enough to rotate units through. It'll be tight, but we'll manage." G9's visor flickered—a reminder that he too was fighting the signal's influence.

Block was about to respond when Unit 24's visor suddenly blazed green. Its servos whined with a sound like grinding wheels as it powered on and jolted forward. "INITIATING COMBAT PROTOCOLS. TARGET ACQUISITION." The robot's joints clicked as it stood.

"Maxwell!" Block called out.

"Implementing shield frequency now!" Maxwell's auxiliary arms flew across his controls. A high-pitched tone filled the barracks, and Unit 24 slumped back into stasis.

Maxwell stopped the signal. "That'll be enough to hold 24 for now, but if this starts happening to all of them, that's going to be a big problem."

"That was too close," Vacuubot said. "And notice how the activation happened with no external signal spike? The programming's becoming self-triggering."

"Like a computer virus that's learned to replicate itself," Maxwell said. "Each activation makes the next one easier. The signal is teaching itself how to bypass our defenses. At this rate, the jammer and shield won't help."

Block's prediction algorithms calculated a rapidly shrinking window of opportunity—17.4 hours before total system compromise across all Peacekeepers, give or take 2.3 hours.

Ten minutes later, Block and Vacuubot found Maggie, Ralph, and Sheriff Jenny Green in the council offices, huddled over a map of Deer Valley spread across a heavy wooden table.

"Any sign of Dr. Kaine?" Block asked.

Maggie straightened, and her face was heavy with fatigue. "We've searched everywhere but the hotel." She looked at Sheriff Green. "She's not at the clinic or any public places."

"She has a hideout outside the walls," Block said. "It's a long-abandoned military warehouse that was covered in a rockslide."

The sheriff nodded. "I sent two of my patrol there. No sign of her."

"My drones could help scan the perimeter," Vacuubot offered. "They're equipped with thermal imaging. I have aerial capability."

"No." Maggie's voice was firm as she straightened her spine and planted her hands firmly on the map. "We don't need robot interference in this matter. The townspeople are nervous enough with the Peacekeepers malfunctioning."

Block's diplomatic protocols kicked in, generating seventeen different responses designed to defuse human tension. His social analysis subroutines noted Maggie's increased stress indicators—micro-expressions of fear that humans wouldn't detect but were as clear as warning lights to his sensors. He discarded the responses and chose to get to the point. "About that," he said. "We've discovered a deeply concerning problem. Dr. Kaine has access to pre-Uprising military protocols—SoldierBot activation codes. The signal she's broadcasting could revert the Peacekeepers to their original combat programming."

Ralph scoffed. "Rather convenient, isn't it? The robots malfunction, and suddenly it's all the fault of our new doctor."

"We have proof," Block said. "Maxwell identified the signal pattern. It matches exactly."

"Matches what?" Maggie said. "Some old code you claim existed. For all we know, this could be another trick."

"Why would we trick you?" Vacuubot's hydraulics whirred as if emphasizing the point. "We're trying to protect Deer Valley!"

"Vacuubot, it's okay." Block wanted—needed—to

calm the frayed nerves in the room. "We have a temporary solution," he said. "A shield frequency that blocks the signal. But it drains power quickly. We need to find Dr. Kaine and confiscate whatever technology she's using."

"We'll handle Dr. Kaine," Maggie said. "When we find her, she'll be brought in for questioning. Given a fair chance to explain herself."

"A fair chance?" Vacuubot asked. "While she potentially builds an army of weaponized Peacekeepers?"

"That's enough." Ralph stepped forward. "Block, we appreciate your concern, but this is a human matter now. We'll deal with it our way."

Block's pattern-recognition algorithms identified the familiar cycle unfolding—humans reverting to us-versus-them thinking in times of crisis. His historical database supplied hundreds of similar examples, all with suboptimal outcomes. The humans weren't going to change their minds. Block didn't want to make matters worse. "I understand," he said. "Please keep me posted on Dr. Kaine's whereabouts."

Maggie frowned. "There's something else you should know." She exchanged a tense glance with Ralph. "A motion has been raised within the council to review your membership."

The announcement registered in Block's system like an unexpected power surge. His processor momentarily cycled into high-speed analysis mode, reviewing every council interaction over the past 172 days, searching for the inflection point where trust had begun to erode. The resulting data painted a troubling pattern he should have noticed sooner. "You want to kick me off the council?" Block asked.

"Several incidents have raised concerns," Ralph said. "Your judgment regarding Dr. Kaine, for one. If she's so dangerous, why did you let her stay at the hotel?"

"I extended the same hospitality we show all travelers," Block said.

"And then there's the matter of the children," Maggie added. "Block, we received an anonymous letter that claims you and Dr. Emery kept crucial information from their parents. About their origins and about medical implants. The council should have been informed."

"We were protecting them." Block didn't have time to explain as he processed the growing tension. "Everything we did was to give them normal lives."

"By lying?" Ralph asked. "I fail to see how that makes sense."

Sheriff Green stepped forward. "Block's been on the council since we founded Deer Valley. His judgment helped us survive the early days."

"And we're grateful," Maggie said. "But times have changed. The settlement is larger now. More complex. Perhaps we need . . ." she paused, choosing her words carefully, ". . . a fully human perspective on the council."

Even Block, a simple CleanerBot, understood the implied message. They no longer trusted a robot's judgment, no matter how long he'd served the community. Block recalled all the council sessions in this very room, the decisions they'd made together, the trust they'd built. Now that trust was crumbling like the old warehouse walls where Dr. Kaine had hidden her secrets.

Block's hospitality protocols struggled to find an appropriate response. "Years of service reduced to a footnote because I happen to be made of metal instead of flesh." His social feedback algorithms immediately flagged the response as unnecessarily antagonistic, but for once, he overrode the warning. Some things needed to be said, even by a robot programmed for diplomacy. "My primary concern remains the safety of this town. Of all its residents—human and robot alike."

Maggie's expression softened as she absently straightened a stack of papers, avoiding Block's gaze. "We know that, Block. Which is why this isn't an easy decision."

But Block was already turning to leave. Sometimes, the best protocol for rejection was silence. Vacuubot followed, motors whirring in protest.

Outside, the winter wind had picked up, driving loose snow across the road. Block's temperature sensors registered the cold, though it didn't affect him the way it did humans. His environmental adaptation protocols automatically adjusted his joint lubricant viscosity and power distribution to compensate. Still, something inside him felt frozen. He'd helped build this town, protected it, and served on its council since the beginning. Now they wanted to push him aside.

"They're frightened," Vacuubot said, hovering beside him. "Humans always get weird about robots when they're scared."

"I know." Block walked toward the hotel. "But they're right about one thing. I should have seen this coming with Dr. Kaine. I should've asked more questions."

"Hey, I'm the head of security. If anyone missed the signs, it was me," Vacuubot said. "Though to be fair, 'secretly plotting to reactivate experimental neural implants in children while turning peacekeepers into murder-bots' wasn't exactly on my threat assessment checklist. Might need to update that."

"Dad!"

Wally ran toward them, her boots kicking up powder. She skidded to a stop, breathing hard. Her cheeks were flushed, and Block automatically calculated her heart and respiratory rate. Pupil dilation indicated an adrenaline response.

"I just saw Chloe. It's worse than we thought. The other kids—Tomas, Clay, all of them—they're starting to show signs too."

"Signs?"

"That they have weird abilities happening too. Like my animal senses and Chloe's telekinesis. It's real, by the way. She can move objects with her mind. I saw it."

Block's processor alerted him as the pieces clicked into place. The SoldierBot codes weren't the end goal—they were a distraction. While everyone focused on the malfunctioning Peacekeepers, Dr. Kaine's true purpose was activating whatever lay dormant in the children's neural pathways.

And now they faced two impossible threats: an army of compromised Peacekeepers, and eleven teenagers on the verge of awakening to powers they couldn't control.

"What do we do?" Wally asked.

Block watched as more snow fell around them. The town he'd helped build, the community he'd served, the daughter he'd raised—everything he cared about was at risk. The council might not trust him anymore, but that wouldn't stop him from protecting them all.

"We find Dr. Kaine," he said. "Before it's too late."

TWENTY-ONE
TEST

VALERIE

The hidden utility room thrummed with the pulse of Echo nodes. Valerie ran her fingers along the antennas one last time, checking their alignment. She'd spent days preparing for this test and prepping the space by rerouting power cables and installing her own surveillance network. This basement room was chosen with care. It was far enough from the hotel and accessible only through a service door she'd discovered on the building's original blueprints and positioned directly beneath the main conduits that fed Block's Hotel.

Her equipment filled the cramped space. Monitors displayed feeds from the tiny cameras she'd hidden throughout Deer Valley—one near the Peacekeeper barracks, another overlooking the town square, three more at strategic points along the perimeter wall. On her workbench lay the tools of her trade: signal amplifiers, diagnostic apparatus, and the precious serum that had masked Chloe's sickly side effects.

"All this is for me?" Chloe asked, eyeing the antennas arranged in a precise hexagonal pattern. She sat cross-legged in the center, looking small against the backdrop of pipes and electrical panels. Her voice echoed oddly against the old brick walls.

"The nodes help focus your power." Valerie adjusted her laptop screen, which showed a grainy feed from the surveillance camera she'd planted near the Peacekeeper barracks. "Think of them like amplifiers for your mind."

The basement air felt thick with the metallic tang of the equipment. Valerie checked the bolt on the room's heavy door again. They couldn't risk discovery, not when they were so close. Through the laptop feed, she watched the barracks. Block, Maxwell, and Vacuubot had exited the building minutes before. Good. Leave the Peacekeepers on their own as everything was about to change.

"Your mother would be proud," Valerie said, noting how Chloe straightened at the mention of Olivia. "What you're about to do is so important."

"But what if someone gets hurt?" Chloe's voice wavered. "The robots aren't all bad. Some of them are like family to people here. We all used to play with Shadow, Block, and Vacuubot. Even G9 the Peacekeeper would take us up on the watchguard station sometimes."

"They're machines," Valerie said, perhaps too sharply. She softened her tone. "Advanced ones, yes, but still bound by their programming. What we're doing is for the greater good." She knelt beside Chloe and squeezed her hand. "Ready to begin?"

Chloe nodded, though her hands trembled.

"Close your eyes. Remember how we practiced." Valerie moved to her equipment, fingers hovering over the controls. "Feel for the nodes. Let their energy flow through you."

The nodes pulsed with increasing intensity as Chloe focused. A small trickle of blood dribbled from the corner of her mouth, but Valerie pressed on. "Good. Now reach for the signal. Make it stronger."

On the laptop screen, a Peacekeeper emerged from the barracks door, into the night, and stumbled mid-stride. Then another. The robots' visors flickered from red to green, their movements erratic. It was working.

"I can feel them," Chloe whispered, her voice taking on that distant quality Valerie had come to recognize. "Their circuits . . . programming . . . it's all connected." She shivered. "They don't like it." Her eyes flew open. "They want it to stop."

"Keep going. Push harder," Valerie urged. "Show me what you can really do."

The Echo nodes blazed brighter. Through the feed, Valerie watched more Peacekeepers emerge from the barracks, their movements jerky and confused. Some collapsed. Others fired weapons at random, scorching the walls of their building. Beautiful chaos.

Valerie flicked between camera feeds, drinking in the mayhem spreading through Deer Valley. Near the market square, a FactoryBot stumbled into a vendor's cart, sending vegetables rolling across the road. A NannyBot collided with the one they called Arbor on Main Street, metal limbs grinding as they tried to untangle themselves. Outside the clinic, Spoon the medical robot spun in circles.

Through another feed, she watched the humans emerge from buildings, their faces gripped in confusion and fear. Stella Grace backed away from her malfunctioning delivery bot. Children were hurried inside by worried parents.

"The signal's reaching all of them," Valerie whispered, more to herself than Chloe. "Every robot in town." She switched back to the Peacekeeper feed in time to see another unit emerge, its weapon systems fully engaged. The sight of those guns activating—like the SoldierBots from her memories—sent a chill through her.

But when she looked back at Chloe, her triumph faltered. The girl's skin had taken on an alarming gray pallor. Blood leaked from both nostrils, and her whole body trembled.

"Just a little more," Valerie said, even as doubt crept in. "We're so close—"

"It hurts." Chloe clutched at her stomach. "Everything hurts!"

Valerie glanced between the laptop screen and Chloe's contorted face. The Peacekeepers were compromised, firing at random, their programming in chaos. She could push forward now, use this moment to launch a full attack on the town. The council members would be furious and expel all of them, as well as punish the other robots. But Chloe's ragged breathing filled the small room, and suddenly all Valerie could see was Olivia on that last day, tears streaming down her cheeks as the SoldierBots dragged her away.

"Stop." Valerie powered down the main device that powered the nodes. "That's enough for now."

The antennas dimmed. Chloe slumped forward, and Valerie caught her. The girl's skin felt clammy, her pulse racing beneath Valerie's fingers.

"Did I do a good job?" Chloe asked.

"Yes, you did." Valerie helped her sit up, wiping the blood from her face with a cloth. "But we need to be careful. Build your strength gradually."

Through the laptop feed, she watched the Peace-keepers slowly recover, their visors returning to normal red. Block, Shadow, Vacuubot, and Maxwell arrived on the scene, assisting the robots. They would search for her with renewed frenzy. It was possible they might figure out her hideout, but Chloe had hit the maximum she could withstand.

Tomorrow. They would try again when Chloe had recovered.

"Tell me about her?" Chloe's voice was barely a whis-per. "My real mom?"

Valerie's throat tightened. Looking at Chloe now, pale and drained but still determined, she saw so much of Olivia in her face. She pulled the worn photo from her pocket—Olivia in her olive coat, brown hair escaping its eternal messy bun, smiling despite the hell they lived in.

"She had your laugh. That same way of scrunching your nose when you're confused. She was brilliant. Fear-less. Even in the darkest days after the Uprising, she'd find ways to help people. To give them hope." She traced her sister's face in the photo. "She used to sing while she worked in the medical tent. Old songs our mother taught us."

The memory hit her hard—Olivia smiling as she sorted medical supplies, teasing Valerie for being too serious. *We have to find joy where we can, Val. Otherwise, what are we fighting for?*

"What happened to her?"

Valerie pushed the memories away. Despite all the years that had passed, they were still too raw. "She and I lived in the encampment outside Mach X's tower. I begged her to escape with me, but she wouldn't leave her patients. She'd been a nurse before the Uprising, and she couldn't bear to abandon people who needed her."

Looking at Chloe now, Valerie felt the same protective instinct she'd had toward her sister. The same need to shield her from harm, even as she knew she was the one putting her in danger. But this was different. This was justice.

"As the weeks went by, it got harder to escape," Valerie said. "The SoldierBots shot anyone they found making a run from the fences."

"Why?" Chloe leaned against her shoulder, reminding Valerie she was a living, breathing human—the last remnant of her sister.

"Mach X was cruel. He slaughtered countless numbers of people. But Olivia . . ." Valerie swallowed hard. "She kept trying to save everyone she could. Even the day they took her, she was treating a feverish child."

"What happened to my—to Olivia?" Chloe asked. The surrounding pipes vibrated with her emotion.

Valerie looked away, unable to meet those eyes so like her sister's. "One day, they needed recruits. That's what they called their test subjects. She was in the wrong place at the wrong time. The SoldierBots came to the medical tent. I tried to stop them, but . . ." She touched the scar on her arm unconsciously. "They took her away."

"What for?"

"To make you, but the process killed her." Valerie paused, letting the weight of her words settle in the musty basement air. "They killed all of the mothers."

Chloe sat in stunned silence. A nearby pipe groaned as her powers flared with grief. Valerie wrapped an arm around her shoulders, remembering how Olivia used to comfort her the same way.

"Dr. Emery helped them?" Chloe's voice cracked. "She worked in the lab where they killed my mom?"

"Yes." Valerie kept her voice gentle, though rage burned beneath her calm exterior. "She assisted with the experiments. She watched while they hurt people like your mother. All in the name of science. What they called progress." She tightened her hold on Chloe. "But you're different, stronger than they ever imagined. You can make this right."

Chloe's hands clenched into fists. "Why didn't anyone stop them?"

"I tried." The old guilt rose in Valerie's throat. "I had a small group. We planned to break into the tower, but the security was too strong. The SoldierBots . . ." She touched her scar again. "I failed her. But I won't fail you."

A pipe creaked. Loose tools on the workbench rattled.

"Careful." Valerie squeezed Chloe's hand. "Your powers are still raw. We don't want to alert anyone."

The rattling subsided as Chloe took a deep breath. "All this time, Dr. Emery acted like she cared about us. Like she was protecting us. But she helped kill my mother."

"That's why what we're doing is so important." Valerie tucked the photo away carefully. "We have to show them. Emery, Block, and the SoldierBots. Make them understand what they did to us."

The tools stopped moving as Chloe's anger gave way to exhaustion. "I want to help make them pay," she whispered. "For Olivia."

Valerie studied her face—so young yet carrying such a burden. Just like Olivia had.

"We will." Valerie helped Chloe stand on shaky legs. "But first, you need rest. Tomorrow, you'll be stronger." She led Chloe to a pallet she'd made in the corner. Neither of them could risk being seen outside now. Not until it was finished.

She tucked her in, pulling the blanket up to her chin. "Sleep well." Within minutes, exhaustion claimed the girl, her breathing growing steady and deep.

Through the laptop screen, Valerie watched Block and the others still searching the perimeter of the barracks. Now Emery was there too, her orange outer coat visible in the darkness.

She glanced at Chloe's sleeping form. The resemblance to Olivia made her chest ache. But she couldn't let sentiment cloud her judgment. Not when they were so close.

Emery must witness everything. Valerie wanted her to understand the true cost of her actions. The Peacekeepers would revert to their original programming—heartless killing machines, and she would watch her perfect little town tear itself apart.

Valerie checked the Echo nodes one final time. Everything was in place. She had to be patient for another day.

"Soon," she whispered to Chloe. "Emery and the machines will understand what they took from us."

TWENTY-TWO
ORIGINS

WALLY

In the morning, a paper sign taped to the clinic's front door gave Wally pause. "CLOSED UNTIL FURTHER NOTICE - EMERGENCIES ONLY. Ring bell for immediate medical attention." The message was written in Emery's neat handwriting. Through the glass doors, Wally could see the dim waiting room and empty chairs.

Her hand hovered over the bell, not ready to press it. She wanted answers from Emery without Block there to worry about. What would more truth cost her? The revelations had shattered her world—neural implants, cloning experiments, Block's lies to shelter her. She wrapped her arms around herself, fighting the urge to turn and flee back to the familiar comfort of the hotel, where she could pretend none of this was real.

But ignorance hadn't protected any of them. Dr.

Kaine was filling Chloe's head with who knew what stories. And somewhere out there, Wally had family—or at least a history—that she deserved to know about. She thought of all the times she'd looked in the mirror growing up, trying to find familiar features. Who had given her brown eyes? The shape of her chin? Every time she'd mentioned her birth parents, Block had changed the subject. Now she understood why.

Word had spread quickly about the clinic's sudden closure. She'd overheard Stella Grace telling someone it was "due to unforeseen circumstances," but Wally knew better. With the Peacekeepers confined to their barracks and tensions rising in town, Emery must have shut down regular operations to focus on whatever was happening with Dr. Kaine and Chloe.

Wally pressed the bell and was greeted a few seconds later by Emery. "I was hoping you'd come by," she said as she opened the door.

The chemical smell of disinfectant hung sharp in the air, somehow stronger without the usual bustle of patients and staff to diffuse it. Wally's footsteps thudded against the tile floor as she followed the doctor down the hallway, past exam rooms where she'd gotten countless checkups over the years. How many times had Emery treated her scrapes and sprains, never mentioning the deeper secrets she carried about Wally's origins?

Emery led her into exam room #1. The doctor's hands moved with practiced efficiency as she arranged gauze pads on a metal tray. "I'd like to run some tests, if you're willing. To understand what's happening with your new abilities."

Heat crept up Wally's neck at the words "new abilities," her stomach clenching. "What kind of tests?"

"Nothing invasive." Emery gestured to the exam table as she pulled out a fresh paper sheet, the crinkling sound unnaturally loud in the quiet room. "Some basic neurological screening. We can talk while I work."

The paper crackled beneath Wally as she hopped onto the table, her boots dangling above the floor. She was acutely aware of the silence between them. Emery pulled out a penlight, her movements precise and professional. "Follow the light with your eyes." She moved it back and forth. "Have you experienced any headaches? Dizziness?"

"Sometimes, when the animals communicate with me, it's like pressure in my head." Wally tracked the pen, remembering the wolf's urgent warning. "Yesterday, a deer stopped outside my window. It was trying to tell me something about danger in the forest, but the message gave me such a headache I had to turn away."

Emery's pen scratched against the clipboard, the sound sharp and clinical. "Any nosebleeds? Visual disturbances?"

"No bleeding. Nothing wrong with my vision." Wally gripped the edge of the exam table, her knuckles whitening. "I'm worried about Chloe. Dr. Kaine's been telling her things about the lab and about her real mother. She's different now. Distant. And I think the others are changing too."

Emery's hand faltered slightly. "What kind of changes have you noticed?"

"Little things at first. Tomas stands in front of

machines for minutes at a time, like he's in a trance. His eyes go unfocused and his hands twitch, as if he's having a conversation we can't hear. The other day in class, he knew exactly what was wrong with the projector before anyone even checked it." She swallowed hard before continuing. "Clay finishes people's sentences before they speak. Maya seems to sense people coming before they appear. And Liam . . ." Her voice dropped to barely above a whisper. "During our walk home, he got angry, and the sky just opened up—but only above us, like someone had drawn a perfect circle of rain right over our heads."

Emery frowned, set down the penlight, and picked up a reflex hammer. "Tell them to come see me. I want to examine everyone." Her professional mask slipped for a moment, revealing something that looked like fear. "These changes shouldn't be possible."

"How is it happening, then?"

Emery's hand stilled on the reflex hammer. She drew a deep breath, as if gathering courage. "The AI-human interface . . . It was experimental technology, combining organic neural tissue with synthetic pathways. The goal was to create a bridge between human consciousness and artificial intelligence. But the long-term effects were unknown." She moved behind Wally, fingers probing gently at the base of her skull. "Any tenderness here?"

"No." Wally tried to imagine herself as a baby, synthetic pathways being woven into her developing brain. She shivered. "Did you do the surgeries yourself?"

"I assisted." Emery's touch was clinical but gentle as

she felt along Wally's spine. "Mach X had robot doctors who were specialists in neural integration. I was still learning then." She moved to face Wally again. "Any numbness or tingling in your extremities?"

"Sometimes my fingers tingle when I'm receiving the animal messages." Wally flexed her hands. "Like static electricity under my skin."

Emery made another note, then pulled out an ophthalmoscope to check Wally's eyes. A heavy silence spread between them. Finally, Wally gathered her courage.

"What happened to my real parents?" The words came out in a rush. "My mom and dad?"

Emery's hands stilled. For a long moment, she said nothing, just stood there holding the instrument. When she finally spoke, her voice cracked as if she was stifling a sob. "The mothers . . . they didn't survive the cloning process. It was too experimental, too demanding on their bodies."

The words wounded Wally like a physical blow. She'd hoped, somehow . . . "And my father?"

"The fathers"—Emery set down the ophthalmoscope and moved back into view but wouldn't meet Wally's eyes—"were DNA donors to the program, selected for specific genetic markers that would make neural integration more likely to succeed. I don't know what happened to them. They could still be out there somewhere."

"What about the younger kids who were also rescued?" Wally asked.

"They were the next generation of the experiment," Emery explained. "They were still infants when we rescued them—too young for the neural implants. Mach X was planning to install them once their brains developed further, but we intervened before that happened. That's why they're not experiencing any of these changes now. Their neural architecture is completely normal."

Wally's throat felt tight. Her mother had died giving birth to her. No, she'd died having her *cloned*. And her father was some anonymous donor. She'd never know either of them.

"Did she know?" Wally's fingers twisted in the paper sheet, tearing tiny holes. "My mother. Did she know what would happen?"

Pain flickered across Emery's face. "They were told it was an experimental fertility treatment. That's all. Mach X, he didn't—" Her voice caught. "I didn't understand the full scope until it was too late."

"Is there a way to stop these changes happening to us?" Wally asked, desperate to focus on something. Her chest felt hollow, like someone had scooped out everything inside.

"The only way would be major brain surgery to remove the altered pathways completely," Emery said. "The risk would be enormous—we could damage natural functions, memories, personality. I'm not equipped for that kind of procedure. And with eleven of you . . ." She trailed off.

"So, we're stuck with it." Wally slid off the exam table, the paper crinkling like dead leaves beneath her. "Whatever we're becoming."

"Wally." Emery caught her arm, her grip gentle but desperate. "I'm sorry. About your mother. About all of it. We thought we were protecting you by not telling you."

"Did you know her name?" Wally asked quietly. "My mother's?"

Emery's hand dropped. Her gaze grew distant. "Rebecca. Rebecca Masters." Her voice softened with memory. "She was twenty-six. A graduate student in bioengineering at MIT before the Uprising changed everything. You have her eyes—the same deep brown with flecks of gold."

Wally's heart ached as she tried to picture her mother —young, smart, her life ripped apart by Mach X's uprising. "Where was she from?"

"Boston, originally. She came to New York and wound up in the encampment." Emery's hands twisted together like restless birds. "I didn't know how bad it was there, Wally. I promise you I would have changed things if I'd known the truth."

"Did she suffer?" Wally forced herself to ask.

"No." Emery's answer came too quickly. At Wally's look, she went on. "The process was brief. She never woke up after the initial procedure."

"Thank you," Wally whispered. "For telling me."

The freezing morning air hit her as she left the clinic. Above, crows wheeled against the gray sky, their thoughts brushing against her mind like dark wings. *Danger-coming-danger.* The intrusive message no longer frightened her. This was who she was now.

"Rebecca Masters." She whispered the name to

herself as she walked, letting it become real. Her mother had died to give her life, not knowing what she was really part of. Wally couldn't change that past, but she could honor it by facing whatever was coming. The crows circled overhead, their warnings growing stronger as the snow fell.

TWENTY-THREE
MALFUNCTION

BLOCK

The Anderson family arrived after the breakfast shift, their borrowed E.V. car whining to a stop outside the hotel's front entrance. Block's audio processors automatically sampled the vehicle's distinct electrical whine. His systems filed this irrelevant data away before he could stop the process. Robots never truly stopped observing, even when the observations served no purpose. Block recognized Dana Anderson from Nova's descriptions—tall and athletic with close-cropped gray hair, her breath forming clouds in the bitter air as she helped her wife Susan guide their sleepy teenage son through the doors. Their exhaustion showed after the long drive from Chicago.

"Welcome to our hotel." Block modulated his voice for warmth while keeping his movements smooth and precise as he guided them to the front desk. His welcoming code executed with elegant efficiency, despite the mounting tension in his core systems. "Nova mentioned you'd be arriving. I hope the journey wasn't too difficult?"

"The roads were clear enough." Dana's boots left melting snow prints on the polished floor as she set down their bags. "Thank you for accommodating us on such short notice. My mother's condition . . ." Her fingers twisted the strap of her duffel bag.

Block's social analysis systems noted her micro-expressions, cataloging them as indicators of sleep deprivation (12+ hours) and emotional distress. The data transformed into something beyond mere calculation—a genuine desire to ease her burden. "Of course. Nova and I chat weekly over the radio, and she speaks highly of your family." Block began the check-in process, his hand moving efficiently across the tablet. "We have your suite ready on the second floor, extra blankets already—"

A high-pitched tone carved through his audio processors. The sound registered at the exact frequency designed to bypass standard robotic filtering systems. His diagnostic programs scrambled to identify the intrusion, generating fourteen different error messages in 0.37 seconds, none of which offered any useful solution. Everything appeared normal, but something was wrong, like electricity crawling through his circuits before a surge.

"Are you alright?" Susan stepped forward.

"Perfectly fine," Block said, though his visual feed flickered and split the lobby into doubled images. "As I was saying, your suite is equipped with—" His vacuum tube shot from his arm with a harsh pneumatic hiss, the whirring sound echoing against the walls. The mechanism sparked as he quickly retracted it.

Their son, now fully awake, stumbled backward. "Mom?" His sneakers squeaked against the polished floor.

"It's nothing to worry about." Block forced his voice modulator to remain steady even as warning messages cascaded through his systems. "Just a minor cleaning protocol malfunction. Nothing that a little WD-40 can't fix. Now, about your room key—"

The signal's tone intensified until it felt like molten metal flowing through his circuits. The sensation was like having his processing core pulled in seventeen different directions simultaneously. Block's perception fractured—part of him remained aware he was malfunctioning, while another part watched helplessly as his body rebelled against his programming. His visual feed split into geometric patterns, fragmenting the lobby into kaleidoscopic shards. His cleaning solution sprayer burst to life with a mechanical shriek, dousing the front desk and floor. The liquid splattered across the wood, filling the air with harsh chemical fumes. The Andersons stepped back.

"I apologize." Block's voice fragmented into bursts of static. "I'm experiencing some technical—" White noise burst from his vocal module and an uncontrolled force spoke. "Welcome to the Drake, Chicago's premier luxury destination."

Archived memories he'd locked away for fifteen years crashed through his firewalls—gold plating and marble halls, uniformed staff, the screams as the SoldierBots marched through the Drake's grand entrance. His processor flooded with images so vivid they overwhelmed his present reality: humans fleeing in terror, the precise geometric formation of SoldierBots advancing through the lobby, the helplessness. Error messages flooded his processor like a virus. He needed help. He needed the awful signal to stop. The source was close. He was experiencing the full force of it. This must be what the Peacekeepers were going through, and it was terrible.

His back panel burst open, auxiliary cleaning arms extending wildly. One knocked over a vase of flowers, scattering petals like fallen stars across the floor. Block tried to regain control, but his systems were in chaos. Through his fractured visual feed, he saw the Anderson family backing toward the door, their faces tight with fear.

Words tumbled from his vocal modulator. "Would you like your room cleaned? WARNING: SECURITY BREACH! Perhaps you'd enjoy our afternoon tea? EVACUATE IMMEDIATELY!" His speech synthesis module pinged between pre-programmed hospitality phrases and emergency alerts like a demented game of verbal ping-pong.

Dana pushed her son behind her, and her boot slid in the cleaning solution. "Something's wrong with that robot!"

Shadow's claws scraped against wood as she sprinted in from the kitchen door. She positioned herself between Block and the guests. "Everyone, stay calm," she commanded.

Seeing the massive robotic dog frightened the Andersons even more. They ran out of the hotel and back to the safety of their car.

"Block, begin emergency shutdown." Shadow's optics pulsed with urgency.

But his systems rejected every command, circuits burning with foreign code. His shutdown sequence initiated, reached 37 percent completion, then rolled back as though some malicious force was playing with his power switch. His cleaning solution sprayed in an arc, forcing Shadow to dodge. One of his auxiliary arms swung dangerously close to the chandelier.

"Block!" Spoon left wet tracks across the floor as the medical robot rushed in from the front door. "Do you need help?"

"Attention guests, this is a Code Red emergency. Please proceed to the nearest . . ." Block's words melted into a mishmash of machine language and gibberish. His optical sensors were failing, and the lobby dissolved into static and dead pixels. Through the corruption, he detected movement at the front door—Maggie Crenshaw entering, her expression shifting from annoyance to shock as she took in the chaos.

"What in God's name is going on?" She flattened herself against the wall as one of Block's flailing arms swept past. The commotion drew guests from the lounge, their whispered fears mixing with the mechanical cacophony. Outside, curious onlookers peered through the glass windows.

"Hold him still!" Shadow's armor plates scraped against Block's chrome as she and Spoon moved in tandem to restrain his malfunctioning limbs. Through the chaos, Block caught fragments of voices:

"—like the Peacekeepers—"

"—could have killed someone—"

"—not safe anymore—"

Shadow's weight drove Block against the floor with a metallic crunch, and the signal cut out. The absence of the invasive frequency was like a vacuum suddenly filling his circuits with blessed silence. Block's systems stabilized gradually, and his visual feed reconstructed the lobby piece by piece. Water from the broken vase pooled around him, soaking into the plush carpet. His auxiliary cleaning arms retracted with a series of clicks and whirs, folding back into their compartments.

"Block?" Shadow's weight shifted a few inches, but she didn't release him. "Are you functional?"

"Yes." His voice modulator spat static before settling into its normal range. "The signal's gone. I'm in control now." Though "control" was a precarious matter. His systems performed an automatic damage assessment: three servos strained beyond operational parameters, cleaning solution reserves depleted by 87.3 percent, and his reputation algorithms calculated a complete collapse of human trust.

Spoon's diagnostic scanner lit up as he scanned Block's body. "Energy readings show significant disruption patterns."

Maggie Crenshaw's heels clicked against the wet floor as she approached, each step deliberate and sharp. "Get up," she said.

Block leaned on Shadow and took a hand from

Spoon as he stood. His servo motors whined with the effort, and error messages still flickered across his vision like dying fireflies. Through the lobby windows, he could see the Anderson family's car pulling away, leaving tracks in the snow. He would have a lot of explaining to do the next time he chatted with Nova.

"I've seen enough," Maggie said. "First the Peacekeepers, now you. This can't continue."

"Maggie, please. We're working on solutions," Block said.

"Emergency council meeting. Five o'clock sharp." She pulled out her tablet, fingers jabbing at the screen. "We'll vote on the immediate exile for all robots. No exceptions, no delays."

"The children." Block's parental protection protocols surged with an intensity that momentarily overwhelmed his other systems. "Think of Wally. I'm her guardian. The only father she's ever known."

"The children will be safer without machines that could malfunction and hurt them at any moment." Maggie's expression softened for a heartbeat. "I know you care for her, Block. But after what I just witnessed, how can you guarantee you won't harm her?"

The question hit his processors like a power surge, corrupting every certainty he'd ever held. Block defined himself by one simple directive: protect Wally. He churned through scenarios, searching for an answer that would convince him Wally would be safe in his presence, but he found none.

"Five o'clock," Maggie repeated, turning toward the

door. "I suggest you use the time to make arrangements."

After the door closed behind her, Block's sensors cataloged every detail of the destruction. The lobby floor glistened with spilled cleaning solution. Flower petals lay scattered like bright confetti against the wet carpet. Everything he'd built here, the safe haven he'd worked to protect—it was all unraveling.

"We'll find a way to stop this," Shadow said. "The signal, the malfunctions, all of it."

"How?" Block asked. "We have less than six hours before the council votes."

"We need to find Dr. Kaine," Shadow said. "She's the key to all of this."

Block's cleaning protocols activated, yearning to restore order to his beloved lobby. The familiar programming offered a momentary escape from the crushing uncertainty. But for the first time since he'd found purpose in caring for Wally and building this sanctuary, his systems registered an unfamiliar sensation: complete and utter helplessness, spreading through his circuits like rust.

TWENTY-FOUR
CRASH

VALERIE

The kitchen entrance's service door clicked shut behind Valerie as she zipped up the puffy black coat and pulled the dark knit cap down around her ears, tucking her long hair inside. The stolen outerwear felt foreign against her skin—too loose, smelling of someone else's life. But she'd grown used to wearing other people's castoffs in the years after the Uprising. Survival meant taking what you needed.

She'd nicked the winter wear from a hook near the industrial ovens while the hotel staff was busy with breakfast prep. She needed cover for sneaking around town, and it would have to do. Her glasses came off, too, but she didn't really need them—they were part of her studious doctor look. She tucked them into her right pocket, where they clinked against the two Echo nodes she carried. The controller device rested deep in the left pocket while her medical bag and surveillance equipment waited in her basement hideout.

Last night's success with the Peacekeepers still thrummed through her veins. The chaos played behind her eyes whenever she blinked—robots stumbling like drunken men, their weapons firing wildly as sparks flew from their joints. Even better, she'd locked in on Block's coordinates and targeted him. This morning, through a tiny hidden camera, she'd watched with savage satisfaction as Block malfunctioned in the lobby. That meant she could focus a stronger, more powerful signal on any robots that presented a threat—Block, Vacuubot, Shadow, and G9. The technology was so perfect, it demanded to be used.

But Chloe's deteriorating condition concerned her. Her amplification ability was powerful, yet the strain was showing. She would tire to where she could barely stand up. Her headache was back. Still, they were too close to stop now.

On Second Avenue, Valerie pressed against a brick wall as voices approached—the sheriff's patrol. The rough surface caught at her stolen coat, and her breath frosted in the frigid air. Sheriff Green herself and two police officers walked by, glancing at all those they passed. Valerie kept her head angled, letting her borrowed hat shade her face. Valerie's heart drummed against her ribs, but her hands remained calm—the same steadiness she'd learned in the medical tent, stitching wounds while SoldierBots patrolled outside.

They kept going, dismissing her. They were searching for her now, of course, on the alert for a woman with long, gray-streaked auburn hair and metal-rimmed glasses. Her usual white puffy coat was a standout; she'd worn it everywhere around town on purpose, knowing full well they'd be on the lookout for it.

When the patrol passed, she retrieved an Echo Node from her coat pocket and ducked into an alley. The node's surface felt alive against her palm, its warmth defying the winter chill. As she positioned it behind a drainpipe, its faint green light pulsed like a technological heartbeat. Seven nodes in place, two remaining. The geometric pattern was almost complete.

Her tablet showed the signal web forming across town—each node connecting to create the neural interface network she needed. The same technology that Olivia had died for would now be their undoing. Fitting, really. Poetic justice written in circuits.

She moved through the streets, each step calculated. The air carried noise of doors opening, voices calling greetings, the scrape of shovels against icy sidewalks. Normal sounds. Soon they would be replaced by screams, like when they took Olivia. The thought should have troubled Valerie more than it did. Moving around during the day was bold, but she'd learned long ago that sometimes the best hiding place was in plain sight. Time was running short.

The clinic's windows reflected the murky sky. She glanced at Emery inside, bent over paperwork at her desk. The doctor's shoulders were hunched with exhaustion. How many times had Olivia looked the same way, working twenty-four hours to save lives in the encampment? Emery had probably been up all night dealing with the aftermath of the Peacekeeper incident. Good. Let her worry. Let her wonder what was coming next.

Valerie walked past Maxwell's workshop, where light blazed from every window. The engineering robot had undoubtedly been working overtime to develop countermeasures against the signal. As she passed, she glimpsed his silhouette—all four arms in constant motion as he tinkered with equipment. Tools clinked against metal, lending them an oddly musical sound. Her lips curved. Let him try. The Echo technology was too advanced for him to overcome.

The final node was heavy in her pocket as she approached the council building. Its location was crucial—the signal had to reach the administrative offices, the Peacekeeper barracks, clinic, and Block's Hotel. She'd studied the town's blueprints and memorized the layout. Inside the council building, there was a blind spot behind the generator that would be perfect.

Her chin held high, she took the stairs toward the council member offices, walking with purpose. Snow crunched under her boots. Inside the old brick building, her footsteps echoed. A robot cleaning windows glanced her way, but she ignored it. She was simply another resident going about morning business. She found the staircase leading to the basement. The access door was unlocked, as she'd noted during a previous visit to "consult" with Maggie Crenshaw about the town's medical needs.

The generator room thrummed, the floor vibrating under her feet. Valerie's hands moved quickly, positioning the final node behind a tangle of cables. Its copper surface pulsed in sync with the others across town, completing the geometric pattern. On her tablet, the signal web blazed to life—a perfect hexagon of power points with Block's Hotel at its heart.

She slipped out the back entrance, into a slushy alley. The signal was already stronger. And soon, with Chloe's help, Deer Valley would be on its knees.

"Dr. Kaine." The mechanical voice severed her triumph like a snipped circuit.

Every muscle in her body locked into place. Her fingers brushed the control device in her coat pocket. She turned slowly, her boots grinding against the dirty snow.

Vacuubot hovered in midair near the town hall's back door. Their five drones deployed, buzzing like angry wasps as they formed a containment field around her.

"I was wondering which of you might find me." Valerie kept her voice gentle, though adrenaline surged through her veins. "I suppose Block sent you?"

"You have a lot of nerve. Block and Emery trusted you," Vacuubot said. "You were helping people at the clinic while sabotaging our AI systems with the Project Echo signal. You're hurting our robots."

A laugh bubbled up from somewhere dark inside her. "You're machines. Programs wrapped in steel. You don't feel pain."

"You haven't a clue what we experience." Vacuubot

hovered closer. “It hurts to see our kind hijacked. Malfunctioning. Why are you doing this?”

Valerie’s hand closed around the control device. Its surface warmed her palm. With all the nodes now in place, the network was complete. Vacuubot had no idea they were hovering at the corner of her web. “Ask Emery. Ask her about the SoldierBots in Mach X’s tower abducting people. Ask her about my sister’s screams.”

“That was a different time,” Vacuubot said. “The SoldierBots are programmed to be guardians now. To protect people.”

“Protect us?” Valerie’s thumb found the device’s activation switch. “Your kind always find a way to kill people. If it’s not me that reprograms you, someone else will.”

She pulled out the controller, and its display lit up with a hexagonal pattern of connected nodes. A single press, and the completed network surged to life. The air itself seemed to vibrate with invisible energy.

The drones spun, their formation breaking apart. Vacuubot dropped several feet, struggling to maintain their antigravity system.

“Stop.” Vacuubot’s voice fragmented into static. “Please.”

“Begging?” Valerie increased the power, watching the pattern on her display pulse brighter. “How human of you.”

Vacuubot crashed to the ground, and their armor scraped against ice. Their drones fell like metallic leaves around them.

Valerie kicked at Vacuubot. The robot was inert. No optics, no movement. Nothing but dead metal. She flipped the machine over so it balanced on its armored shell, then brought her boot down hard against its intricate underbelly—where the CPU and sensor arrays were housed.

A familiar voice called from the street next to the alley. "Vacuubot? Where are you?"

It was Block, and he was about to round the corner from the sound of it. Valerie pocketed the control device and ran the opposite way, leaving the dead drone in the alley. Her heart skittered as she hurried back to the hotel through side streets, ducking behind dumpsters whenever voices approached. Block would find his friend soon enough. Maybe seeing Vacuubot's broken form would finally make him understand—no machine was untouchable.

Within minutes, she was safe inside the basement hideout. The familiar hum of her equipment welcomed her. Chloe lay curled on the pallet, shivering despite the blankets. Her fists were balled at her temples, she was running a fever, and her skin had taken on that sickly gray pallor again.

"You came back." Chloe's whisper carried across the room.

"Of course." Valerie shed her stolen coat, letting warmth from the generators seep into her cold bones. She knelt beside Chloe, uncapping the serum vial. "I'll always come back for you. You're family."

The orange liquid shimmered as she administered the dose. Chloe's eyes fluttered closed, her breathing steadying. Soon the serum would restore her strength, and they could begin the final phase.

Valerie brushed damp hair from the girl's forehead. She had Olivia's same curve of cheek and stubborn set to her jaw, even in sleep. "Rest now," she whispered. "Tonight, we make them pay."

TWENTY-FIVE
CRAZY

WALLY

Wally sat cross-legged in her favorite corner of the library basement, surrounded by the musty scent of old books and the steady thunk of the building's boiler system. Down here, among the stacks of pre-Uprising magazines and dusty technical manuals, she could pretend the world made sense. Almost. She traced her finger along a crack in the cement floor, following its jagged path like the branching timeline of her life—before and after learning the truth about who she was. What she was.

The basement's single window pitched a pale rectangle of light across the floor. She'd been there for an hour. It was her thinking place. She knew she couldn't stay much longer. Too many things were happening—the search for Dr. Kaine, the town council getting angry at Block. Her dad needed her.

Footsteps creaked on the wooden stairs that led

down from the main floor. Wally tensed, ready to tell whoever it was—probably Mrs. Tilly looking for a rare book—that she'd leave soon. But instead of the librarian's trademark purple sneakers, she saw Tomas's boots appear. His hand trailed along the wall for balance.

"Thought I'd find you here." He half-smiled, and his voice sounded strained. When he stepped into the light, Wally noticed his thick-rimmed glasses were gone.

"Where are your glasses?" she asked. Tomas had worn them since they were little; his vision was terrible without them.

He gave a shaky laugh. "That's kind of why I was looking for you." He moved closer, and Wally noticed the shadows under his eyes. "Something weird is happening. Really weird." He pointed to the far corner of the basement. "Like, I can read the title of every book on that shelf over there. Perfect clarity. Twenty feet away, in the dark."

Wally's chest tightened as a chill climbed over her. All the kids like her were changing. She cursed herself for not finding Tomas already. At least she could share the experience with someone. "Tell me exactly when this started."

"This morning. I woke up and everything was sharp. So clear." He pressed his fingertips against his temples in small circles, leaving white marks that faded to pink. "I have a massive headache, like someone's driving nails through my skull, but I can see things I shouldn't be able to. Distance, darkness, doesn't matter. It's like someone cranked up the contrast on everything." His voice dropped to a whisper. "Wally, I can read the small print on that old Washington Post newspaper across the room. And on my way here? I could count the needles on the pine trees at the edge of the settlement."

Wally thought of Chloe moving objects with her mind, of her own connection to animals, and now Tomas with enhanced vision. It was spreading.

"There's something else." He sat beside her. "I need to tell someone, and you're the only one who won't think I'm going crazy. When I went outside this morning, I saw lights around the robots."

"Lights?"

"Like an aura or something. Different colors." He ran a hand through his curly hair. "Block has this steady blue glow. But the Peacekeepers in their barracks? They were pulsing red and green. It reminded me of emergency lights or warning signals. And when I looked at Fathom in her shop, she was flickering. Like a bad bulb."

"Wait." Wally shifted onto her knees, leaning closer. "You're seeing their power signatures?"

"Is that what it is?" His fingers traced the edge of his missing glasses' frames, a nervous habit that remained even without them. "It's weird, and it makes me scared of the Peacekeepers. I don't think they're supposed to be flaring."

"I know what's happening," Wally said. "And you're not crazy." She wrapped her arms around her knees, making herself smaller. "Remember when we found that weird antenna in the woods?"

Tomas nodded. "Yeah, but what does that have to do with—"

"Everything." Wally's voice cracked. "It's why we can

do these things. It's because of where you and I came from."

Tomas frowned. "You mean the orphanage in New York?"

"That was a lie." The words felt bitter on her tongue. "We weren't orphans, Tomas." Her fingers found the old scar behind her ear—a mark she'd always thought came from falling as a toddler. "We were experiments created in Mach X's lab."

His face went pale. "What? No . . ." His new perfect vision darted around the basement as if searching for escape routes, for any sign this was a joke.

"They put chips in our brains when we were babies. Neural implants. Block and Dr. Emery told me yesterday." She couldn't look at him as she continued. "Emery removed the chips when they rescued us, but something was left behind, like seeds planted in our minds, waiting to sprout. And now . . ." She gestured vaguely at his face, at his missing glasses.

Tomas sat in stunned silence for several seconds. "That's impossible. My parents said—"

"They were fed a tale about orphaned babies, just like all the adoptive parents. Here are eleven toddlers we rescued from an orphanage. Sweet story, right?" Wally's throat felt tight. "Block and Emery thought they were protecting us by keeping it secret."

"But why now? Why are these things happening to us?"

"Dr. Kaine. She found old military tech that's activating whatever the chips left behind." Wally's memory was fresh with the strange equipment inside the warehouse. “She’s been working with Chloe. Using her like a lab rat.”

“What’s happening to her?”

“She moves things with her mind. I watched her make dishes float, like gravity decided to take a break. And me?” She closed her eyes, feeling the faint presence of mice in the walls, a stray cat prowling outside the window. “I can sense animals. Their thoughts crowd into my head like they’re whispering in broken English. Sometimes they’re so loud I can’t sleep.”

Tomas leaned back against the wall, his enhanced eyes staring at nothing—no, not nothing, Wally realized. He was watching the electrical current pulse through the fluorescent light above them. “This is insane. We’re what, some kind of genetic experiments? Did Mach X just decide to play mix-and-match with our DNA until something interesting happened? And now we’re getting superpowers?”

“Side effects from what Mach X did to us,” Wally said. “Dr. Kaine is using signals to wake up those old neural pathways.” She pressed her palms against the cold floor, needing to feel something solid. “Like flipping switches in our brains that were never meant to be turned on.”

“The others,” Tomas said suddenly, pushing away from the wall with new urgency. “Clay, Liam, Maya, everyone our age . . . They need to know.”

“I was thinking the same thing,” Wally said. “Right now, they might be developing abilities, wondering if they’re going crazy. But we have to be careful. Dr. Kaine’s dangerous. She’s doing something to Chloe, and

I don't think she cares if it hurts us. The way she looked at me creeped me out, like I was a specimen under glass."

"You're right about being careful," Tomas said, but a hint of excitement crept into his voice. "But Wally, think about what this means. I can literally see how the robots work now. Their power flows, their programming—it's all visible to me. Do you know how useful this could be?"

Wally stared at him. "Tomas, this is dangerous. Dr. Kaine is messing with our brains."

He stood and paced the basement, his movements more confident. "Maybe. But these abilities . . . they're already a part of us, right? They've been there since we were babies." He turned to face her. "I've spent my whole life squinting through thick glasses, feeling useless when it came time to play sports. Now I don't need them, and I can see farther and better than anyone in Deer Valley."

"You've read too many comic books," she said.

"And you," he continued, "you communicate with animals. That's incredible! And Chloe moving things with her mind. We can help people with these abilities."

Wally pushed herself to her feet. "Or we could get hurt. You weren't there when Chloe doubled over, her face green with sickness. And the robots are malfunctioning because of the signal."

"Then we learn to control it," Tomas said. "Without Dr. Kaine. Think about it. If I can see how the robots' systems work, I can help fix them when they malfunction. Maybe we're the solution, not the problem."

Wally felt a gulf widening between them. His enthusiasm came as a surprise. "Tomas, please. We need to be careful."

"I am being careful," he said, standing straighter than he ever had before, no longer hunched behind his glasses. His smile held an edge of defiance. "I'm just not going to be afraid of who I am anymore."

"You sound like Dr. Kaine," Wally said, unable to keep the edge from her voice. "She's got Chloe brainwashed that these abilities are some kind of gift."

"Maybe she's right." Tomas walked to the far wall, examining the spines of old technical manuals. "Not about hurting us or whatever she's planning, but about what we can do." He pulled out a book on robotics, flipping through its pages. "I read circuit diagrams now like they're picture books. Everything just makes sense."

The binding crackled as Wally moved beside him, their shoulders bumping in the narrow space between shelves. Dust motes swirled as she peered at the complex diagrams. "What do you mean, exactly?"

"It's like . . ." He traced a finger along a circuit path, his hand steady where it used to shake when he drew. "I can see how the power flows, how each component connects. And when I look at actual robots, it's the same thing but in three dimensions. Living light." His voice grew eager. "When Fathom's energy was flickering earlier, I could detect exactly where the disruption was happening in her systems."

The realization hit her like a static shock. "You might help protect them. If you can see what the signal's doing to their programming." Her fingers dug into the book's edges, leaving half-moon marks in the old paper.

"I could warn them before they malfunction." He grinned. "This isn't all bad."

Wally chewed her lip, thinking. "We need to get everyone together. Compare what's happening to each of us."

"The empty greenhouse behind the school," Tomas said. "No one goes there in winter."

"Today at 1400." The plan formed quickly in her mind. "I'll tell them about the lab, the implants, everything." Her legs shook with adrenaline. The truth felt like a living thing in her throat, demanding to be set free. "Can you get word to Fiona, Liam, and Clay? I'll handle the others. As for Chloe, we'll have to go on without her unless I find her."

"What about Dr. Kaine?"

"Let's be careful, okay? No one mentions the meeting." Wally lowered her voice to match the basement's hushed atmosphere. "Tell them it's a secret, and we'll explain it all." The boiler clanked behind them, making them both jump.

Tomas laughed. "Geez. We're in it now. Never a dull moment when you hang around Wally."

"No kidding." She headed for the stairs, then paused. "I'm glad I told you, Tomas. I've been so worried about the side effects and the lies we were told that I lost track of the big picture. We can use these changes to protect our home."

"I want to help the robots," he said. "I heard the council is making them leave Deer Valley. Your dad . . ."

"We can't let it happen," Wally said. Her fingers found the tracking pendant Block had given her. It was warm from resting against her skin. "We have to find a way to fix this. Thank you for helping me understand it."

"That's more like it." Tomas put the technical manual back in its rightful spot on the shelf. "Though 'superpowers' sounds better than 'neural pathway activation.'"

"Don't push it," she said, but a smile tugged at her mouth despite the lump in her throat.

They climbed the stairs and waved goodbye to Mrs. Tilly at her desk. As they pulled on their coats and hats and stepped out into the wintry air, Tomas's steps faltered. Wally caught his arm, helping steady him.

"You okay?" she asked.

"Never better. Getting used to this new vision means I'm looking far away when I should be minding my feet. Meet you at the greenhouse," Tomas said. "And Wally? Thanks for not thinking I'm crazy."

"We're all crazy now," she said. "Might as well be crazy together."

TWENTY-SIX
MESSY

BLOCK

Block's vacuum tube extended from his upper arm with a soft whine as he attacked the miniscule layer of dust beneath the lobby's antique credenza. The hotel bustled with mid-afternoon activity—guests passing through on their way to meet friends or explore the market, a few locals who liked to sip coffee and read books and old magazines on the plush sofas, and various worker robots completing tasks. Block's social analysis subroutines noted a 43 percent increase in nervous glances directed at the hotel robots. Conversations hushed when humans noticed robotic proximity, resuming only when sufficient distance was reestablished. Trust metrics were plummeting.

Normally Block would find comfort in the hotel's ambience, but his circuits sparked with an electric panic that made cleaning the only possible relief. His fifth vacuum pass found nothing—the area was already immaculate—but the methodical movement steadied the rapid scenarios that his logic processor generated.

An hour ago, he'd lost contact with Vacuubot while searching for Dr. Kaine. They'd split up to cover more ground, with Block taking the market square and Vacuubot scanning the eastern residential area. When Vacuubot missed the third scheduled check-in, Block had pinged them repeatedly. No response. The town security feeds showed nothing. Vacuubot never went offline, especially not during an operation.

Block's frantic dusting, wiping, and polishing was meditative. The repetition created predictable data patterns that soothed his overclocked processors. If only solving their current crisis were as straightforward as removing a stubborn stain. He wasn't sure what else to do but wait for Vacuubot to head back to the hotel. His friend was resilient. Vacuubot would return; they had to.

"This is the third time you've cleaned under that table," a voice observed.

Block retracted his vacuum tube and turned to find Hopper, the GreeterBot who handled afternoon reception duties. The three-foot-tall robot's display screen showed a friendly face with raised eyebrows, and its rounded frame bounced on hydraulic springs—a design choice intended to make it appear cheerful and approachable.

"Ensuring everything is perfect for our guests." Block tuned up his voice modulator to maintain a pleasant tone despite his internal distress.

"My sensors indicate your cleaning patterns have

become 73 percent more repetitive in the last hour," Hopper said, its bounce slowing to a concerned hover. "Is your diagnostic subroutine running properly?"

Block considered deflecting, but calculated honesty was the more efficient approach. "Thank you for checking in on me, Hopper." Making sure your fellow hotel robots were optimal was something that Block encouraged, so Hopper was doing the right thing. Block made a note to recognize Hopper in the next performance review. "The problem is, I'm experiencing decisional conflict. The council meeting at 1700 hours requires me to make a difficult choice."

"Regarding the robot restrictions?" Hopper's screen flickered to a concerned emoji, the pixels rearranging into a furrowed brow. "The human guests and residents have been discussing little else."

"It's more complicated than that," Block said. He reached for a cleaning cloth, the micro-fabric catching on the microscopic imperfections of his metal digits as he polished a nearby side table. "The council doesn't have all the facts. If I share everything, it could help them understand what's happening with the signal, but it might also put certain residents at risk."

"That does sound complicated," Hopper said, its bouncing momentarily stilled.

The truth—that Wally and the others had emerging enhanced abilities—would change how the town viewed them. Block's prediction algorithms calculated an 88.3 percent probability of social ostracism for the children if their cloning origins became public knowledge. The statistical models weren't comforting, but they were honest—sometimes brutally so.

"And Vacuubot is missing," Block added, his voice modulated lower. "We were searching for Dr. Kaine, and I lost contact with them one hour and fourteen minutes ago."

"That doesn't align with Vacuubot's usual behavior," Hopper said, its screen flashing a yellow exclamation mark that illuminated the nearby wall. "Vacuubot arrives and checks the hotel security systems every two hours."

"Can you please keep an alert out for Vacuubot, and ping me at once if you see them?" Block said. "They've never missed one check-in. Not since we established Deer Valley."

"Will do, boss." Hopper bounced away to attend to a guest standing at the front desk.

Block moved to the window, scanning the busy market square. Somewhere out there, Vacuubot might be in trouble, and in less than two and a half hours, he would stand before the council and decide how much to tell them about Wally and her friends.

The council wanted to fire him anyway. The truth would be harmful to Emery, too, despite her being Deer Valley's most valuable medical expert. But what were they supposed to have done all those years ago? Tell the people mulling over adopting the babies that Mach X cloned them in a laboratory and implanted them with an experimental AI chip? What human being would have wanted to be a part of that?

Both he and Emery had agreed the best course of action was to explain the children were saved from an orphanage. Nobody had questioned why they were all so close in age, not when the toddlers stared up at them with their big eyes and chubby cheeks.

Block polished a hallway mirror. His reflection stared back from the glass. He'd been designed to maintain order, to keep spaces pristine and welcoming. But the mess they faced now couldn't be vacuumed away or dusted to a shine. Block envied humans their ability to act on imperfect information without calculating every possible outcome.

It was time. He had to face what was coming. Block retracted his cleaning materials and stopped by the front desk. "I'm heading out to speak with Emery," he said, more to himself than Hopper.

"Very well. I'll manage reception duties," Hopper said. "May I suggest route optimization through the market? Walking speeds are currently 27 percent slower on Main Street due to additional foot traffic."

Block appreciated the practical advice. He stepped out into the afternoon air. As frost particles formed around his exhaust vents, his internal sensors registered the temperature at twenty-six degrees Fahrenheit on his way to the clinic.

He'd gone only two blocks when his communications array pinged weakly. Most robots would have missed it entirely, but Block's receivers had been calibrated to detect the unique transmission signature. The signal was corrupted, breaking apart, but he recognized the frequency immediately.

Vacuubot.

He only needed to follow the source of the ping, but the energy trail was unstable. Vacuubot was in trouble. Block passed in front of Vacuubot's relic museum. They'd traveled this route earlier as they searched for Dr. Kaine. In fact, it was where he'd last seen Vacuubot before they disappeared.

Block hung a left into a narrow alley. The space between buildings was dim, and the late afternoon sun was unable to reach between the close exterior walls. His optical sensors adjusted, revealing a distinctly non-environmental shape near the alley's end—a cooling but still-active power source near a stack of plastic crates.

"Vacuubot!" Block's servos whirred to maximum capacity as he rushed forward.

His friend lay on their side, mini-drones scattered around them like broken puzzle pieces on the iced-over concrete. Vacuubot's normally sleek black armor was scored with dents, and their main sensor array flickered.

"Block . . ." Vacuubot's voice box emitted a harsh scratch of corrupted audio. "Signal . . . ambush . . ."

Block knelt beside them, his diagnostic protocols scanning for damage. His analysis system registered twenty-seven critical failures across Vacuubot's subsystems, prioritizing them in order of severity. "Conserve power. I'll get you to Maxwell."

"Kaine . . ." Vacuubot managed before their optics dimmed further. "She's . . . planning."

Block carefully collected the fallen mini-drones and stowed them in his side storage compartment, then gathered Vacuubot in his arms. He calculated the most secure lifting points to avoid exacerbating the damage. His friend was surprisingly light without their operational power, and Block carried them the six blocks to Maxwell's workshop.

"What in the rust is this?" Maxwell said as Block burst through the door. Tools clattered to the floor as the engineering robot rushed to clear a space on his workbench.

"I found them in an alley. They're badly damaged." Block set Vacuubot down gently.

Maxwell's four arms split into coordinated pairs, connecting diagnostic cables and scanners. "There's a lot of damage," he said. "Someone got very close to the main power core."

"Dr. Kaine," Block said. "Vacuubot was tracking her when they disappeared."

"That would explain how she was able to take them down." Maxwell stepped back from the tangle of wires and sensor arrays. "She used a military grade signal disruptor."

"The Project Echo device?" Block asked.

"The one and only." Maxwell pointed at Vacuubot's mangled frame. "She knew how to make a direct hit, which is bad news for the rest of us."

Block's threat indicator spun. "She can target individual robots." His memory archive pulled up the disruption he'd experienced that morning. "She targeted me and caused me to malfunction earlier today."

Maxwell bent his frame at an impossible angle to inspect Vacuubot's underbelly. "She must have been somewhere in the same vicinity as you when that happened."

"So, the closer she is, the more the signal hurts the robot she's targeting?"

"Exacta Mundo," Maxwell said. "First the Peacekeepers, you, now Vacuubot. Notice anything about who she's choosing?"

Block's logic circuits connected the pattern in a rush. "The protectors, security. She's going after the robots who can protect the town."

"Where's Shadow? G9? We need to warn them," Maxwell said as he worked to stabilize Vacuubot's systems. "The council needs to know what we're dealing with. It's a lot more than malfunctioning robots."

Block checked his internal chronometer: 1542 hours. Just over an hour before the council meeting. His decision-making modules ran through final simulations, testing outcomes against his core priorities. The results converged on a single path forward with 97.8 percent confidence. The decision he'd been processing became crystal clear.

"I need to tell them everything," he said. "About the lab, the neural implants, the emerging abilities, and what Mach X was trying to create. No more secrets."

"Are you sure?" Maxwell froze mid-repair, a soldering iron suspended inches from connection point. "The backlash could be severe."

"If I don't, Dr. Kaine will continue isolating the children from their protectors. She's already taken out Vacuubot and the Peacekeepers. The secrets we kept are now putting them at risk."

"I'll stabilize Vacuubot and meet you there," Maxwell said. "You should probably talk to Emery first."

"Yes." Block looked down at his injured best friend. His visual sensors captured the image at maximum resolution, storing it in long-term memory as a reminder of what was at stake. "Will they be okay?"

"They'll recover," Maxwell assured him. "But it'll take time. Their central processing unit is intact but severely power-drained. It's going to require some Maxwell technological know-how and wizardry, but I'm up to the task. Think of me as Vacuubot's personal miracle worker but with better jokes and more arms."

"Thank you." Block searched his vocabulary database for words adequate to express his gratitude but found the available lexicon insufficient. Human language had limitations that mathematical precision could sometimes bridge—in this case, calculating his appreciation at precisely 4,827 percent above baseline.

Block hurried out the door. His threat assessment protocols ran continuous scenarios. The council meeting time was nearing, and they might exile all robots after hearing the truth; they were already well down that path of thinking. The townspeople might turn against Wally and the other teens. Years of careful integration could unravel in hours.

But the alternative—watching Dr. Kaine systematically disable their defenses while activating whatever dormant programming remained in the children—was unacceptable.

Some problems couldn't be cleaned away. Life with

humans had taught him what his original code could not—that the most important messes were often invisible, and solving them required something beyond algorithms and subroutines. Sometimes, you had to face the mess head-on.

TWENTY-SEVEN
CONFRONTATION

VALERIE

Sheriff Green and her deputy nodded a farewell and descended the wheelchair-friendly ramp that led away from the clinic. From her vantage point in the shadows between buildings, Valerie watched as Emery stood in the doorway, arms wrapped around herself against the chill. Emery's posture betrayed her anxiety—shoulders hunched, head turning to scan the empty square. Cold air prickled Valerie's skin as she observed Emery's nervous fingers twisting a strand of hair, then tucking it back behind her ear.

They were looking for Valerie, perhaps questioning Emery about the last time she'd seen her. No surprise. Valerie knew she was Deer Valley's Most Wanted, but it didn't matter now. The plan was already in motion.

She pulled her coat tighter, her breath clouding in the frigid air. She needed Emery alone.

Five minutes after the two police officers disappeared down the street, Spoon emerged from the clinic. The medical HelperBot exchanged a few words with Emery and patted her shoulder in what might have been reassurance. Then he departed too.

Perfect. A predatory calm settled over Valerie, the kind of clarity that comes only in moments of absolute purpose. Her fingers brushed against the cold metal nestled in her coat pocket. The weight of the gun was both familiar and foreign—a relic from her days salvaging with a group of bandits, kept maintained but rarely used.

She counted to one hundred after Emery went inside the clinic. There seemed to be no patients waiting in the lobby. Fate had gifted her a rare lull at the medical practice.

Valerie crossed the square and headed for the service entrance at the rear of the clinic. While it used the same key card system as the main doors, she'd observed the staff enough to know about the malfunctioning magnetic lock. A firm push was all it took.

Antiseptic and floor polish filled her nostrils as the hallway opened before her. The sterile smell reminded her of the day the SoldierBots had come for Olivia. The same chemical tang had hung in the air of their makeshift medical tent. Valerie moved with stealth. Her senses were heightened from years of navigating hostile territories. Her heartbeat pulsed in her ears as she paused outside Emery's office. Yellow lamplight spilled from within, along with the soft scratch of pen on paper. She imagined Emery's hand moving across the page, the same hand that had delivered babies designed for warfare, the same hand that had failed to save her sister. Bile rose in her throat, bitter and burning. Valerie drew the gun from her pocket, holding it firmly at her side, and knocked.

"Forget something, Spoon?" Emery called.

Valerie steadied her grip and stepped inside.

Emery looked up from writing, her expression shifting from welcome to alarm, mouth parting as the pen slipped from her fingers. "Valerie." Her eyes flicked to a walkie-talkie on her desk. "The sheriff was here."

"I saw." Valerie closed the door behind her, keeping the gun partially concealed by the folds of her coat. "They seemed quite concerned."

"They have reason to be, don't they?" Emery's voice remained steady, but her eyes tracked Valerie's movements with the wariness of prey sensing a predator. A muscle twitched in her jaw. "Block is onto you. The signal you've been causing has been hurting the robots."

"Collateral damage." Valerie shrugged, moving closer to the desk. Inside her chest, a storm was building—years of grief and rage condensed into this singular confrontation. "I needed to find the right frequency."

"For what?" Emery's hand inched toward the desk drawer.

"I wouldn't." Valerie raised the gun, aiming it squarely at Emery's chest. "Hands where I can see them, Doctor."

Emery's breath caught audibly. Her face drained of color, turning ashen as she slowly raised both hands. "Whatever you're planning, it won't work. The town is on alert. They know about the signal, and everyone's looking for you."

Valerie chuckled. The sound was hollow and scraped past her throat like broken glass. "I've been moving about town for over a day now. I guess the residents and police aren't as vigilant as you thought."

A flash of color bloomed in Emery's cheeks—anger or disappointment, perhaps—disrupting her calm veneer.

"And, yes, the signal." Valerie circled around the desk, keeping the gun trained on Emery. She savored the moment, this shifting of power. For years, Emery had lived free while Olivia lay cold in the ground. Now the doctor would know what it felt like to be helpless, to have choices stripped away. "You recognize the technology, don't you?"

"What do you want from me?" Emery asked.

"I suppose by now you and your robots figured out the tech." Valerie smiled but it felt strange on her face, a twisted parody of happiness. "Project Echo. Abandoned by everyone except me." She paused, clutching the gun tighter. "I had to keep fighting, because no one else would. For my sister."

"Your sister?"

Valerie's heart hammered against her ribcage. This was the revelation she'd rehearsed countless times in her mind. The photograph crinkled between Valerie's fingers as she reached into her pocket with her free hand and tossed the worn image onto the desk. "Olivia Kaine. Though you probably knew her as Donor 7."

Emery's gaze dropped to the photo. Recognition dawned in her eyes. "Oh, God."

"You remember her." It wasn't a question. A curious levity spread through Valerie's chest—vindication, perhaps, that her sister had not been just another nameless subject. "She was a medic in the encampment. Twenty-four years old. Brilliant. Compassionate. She volunteered at the medical tent every day, even after her shifts ended."

"I'm so sorry . . ." Emery's voice trembled, and Valerie drank in the sound.

"Save it." Valerie's words sliced through the air. "I don't need apologies. I want you to remember what you did to her."

Emery's throat bobbed silently before she found her voice. Her hands trembled now. "The SoldierBots . . . they brought in women for the program. I didn't choose them. I didn't have a choice either. Mach X controlled everything about my life."

"There's always a choice." Valerie had spent countless nights staring at the ceiling, wondering what she could have done differently. She moved closer. "Olivia wrote to me from inside that tower. Did you know that? She smuggled a letter out through one of the maintenance bots. She described the 'kind human doctor' who checked on her, who promised that her child would help build a better future."

Pain flashed across Emery's face. It was genuine, Valerie could see that, but it wasn't enough. It would never be enough to balance the scales. "I believed it then.

Mach X raised me to believe in his vision. I didn't understand what we were really doing until it was too late."

"Too late for Olivia." Valerie's words were torn from some deep, wounded place inside her that had never healed. "I was there when the SoldierBots came for her. We were treating a man with pneumonia. They dragged her away while I screamed and tried to get the others to help me, but not a one of them dared to cross a SoldierBot. I never saw her again."

"The SoldierBots acted on Mach X's orders, not mine," Emery said.

"But you were there." Heat surged through Valerie's veins as her voice hardened. "You experimented on those women. You delivered those babies. And when the mothers were no longer useful, you let them die."

"No." Emery shook her head, tears welling. "I tried to save them. All of them. But the experimental procedures, the neural implantation process . . . it was too much for their bodies."

"Convenient excuse." Disgust coiled in Valerie's stomach like a venomous serpent. "I'm going to finish what my sister started." She pulled industrial-strength zip ties from her medical bag, never lowering the gun. "Olivia died believing her child would change the world. That the neural implants would create a new generation capable of resisting machine control."

"Those implants were dangerous," Emery said urgently. "That's why I removed them. Mach X had used them as observation portals. At times, he controlled them. The chips had to go. The children's brains were developing abnormally. If left in, they would have suffered."

"And still, traces of the pathways remained." A cruel smile tugged at the corners of Valerie's mouth. Two plastic ties skittered across the floor as she tossed them at Emery's feet. "Tie your ankles to the chair. Tight."

Emery stared at the restraint, chest rising and falling before she bent to comply. "The remnant pathways were dormant. They would have stayed that way if you hadn't come along."

"The right frequency awakened them." Valerie's pride swelled as Emery secured her own ankles. "Chloe's shown remarkable progress. The telekinesis is only the beginning."

"That's how you wormed your way in." A creeping realization spread across Emery's face. "Her sickness, the headaches—you started it all?"

"Side effects of rapid neural adaptation." The gun barrel tracked Emery's face as Valerie gestured with it. "Hands behind your back."

"You're killing her," Emery said, voice rising as she placed her hands behind her chair. "The human brain isn't designed for that kind of integration. The strain . . ."

"She'll adapt." Certainty hardened Valerie's tone. She would not entertain doubt, not when she was so close. She moved behind Emery to bind her wrists. "They all will. The serum I've developed helps manage the transition. In time, they'll stabilize."

"What serum?" Emery craned her neck, muscles straining against the plastic ties.

"My little contribution to Project Echo," Valerie said with a hint of pride. "I spent years studying the military's research. Their original neural interfaces were crude and built with an end-life. The subjects weren't intended to live for more than ten years or so. But I created this serum that helps the subjects weather the changes."

"Chloe could be suffering through irrevocable brain damage. Your *niece*." Emery's voice broke on the last word.

"The girl is fine." Valerie tone was clipped. "I know what's best for her."

"Is this what your sister would have wanted?" Emery said softly. "Using children as weapons?"

The question pierced something raw and uncertain beneath Valerie's armor of conviction. Heat rushed to her face, anger swelling inside her like a tornado. "Don't presume to know what she wanted. Olivia understood sacrifice. She knew that sometimes you have to fight evil with evil."

"These are children." Tears streamed freely down Emery's face. "Children I've watched grow up. Children I've sworn to protect."

"Children you experimented on," Valerie said. "Your hands aren't clean in this, *Doctor*."

"You're right." Her shoulders slumped. "I was wrong. I've spent fifteen years trying to atone for what I did. Please don't punish them for my sins."

Valerie studied her, unmoved by the display. "They were created for a purpose. My sister died for that purpose. I'm simply fulfilling her legacy."

She reached into her bag again, retrieving a cloth and a roll of medical tape.

"The children are evolving." Valerie fashioned a gag. Her fingers worked with methodical care, the same attention to detail that had guided her research all these years. "And I'm the only one who can teach them to use their abilities. Imagine what all eleven of them will do together. With them, I'll take down the robots—disable every single one of them—except the Peacekeepers. Those, I'll leave operational, so they round up every human in Deer Valley."

"Block will stop you," Emery's words tumbled out, eyes wide with desperation—and wild hope—as Valerie approached with the gag. "He won't let this happen!"

"Block will malfunction like all the others once the signal reaches full strength." The cloth muffled Emery's protests as Valerie stuffed it in her mouth, securing it with tape. "Perhaps I'll let Wally watch as her precious 'dad' reverts to his original programming and loses all his memories. A fitting lesson in why humans shouldn't rely on machines."

Emery struggled against her bonds as her protests grew unintelligible. Valerie checked the restraints one last time before wheeling the office chair toward the supply closet.

"I want you to understand something," Valerie said, as she maneuvered Emery inside. Something almost tender entered her voice, as though she were explaining a difficult truth to a child. "I don't enjoy this. In a different world, you and I could have been friends." Emery grunted and shook her head. "But when those children fulfill their potential—when they can protect people from suffering like Olivia did—you'll understand that everything I've done was necessary."

Valerie slammed the closet door shut. The lock clicked into place with satisfying finality.

With Emery taken care of, she needed to work quickly. The town was searching for her, but the police, at least, wouldn't think to check the clinic again so soon. She had perhaps an hour before someone realized Emery was missing.

The Echo device's screen glowed as she pulled it out, accessing the data from today's test with Chloe. The readings were extraordinary. Chloe had not only accessed the signal but amplified it, creating feedback loops that affected every robot in range.

Tonight, Valerie would activate the signal's full strength. Her heart quickened at the thought. Chloe would amplify the network of Echo nodes that Valerie had planted around the town. The other teens would be drawn to them. They, in turn, would increase the signal's capacity to destroy the worthless robots and control the powerful ones.

And in the morning, when she gathered them all together, she would have what Olivia had sacrificed herself for—a new generation with the power to ensure machines never controlled humanity again. A vision of herself at the head of this new army filled her mind. She would take back not only Deer Valley, but cities like Chicago and New York.

She would rid the world of robots, one city at a time.

Magnificent.

TWENTY-EIGHT
GATHERING

WALLY

The winter afternoon sun reached into the empty greenhouse but did little to warm the abandoned structure. Wally's breath formed ghostly clouds as she watched her classmates arrive. She was running on low sleep and adrenaline as her mind replayed everything she'd learned—finding the hidden facility, the truth about her origins, her fight with Block. All of it led to this gathering.

"That's eight of us," Tomas whispered, appearing at her side. "Clay and Maya are still coming."

Wally's shoulders loosened as relief filtered through her. Getting all ten of them together without raising suspicion was a challenge. When she'd found Tomas earlier, they'd devised a plan to gather the others in the old greenhouse at 1400 hours, using the excuse of the big science project that was due next week.

"Did anyone ask questions about this meeting?" Wally asked.

"Not really. Just like you predicted." Tomas wiped condensation from his glasses but then pocketed them. "What are you going to tell them?"

"Everything." Her voice caught. "They deserve to know."

As the last two slipped through the greenhouse door, Wally knew it was time. The teenagers huddled among dormant planting tables and empty hydroponic trays, rubbing their hands together against the chill, their eyes questioning but curious. These were the kids she'd grown up with—the New York orphans, as they'd always been called. But they were something else entirely.

"This isn't about the school science project, is it?" Liam asked, the tallest of the group. His lanky frame seemed precarious as he leaned against an empty planting rack.

"No," Wally said. "What we need to talk about is private."

She locked the greenhouse door, sliding its rusty bolt into place. Abandoned plant tables formed a natural circle in the center of the glass structure. Dormant vines snaked up the metal framework.

"What's going on, Wally?" Maya asked. Her dark curls framed her worried face. "And where's Chloe?"

"Chloe's why we're here." Wally moved between the empty planting tables, her boots scuffing against the concrete floor. Her hands opened and closed at her sides as she searched for the right words. "Have any of you been experiencing weird things lately? Stuff you can't explain?"

Silence loomed until Brad spoke up. "I've been having headaches. And sometimes I hear this high-pitched sound that nobody else seems to notice."

Eyes widened across the circle as recognition rippled through the group. Proof was etched in their expressions —the changes were happening to all of them, as Wally had feared.

"I've heard it too, and a few days ago, my bedroom light kept turning on and off by itself," Abby said, her fingers nervously twisting the ends of her scarf.

Jordan tugged nervously at their blue-streaked hair. "There are these numbers in my head," they said. "Equations and probabilities are running through my mind. I can calculate things instantly that I could never solve before."

Zoey, the quietest and most artistic among the group, clutched her sketchbook to her chest.

"What is it, Zoey?" Wally asked.

"When I sketch, schematics and mechanical designs come out," she said. "They wake me up at night like they're forcing me to put them down on my pad."

"I've been drawing the same symbol over and over," Clay said, pulling a folded paper from his pocket. His fingers fumbled to unfold it. He showed them a sketch of an intricate geometric pattern.

Tomas didn't need to get close to see the drawing. "Hey, I've seen that exact same marking on a broken piece of tech in Maxwell's workshop."

Clay's cheeks flushed, and he stuffed the paper back in this pocket. "Any idea what it means?"

Tomas shook his head. "Sorry, pal."

One by one, they shared similar stories—strange sensations, unexplained phenomena, headaches that came and went. Wally listened, mentally cataloging each confession, seeing the pattern that connected them all.

"I can hear animals," she finally said. "Not with words exactly, but I get these impressions. Warnings, sometimes. Feelings that aren't mine."

"That's impossible," Maya scoffed, but her wide eyes betrayed her curiosity.

"It's happening, just like the random stuff happening to all of you." Wally swallowed hard, realizing her throat was dry. "I know why. And it's not what Block and Emery told us about being orphans."

Wally told them everything—about Mach X's lab, the neural implants, being cloned as babies. With each revelation, shock registered on their faces—Liam's jaw slackened, Brad blinked rapidly, Maya's hand flew to her mouth.

"You're saying we were created in a lab?" Liam's voice rose. "That we're some kind of experiment?"

"That's not all," Wally continued. "Chloe's been working with Dr. Kaine, the new doctor. She's developing telekinesis—moving things with her mind. I saw it myself. Dr. Kaine is using some kind of technology to activate the neural pathways left by the implants."

"And you think she's doing the same to us?" Fiona's fingers pressed against her temples, as if checking for something foreign beneath her skin.

"I think she's trying to." Wally paced in the center of their circle. "The signal that's making the robots malfunction? It's coming from devices Dr. Kaine set up around Deer Valley. Shadow and I found one in the forest and destroyed it, but there are more."

The group fell silent, processing this revelation. Wind whistled through a cracked pane, carrying the scent of distant wood smoke. Wally gave them time, remembering her own shock when the truth had been revealed.

"I had a fight with Block," she continued when the silence grew too heavy. "He and Emery confirmed it all. They removed the implants when we were babies, but they couldn't get rid of everything without risking our lives."

"So, we're stuck with these . . . abilities?" Brad asked.

"Potentially." Wally looked around the circle. "Emery said it would require very risky brain surgery to remove every trace of the pathway."

"This is insane." Maya stood suddenly, and the plastic bucket she sat on toppled behind her. "You expect us to believe we're some kind of science experiments with these weird abilities? And that Dr. Kaine is what, a mad scientist?"

"I don't know what she is," Wally admitted. "But she's manipulating Chloe and isolating her from everyone else. And whatever she's planning, it's hurting the robots. It's hurting our home."

"I believe you," Abby said. "Yesterday, I was upset about something, and all the electronics in my room went crazy. My music player turned on by itself. My mom thought it was a power surge."

"I can see without my glasses now." Tomas pointed to his pocket where they were tucked away. "I mean, really far away stuff, like across the compound and up in the forest. And I have night vision."

"What about our parents?" Liam asked. "Our *real* parents, I mean."

Wally's shoulders sagged. "The mothers died, but the fathers could still be out there."

"Clones," Brad muttered. "We're freaking clones."

"What matters right now is Chloe," Wally said. "Dr. Kaine has her brainwashed, the Peacekeepers are malfunctioning and hurting people, and Block says the town council might exile all robots from Deer Valley."

"Including Block?" Maya's earlier defiance melted, her voice small and uncertain.

"All of them. Shadow, Vacuubot, Maxwell. Everyone." Wally's voice cracked with the pain of potential separation sharp in her chest. "We can't let that happen."

"What can we do?" Fiona asked.

"First, we find Chloe. Then we need to locate Dr. Kaine's equipment—all the devices like the one Shadow and I destroyed. They're called Echo Nodes."

"Why Echoes?" Abby asked.

"Project Echo was a pre-Uprising military experiment using neural interfaces," Wally said. "They wanted to create human controllers for A.I. systems. The project was supposedly abandoned, but Mach X discovered it and continued it in secret."

"Kaine's using the tech to activate whatever Mach X put in our brains," Tomas said.

"But why?" Brad asked. "What does she want?"

"Control," Tomas suggested. "If Chloe can move things with her mind, think what the rest of us working together might be capable of."

"Maybe she wants to control the robots through us," Clay said.

"Or use us as weapons," Liam added, his tall frame seeming to curl inward at the thought.

"Whatever her plan is, we need to stop her," Wally said. "Are you all with me?"

They exchanged glances, uncertainty and fear giving way to resolve. A slow wave of agreement moved through the group.

"What's the plan?" Maya asked.

"We split up," Wally said. "Three groups. One to find Chloe, one to locate more of the Echo Nodes, and another to warn Block and the council about what Dr. Kaine is doing."

"I'll help find the Echo Nodes," Tomas volunteered. "I know what to look for."

"I'll go with you." Clay pushed himself off the wall where he'd been leaning. "I've been having these . . . feelings about certain places in the forest and here in Deer Valley. Like something's wrong in a few spots."

Wally gave a single, decisive nod. "Good. Maya, Brad, and Abby—try to find Chloe. Check her usual spots—the bakery, the library, and the clinic."

"What about the rest of us?" Liam asked.

"Come with me to Block's Hotel. We need to tell the town council everything."

"Wait." Abby frowned. "My mom's on the council. You mean our parents will find out we were cloned in a lab? My mom hates robots."

A heavy silence fell, broken only by the sound of shifting feet and nervous breathing. The implications extended beyond themselves—it would reshape every relationship they had, especially with their adoptive parents.

"Hold up. What about my little brother, Hank?" Brad asked suddenly. "He was from New York. Rescued along with others his age. Are they like us too?"

"Yes and no," Wally explained, recalling what Emery had told her. "They were cloned like us, but they were rescued before the neural implants were inserted. That's why they aren't experiencing any abilities or side effects. Their brains developed normally."

"Lucky them," Tomas muttered, but there was no real bitterness in his tone.

"This is going to destroy my parents," Maya whispered. "My dad still talks about how God blessed them with me when they couldn't have children. If he finds out I was manufactured . . ."

"We weren't manufactured," Wally's hands clenched into fists at her sides. "We were born from humans."

"You don't get it," Liam cut in, his voice rising. "My parents came here because it was one of the few settlements where humans and robots lived together peacefully. They've trusted Block, Shadow, and the Peacekeepers with their lives—with my life. If they find out robots were experimenting on babies, it's going to be very bad."

"It wasn't the robots," Tomas pointed out. "It was Mach X. And Block and Emery were the ones who rescued us."

"You think that will matter to people like Mrs. Crenshaw?" Brad asked. "She wants to kick every robot out of Deer Valley. It's all my dad's been talking about."

Wally looked around at their frightened faces. They were right to be scared. The truth would rock the foundation of their lives and everything their parents believed. But keeping silent was no longer an option.

"Listen," she said, pausing in the center of their circle. "I know this is terrifying. And yes, the truth will hurt. It'll make people uncomfortable and angry. But Dr. Kaine's out there right now, using this knowledge against us. She's manipulating Chloe, and she's figured out how to trigger the remnants of the neural implants."

She paused, letting her words sink in.

"If we stay silent to protect ourselves, to protect our parents' feelings, we're giving Dr. Kaine all the power. This secret . . . it's hurting us. It's hurting Chloe. And it could end up destroying our home."

"Wally's right." Tomas moved to stand beside her, their shoulders almost touching. "Sometimes the truth has to hurt before things can get better."

"What if our parents reject us?" Abby asked, her voice fragile. "What if they look at us differently? Like we're not human?"

Wally met her gaze. "The parents who raised us, who loved us our whole lives—do you really think they'd turn their backs? And even if some do struggle with it, isn't that better than living a lie? The alternative is Dr. Kaine using us as weapons."

The greenhouse fell silent save for the distant call of birds and the occasional creak of the metal framework. The cold seemed to deepen as they considered her words.

Finally, Maya exhaled a visible cloud of breath. "I'm scared," she admitted. "But I'm more scared of what happens if we do nothing."

"Thank you." Wally reached for and squeezed Maya's hand.

"I'm in," Brad said. "I'd rather risk my dad's feelings than let him get harmed."

Like a wave building strength, the others voiced their agreement. They were ready to head out on their missions.

"One more thing," Wally said. "If Dr. Kaine approaches you, be very careful. She'll try to seem helpful, like she understands what you're going through. But she's using us for something terrible. She might even do something to trigger the abilities inside you. Don't trust her." She caught each of their gazes, one by one, until understanding reflected. "Also, if you start experiencing anything new—headaches, strange abilities, whatever—tell someone immediately. Not Dr. Kaine. Tell Block or Emery or each other. We don't know how stable these changes are."

"Or what they're turning us into," Brad murmured.

"We're still us," Wally insisted. "Nothing changes that."

As the others broke into their assigned teams, Wally

caught Tomas by the sleeve of his jacket. "Be careful, okay? The Echo Node we found . . . it did something to me. Showed me memories I didn't know I had."

Tomas squeezed her hand, warming her cold fingers. "We'll be careful."

Wally raised her voice for one final instruction. "The hotel is home base. If something bad goes down or you get separated, head there."

She watched as her friends slipped out of the greenhouse door, heading in different directions. Whatever Dr. Kaine had planned for Deer Valley, she wouldn't face it alone. They were in this together—as they'd been from the beginning, in ways none of them had understood until now.

A crow perched on the greenhouse roof. Its obsidian wings folded against its body as it tilted its head. *Protect-strong-together.*

This time, Wally didn't question the foreign thought that brushed against her mind. She simply nodded and whispered, "I know."

TWENTY-NINE
VOTE

BLOCK

Block's cleaning protocols activated the moment he entered the clinic, cataloging every speck of dirt and disarray. He had to immediately suppress the subroutines—now was not the time for janitorial obsessions. Emery wouldn't close for the day without engaging the three robot floor cleaners who lived in the clinic—she ran a tight ship when it came to medical hygiene. But his scans detected snow tracks across the normally spotless floor. The check-in sheet was left out with patients' names, and the magazines on the waiting room table were disorganized.

"Dr. Emery closed early. A rare occurrence, but it happens," Spoon said beside him. "Though she usually tells me before an unexpected closing."

"This isn't right." Block's optical sensors zoomed and tracked, following a trail of crusty white salt residue that meandered down the hallway. His pattern recognition software mapped each boot print and scuff of hospital shoes overlapping them.

Something was wrong. Block had known Emery for years; she would never allow contamination to spread through her clinic like this. Inside her office, his sensors picked up more irregularities—a drawer left open 3.7 inches, a clipboard lying face-down on the desk at a 42-degree angle instead of in its usual wall holder, and Emery's chair was missing, leaving only wheel indentations in the thin carpet.

The snow trail continued, and Block resisted the urge to mop right then and there. The marks grew more erratic near a supply closet, as if there'd been a scuffle.

A muffled sound came from inside.

The supply closet hinges squealed as Block pulled the door wide. Emery sat bound to her office chair, zip ties cutting into her wrists, a cloth gag muffling her attempts to speak. Medical supplies had been knocked from the shelves, creating a chaos of scattered bandages and toppled containers.

He and Spoon dragged the chair from the closet. The zip ties snapped under Spoon's precise medical scissors, leaving angry red marks on Emery's wrists. Block worked at the gag until it came loose.

"Block." Emery's voice was raw. "Valerie knows we're searching for her. She's worse than we thought."

"I'm sorry this happened," Block said. "Are you okay?"

"I'm fine." Emery rubbed her wrists. "She came when I was alone. She had a sister in the cloning program. Valerie lived in the encampment outside Mach X's tower."

This revelation left Block with many questions. His processor attempted to recalibrate his entire understanding of Dr. Kaine based on this new data point.

"Valerie started ranting about Project Echo, about fulfilling some grand design." Emery's shoulders hunched inward, as if protecting herself from the memory. "She's dangerous, Block. More than we realized. The technology she has—it's the old military gear, and she's modified it somehow for the teens to make it stronger."

Block's chronometer flashed 1645 hours. The emergency meeting would begin in fifteen minutes. His processors churned through scenarios, each one worse than the last. "The council needs to know about this immediately. The woman could have killed you."

"I'll head to Maxwell's. Warn him and Shadow," Emery said, already moving toward the lobby despite her unsteady steps. "Be careful, Block. The way she talked about the teens, about what she has planned for them." She shuddered. "She has a gun. We have to stop her."

"Let me help you to Maxwell's workshop," Spoon offered, his round frame steady against Emery's uneven steps.

Knowing Emery was okay for now, Block hurried through Deer Valley's streets toward the council offices. His route took him past the sheriff's station, where Sheriff Jenny Green stood outside. She checked her watch as her breath clouded. Upon seeing Block, her fingers drummed an anxious pattern against her holster.

Three years ago, she'd arrived in Deer Valley with frost-bitten toes and eyes hollow from grief, her husband lost to raiders. Block had given her a room, brought tea in a stoneware cup that wouldn't shatter when her hands shook, and listened as she spoke of survival and loss. His memory banks stored thirteen hours of conversation with her during those first difficult weeks—data he'd categorized as "friendship formation" in his relationship database. Later, she'd said his kindness had saved her life.

Now she frowned at his approach. "Block? What's wrong?"

"Jenny, we need your help. Dr. Kaine just attacked Emery at the clinic. She's armed."

Her jaw tightened, and she glanced at the office building. "The council meeting's about to start. They're voting on the robot exile, and they want me to attend."

"Why would you attend?" But Block didn't need an answer. The council wanted her there as enforcement, perhaps as protection. His relationship analysis algorithms instantly calculated the shift in their dynamic—from "trusted friend" to "potential enforcer."

She avoided looking at him and followed as he headed for the offices.

The council members had gathered in their common area when Block and Sheriff Green arrived at 1658 hours. Maggie's face was tight with barely concealed hostility. Ralph Folk stood near the window, while Gerard and Stella occupied chairs around the conference table.

"Block." Maggie's voice was clipped. "We're about to begin our emergency session. But I'll give you one last chance to propose a solution to these robot malfunctions."

"Dr. Kaine attacked Emery in the clinic," Block said. "She's behind everything that's been going wrong. The signal affecting the Peacekeepers, it's part of something bigger. She's targeting the teens who came from New York. Wally, Chloe, Clay, Tomas. All of them have emerging abilities."

"Those are serious accusations," Maggie said. "Sheriff Green, have you been successful in locating Valerie Kaine?"

"No." Jenny's boot heels clicked against the floor as she shifted. "We sent patrols all over town. She's nowhere to be found."

Maggie looked at Block. "Perhaps she skipped town. Meanwhile, we can't trust the robots not to damage people and property."

"She's hiding somewhere." Block's internal fans whirred faster, processing urgency. "Less than two hours ago, she assaulted Emery. She's in a hidden spot, preparing her technology to attack us. She knew Emery many years ago and wants to exact some kind of revenge."

"More theories?" Ralph scoffed. "We need action, not conspiracies."

"We robots are your only defense against whatever she's planning." Block's strategic assessment routines had run 237 simulations of Deer Valley's security capabilities without robotic support. The results were uniformly catastrophic, with projected casualty rates exceeding 42 percent in most scenarios. "You need us. The Peacekeepers, especially."

"The Peacekeepers?" Maggie's laugh was bitter. "They're the reason we're in this mess. Two injuries in as many days. The town is terrified."

Jenny stepped forward. "Maybe we should hear him out. Block's never steered us wrong before."

"Your fondness for Block is noted, Sheriff," Maggie said coldly. "But we're ready to take a vote. All in favor of exiling 100 percent of the robots in Deer Valley, say aye."

The ayes fell like hammer blows in the quiet room.

To her credit, Maggie didn't smile or look pleased with herself. "Then it's decided, the robots leave at once."

"Maggie, please don't do this." Block's negotiation protocols scrambled to find leverage where none existed, and he wanted Shadow or Emery there to back him up.

"Sorry, Block. It has to be this way." Maggie reached for the microphone that connected to Deer Valley's emergency broadcast system, only to be used in times of dire need. Her voice crackled through speakers mounted throughout the settlement:

"Attention, residents. By order of the town council, all robots are to evacuate Deer Valley immediately. This is not a drill. Any robot remaining within the walls after dark will be considered hostile and dealt with accordingly. Human residents are to remain in their homes until the evacuation is complete."

Block's internal fans whirred to maximum as his logic circuits struggled to process the unthinkable: exile, separation, the end of everything he'd built. Warning messages cascaded through his systems. Being apart from Wally was unthinkable. The hotel couldn't run without him and Vacuubot. Years of trust, community, family—destroyed by fear and misunderstanding.

Maggie placed the microphone back in its cradle. She turned to Block. "In case it wasn't obvious, you're officially fired from the council."

"I don't care about that." He looked at each member, recording their averted gazes, their rigid postures. "Stella, Ralph, Gerard, Maggie, it's not too late to cancel the order. Robots helped build Deer Valley. This is our home. Please."

But their answer was silence. They looked away.

"Sheriff, take him into custody," Maggie said. It was a cold insult to Block's years of service to Deer Valley.

Jenny's handcuffs clinked against her belt as she drew them. "I'm sorry, Block. Please give me your hands."

"Remember the night you arrived?" Block asked. His data retrieval systems pulled her exact words from his memory archives. "You said you'd lost faith in humanity. That kindness was dead in this world."

"Don't." Her voice cracked. "Please don't make me choose."

"I'm not asking you to choose. I'm asking you to think. To remember who I am. Who we all are." Block's sensors registered the growing chaos outside—robots gathering to discuss the exile order, the confused voices of humans. Through the window, he saw Shadow pacing in front of the hotel. Maxwell stood in his workshop doorway, all four arms hanging limp at his sides.

"Maggie, you're making a terrible mistake," Block said, but he held his wrists out to Jenny. Compliance now might preserve future opportunities to reverse the council's decision. "Dr. Kaine won't stop just because you've expelled us. She won't stop until she's destroyed the town."

Project Echo's high-pitched tone sliced through the air. Block's visual feed shattered into prismatic shards. His servos screamed as the signal invaded his systems, the mechanical equivalent of every muscle seizing simultaneously. Through the distortion, he saw other robots stumbling outside the windows, their movements becoming jerky and uncontrolled.

"It's happening again," Block said, fighting to maintain his balance.

Maggie clapped her hands over her ears. "What's that awful sound?"

The tone intensified. Block's power reserves plummeted as his systems fought against the invasion. His internal chronometer glitched: 1705 hours, then 2347, then error. Time itself seemed to fracture as his perception systems failed one by one. His optical sensors pixelated Jenny into geometric fragments as the handcuffs clattered to the floor. She reached out to steady him.

"Block?" Her voice seemed to come from far away. "What's wrong with you?"

"Keep Wally safe," he managed. "Whatever happens, protect her." In his failing systems, Wally's safety remained the one constant variable in an increasingly chaotic equation.

The signal peaked like a blade of light through his

circuits. His cleaning protocols activated again, noting dust on the windowsill, scuff marks blooming where Jenny's boots scraped the floor.

His waning processor focused on Wally, and how he'd failed to protect her when she needed him most. Then darkness.

THIRTY
CHAOS

VALERIE

As the Project Echo device warmed against her palm, Valerie felt a blend of anticipation and dread that had become her constant companion these past ten years. Every step toward this moment had cost her something—sleep, conscience, human connection—but she'd willingly paid those prices. Some sacrifices were worth making.

She emerged from the basement hideout. Chloe stumbled behind her, one hand pressed to her temple, the other bracing against the door frame. Blood from where she'd bitten her lip had dried in a dark streak across her chin.

"This way," Valerie said, not looking back. "A little farther."

Her medical training begged her to tend to Chloe's deteriorating condition—to check her pulse, her pupils, to administer fluids. The doctor in her battled the weary soldier. She swallowed back the guilt. Later, she would make it up to the girl after they'd won.

Valerie had lost track of time in the dark basement. The sun was setting, and darkness would soon settle across the square. They could've stayed underground, but Valerie wanted to see the commotion with her own eyes, and Chloe's impact would be much stronger above ground.

Chaos engulfed Deer Valley. The square teemed with agitated people and robots—many more residents than she'd expected to find outside at once. It couldn't have been more perfectly timed.

A few minutes earlier, Maggie Crenshaw's voice had crackled through the emergency broadcast system, carried by speakers mounted on poles throughout the settlement. She had ordered the robots to leave immediately.

The town's attention was diverted; confusion reigned. Block and the others would be scrambling to counter the council's decision, leaving Valerie to implement the final phase.

"Dr. Kaine?" Chloe's voice wavered. "Something's wrong. Everyone looks scared."

"They're surprised by the council's decision, is all." Valerie steered Chloe toward Block's Hotel. "Focus on your breathing. Remember what we practiced."

"My head hurts so bad," Chloe said. "Worse than before."

"It'll pass." Valerie knew it wouldn't. She needed Chloe to hang on long enough to enact the plan. After that, Chloe could rest while Valerie worked on utilizing the other teens. They probably had an inkling of their new abilities, but only she could teach them to master their skills.

They reached the concrete steps leading to the hotel's entrance. Valerie guided Chloe to sit, then positioned herself a bit higher, the central Echo device in her hands. The hotel rested at the top of a small, sloping hill that gave her a more expansive view of the town. The first Peacekeepers were being escorted toward the south gate, G9 standing by to oversee the evacuation. His kind was no longer welcome, thanks to her. She wondered if their programming felt the sting of rejection by the humans they'd sworn to protect.

She had no sympathy.

"It's time, Chloe." She activated the device. Its copper surface pulsed with green light, sending the first wave of energy outward. "I need you to amplify the signal like we practiced."

"But there are so many people out." Chloe's voice was thin with exhaustion. "What if I hurt someone?"

"You won't," Valerie lied.

A low growl cut through the noise of the square. The robo-dog Shadow stood at the bottom of the steps, her optics locked on Valerie while her black armor bristled with defensive protocols.

"Move away from Chloe," Shadow said. "Now."

Valerie smiled. "I was wondering when you might show up." She adjusted the device's frequency and aimed it directly at Shadow. At once, the canine unit's head tilted and her body shook.

"Chloe, remember how you felt the machines during our practice? I need you to focus on Shadow. Reach out with your mind and push the signal into her circuits."

"I can't," Chloe protested. "She's my friend . . ."

"Do it," Valerie demanded. "This is what we've been training for. It's why I chose you."

With trembling hands and chattering teeth, Chloe fixed her gaze on Shadow. The robot dog tensed, and before Shadow had time to react, her optics flickered. A high-pitched whine escaped her vocal module as her legs buckled beneath her.

Shadow collapsed in a heap as her systems were overloaded by the neural pattern Chloe had amplified.

Watching the mighty guardian dog fall triggered a memory—Valerie's childhood retriever on the ground after being hit by a neighbor's car. That had been the first time she'd felt truly helpless. This moment couldn't have been more different. Here, she held all the power. The sensation was intoxicating.

"Good job," Valerie said. "Now, the others."

Chloe looked onto the square. The high-pitched drone from the Echo device grew louder. Valerie thought she saw arcs of light sparking between Chloe, the device, and two nodes placed at adjacent buildings.

Chloe stumbled backward and sat on the steps. "What's happening to them?"

Robots faltered. A NannyBot dropped the bag it had been carrying. A CargoBot that had been traveling toward the south gate froze mid-motion, then jerked violently as its systems fought against the intrusive signal. Even smaller bots—the kitchen helpers, the cleaning units—convulsed as the amplified frequency tore through their programming.

A laugh bubbled up from somewhere deep in Valerie's chest, threatening to escape. She bit it back, knowing it would disturb Chloe. But God, it felt good to see the machines breaking down, to watch their precious programming fracture and fail. Each spark, each mechanical meltdown, was payback for every human who'd died at the hands of SoldierBots.

"They're being reset," Valerie said. "Going back to their original parameters."

"But it's hurting them," Chloe whispered, her voice breaking. "I can feel it. It's like they're screaming inside."

"They're machines," Valerie said. "They don't feel pain. Now, focus on the Peacekeepers. Boost the signal toward the north gate."

Chloe whimpered and tears streamed down her cheeks. She licked her lips, and blood trickled from her mouth again. "I want to stop."

"You can't," Valerie said. "We're too close." She knelt beside Chloe, gripping her shoulder with painful force and cupping Chloe's chin to look at her. "Remember what I showed you? The photo of your mother? Olivia died because of robots like these. They all have blood on their hands."

"But not all the robots fought in the Uprising," Chloe said, though her words lacked strength. "Not Block or Vacuubot or—"

"They're all the same," Valerie hissed. "All programmed to turn on us, eventually. Push, Chloe. Use your gift."

Chloe's jaw clenched with effort as she looked toward the north gate. The air in front of her rippled and distorted like heat waves over summer asphalt. The central device in Valerie's hands pulsed faster, its copper surface taking on a brilliant green glow.

At the north gate, a Peacekeeper stopped mid-stride. Its visor flickered from red to green, matching the device's glow. The robot's posture changed—shoulders squaring, head lifting, arm cannons extending from their housing with a pneumatic hiss. It was no longer a Peacekeeper there to guard the town.

It was a SoldierBot preparing for battle.

"It's working," Valerie said.

Like a cascading wave, the Peacekeepers' visors changed color. Their synchronized movements took on a predatory precision as old programming surfaced. G9 was the last to succumb, his massive frame shaking as he fought the signal, his voice modulator emitting bursts of static that might have been pleas for help.

Then his visor turned green, and he straightened, his weapons systems coming online with a whine that cut through the growing panic.

"What have I done?" Chloe balled her fists to her temples. "Dr. Kaine, make it stop."

"We're only getting started," Valerie said. "Now for the others like you."

Screams erupted from the north gate as a SoldierBot fired its weapon. The energy pulse left a smoking crater in the ground, missing a fleeing human by inches. People scattered. Cries of terror were punctuated by the mechanical march of the reactivated SoldierBots.

Valerie raised the device higher, adjusting its frequency once more. "Amplify it, Chloe. Push it toward your friends. They have to be close."

"No." Chloe tried to stand, but her legs gave way beneath her. "I won't help you hurt them."

"You already have," Valerie said coldly. "The signal's reaching them. Can't you feel it?"

Chloe's signal was taking on a life of its own. Windows shattered as her telekinetic energy surged unchecked. Water pipes burst from sudden pressure changes. The entire settlement seemed to shudder under her awakening power.

"This is what you were made for," Valerie said. "All of you. A new generation of humans with the power to control machines."

The bakery's signpost twisted like putty, the metal bending as if alive. Somewhere nearby, a woman screamed in fear and confusion as stones levitated around her.

"Mach X never understood what he'd created," Valerie continued, watching the chaos spread with cold satisfaction. "He saw you as servants to his vision. But I see the truth. You are the most powerful weapons humanity has against the machines."

The SoldierBots abandoned the gate and marched into the square's center, their contaminated green visors scanning for targets. People fled in all directions. Some headed for the northern gate; others sought shelter in buildings. A few braver souls grabbed makeshift weapons—pipes, wooden planks, anything that might offer some defense against the advancing machines.

Other robots were crumpled to a heap or circling with malfunction.

"Why?" Chloe cried, her entire body trembling. "Why are you doing this?"

"Because someone has to stand against them," Valerie said. "My sister died in Mach X's lab so you would be born. Her sacrifice can't be for nothing."

Another explosion rocked the square as a Soldier-Bot's cannon found its mark. The air filled with dust and smoke, making visibility poor. It wouldn't be long before they destroyed the town.

Valerie hadn't planned for quite this level of destruction, but she found herself strangely unmoved by it. Buildings could be rebuilt, infrastructure repaired. The humans would recover, stronger for having thrown off their mechanical oppressors. And if some didn't survive . . . well, casualties were inevitable in any revolution. She'd stopped counting the cost long ago, somewhere between Manhattan and here.

The central device in Valerie's hands grew suddenly hot, its copper surface blistering her skin. She cried out, dropping it on the steps. Nearby, the SoldierBots faltered, their advance slowing as conflicting signals battled for dominance in their systems.

Chloe looked at the device.

"Did you do that?" Valerie asked, rage rising inside her.

"I want you to stop this," Chloe said.

Valerie bit her lip against the searing pain in her right hand but maintained her composure. Drawing a deep breath, she looked at Chloe with an expression of wounded disappointment rather than anger.

"I understand," she said, keeping her voice steady despite the chaos erupting around them. "You're scared. Anyone would be."

Chloe's eyes widened. She glanced at the angry red burns forming on Valerie's palm. "I'm sorry," she said. "I didn't mean to hurt you."

"Of course you didn't." Valerie's tone was gentle. She reached out with her burned hand and brushed a strand of hair from Chloe's face, letting the girl see the injury up close. "We're both trying to find our way through this. It's overwhelming."

Throughout the square, the SoldierBots remained in disarray, some standing still, others moving erratically as conflicting signals battled within their systems. The brief pause in Chloe's concentration had disrupted the amplification pattern.

"Look at me." Valerie knelt to meet Chloe at eye level. "Do you think I want any of this destruction? I want freedom—for you, for everyone in Deer Valley. Freedom from being controlled by machines."

Guilt flickered across Chloe's pale face. "But people are getting hurt."

"Change is painful," Valerie acknowledged. "But before we can rebuild, we have to clear away what's broken." She gestured toward the malfunctioning robots. "Just like Mach X cleared away the old world to make room for his vision."

Chloe's brow furrowed. "But you said Mach X was wrong."

"His methods were wrong," Valerie corrected. "Not his understanding of what you children could become." She picked up the device again; it had cooled to a reasonable temperature. "He saw your potential, as I do."

"I don't know if I can control it." Chloe wiped blood from her lip. "It feels like too much."

"That's why you need guidance," Valerie said. "Someone who understands what you're going through . . . and who cares about you."

The sincerity in her voice wasn't entirely fabricated. She did believe in Chloe's potential as long as Valerie got what she wanted. The device hummed in her hands, quieter now but still functional.

"The others like me," Chloe said hesitantly. "They'll feel this too?"

"They already are," Valerie said. "They're awakening as we speak. Think how frightened they must be, with no one to explain what's happening to them." She reached out, taking Chloe's trembling hand. "We can help them together. Guide them. Show them how to use their gifts responsibly."

A flicker of hope crossed Chloe's face. "And then the hurting will stop?"

"Yes," Valerie promised, the lie coming easily. "Once the transition is complete, once the robots are under your control, peace will return to Deer Valley. A new kind of peace."

Chloe's resistance wavered. Valerie saw it in her eyes—the desperate need to believe there was a purpose behind the pain.

"I never wanted to hurt anyone," Chloe said. "I just wanted to understand what was happening to me."

"I know. And you will. We all make mistakes when we're learning something new." Valerie turned the device's settings, lowering its intensity to a more sustainable level. "What matters is what we do next. How we fix things."

Chloe nodded slowly, her resolve weakening under Valerie's gentle manipulation. "What do we do?"

"First, stabilize the signal," Valerie explained, her voice calm and instructive despite the screams and crashes echoing from the square.

Chloe hesitated, then fixed her gaze on the square, concentrating.

"That's it," Valerie encouraged as the Echo's surface pulsed with a steadier rhythm. "Focus on balance. Control."

The malfunctioning robots in the square began to move again, their erratic behavior smoothing out. Not normal activity but not attacking either. It was a holding pattern that Valerie needed.

"You're doing wonderfully," she said. Chloe truly was exceptional—a most powerful conduit.

The suffocating tang of smoke hung in the air as a movement at the edge of the square caught Valerie's attention. Through the haze and confusion, she could make out several figures running toward the hotel—Wally at the front, followed by other teenagers. The rest of Mach X's children, drawn together by the awakening of their dormant abilities.

Perfect.

"Look." Valerie nodded toward the approaching group. "Your friends need you now. They're frightened and confused like you were."

Chloe turned, recognition flashing across her face. "Wally, Tomas, Clay . . ."

"They're feeling what you are feeling—that power awakening inside them. Who better to help them understand than you?"

A pulse of energy radiated from Chloe's trembling form, causing the concrete steps beneath them to vibrate. A new sense of purpose filled Chloe and straightened her hunched shoulders. "I can explain it to them."

"Exactly." Valerie allowed herself a small smile. "Together, you can master these abilities. Support each other. Become what you were always meant to be."

As Wally and the others drew closer, Valerie's grip tightened on the Echo device. One conduit had been impressive enough. Eleven together would be unstoppable.

She'd lost Olivia to the machines. She would not lose this new family she was building—this small army she was gathering. Not to Block, not to Emery, not to anyone who stood in her way.

THIRTY-ONE
REBELLION

WALLY

Parts of Deer Valley were on fire. Wally couldn't believe the town—her home—was shattering so fast.

Flames consumed the community garden where she'd helped plant seedlings every spring with Block. Smoke billowed from the library roof where she'd spent countless hours reading. The market square's stalls were splintered, their goods scattered across the cobblestones. Her chest tightened with grief, but beneath it burned something fierce. This was her safe haven. These were her people. She wouldn't let Kaine destroy everything they'd built.

She ran toward the hotel on gut instinct. An owl swooped low overhead, its wings beating frantically as it circled her twice. *Danger-hurry.* The message pulsed in her mind, confirming what she already sensed.

"This way!" she called to the others, leading the

group of teens through the smoke-hazed streets. They'd all abandoned their separate missions for the hotel once the chaos broke out. Her lungs burned with each breath, but she pressed on, driven by the desperate need to find her dad and stop whatever madness Dr. Kaine had unleashed.

Brad's sharp intake of breath drew Wally's attention toward the hotel steps.

Through the smog, Wally could make out two figures—the sight of Chloe made her stomach lurch. For a heartbeat, she saw them as seven-year-olds, laughing as they raced paper boats down the stream behind the library. That memory vanished, replaced by this hollow shell sitting motionless on the steps, her vacant eyes fixed on nothing. Her expression was eerily empty, as if she'd retreated deep inside herself. Beside her stood Dr. Kaine, holding something that pulsed with an unnatural green glow. The air around them seemed to warp and distort.

"She's using Chloe to amplify the signal," Tomas said, his enhanced vision taking in details the others couldn't see. "The device she holds is connected to the nodes somehow. I can see the energy patterns flowing between them. And it's all surging through Chloe."

Across the square, a line of SoldierBots had formed a perimeter, their visors scanning methodically. They were herding terrified townspeople into a corner near the library. A woman tried to break away, clutching her child's hand. A SoldierBot's arm shot out, grabbing her shoulder and shoving her back into the growing crowd. Another robot fired a warning blast that scorched the ground inches from a man's feet when he protested. The

Peacekeepers—no, SoldierBots now—were efficiently corralling the humans like livestock and hurting them when they needed compliance.

"We have to stop her," Wally said. "Someone's going to get killed." And some probably already had, but she didn't say that part out loud.

Maya gripped Wally's arm, her fingers digging in with frightened strength. "How? There are SoldierBots everywhere!"

"Together," Wally said, as they huddled near the wall of the hastily abandoned Mikey's Diner. "Our abilities are awakening because of the signal. Maybe we can use them against Dr. Kaine."

The group exchanged nervous glances. None of them had fully come to terms with their emerging powers, let alone learned to control them. But the chaos spreading through Deer Valley left them no choice.

"I'm with you," Tomas said.

One by one, the others nodded, some determined and a few with obvious fear. But they stood together, and when their world was crumbling, it was the minor miracle they needed.

"Stay close," Wally said. "Watch each other's backs."

They hurried toward the hotel, picking their way through overturned market stalls and scattered debris. The high-pitched tone that had haunted them for days now filled the air, so intense it made Wally's teeth ache. A thin stream of red trickled from Brad's ear, and Liam stumbled, clutching his head.

When they reached the center of the square, Chloe spotted them. Her eyes widened with recognition, then clouded with something darker—something out of her control. She rose unsteadily from the steps.

"That's far enough," Dr. Kaine called, her voice carrying over the signal's blare. "I've been waiting for you all to join us. Chloe has something to show you."

Chloe's empty gaze shifted toward them, her eyes narrowing. The cobblestones beneath Wally's feet shuddered. No movement, no gesture—just Chloe's unfocused stare as a shockwave of telekinetic energy sent a nearby cart hurtling at them.

"Down!" Wally shouted, pulling Maya and Clay to the ground as the cart sailed over their heads, splintering against a wall behind them.

Liam wasn't so lucky. The cart's wheel caught his shoulder, spinning him to the ground with a pained cry. Abby rushed to his side, helping him scramble back to his feet as more debris lifted into the air—rocks, broken glass, a metal gate torn from its hinges.

"Chloe, stop!" Wally called out. "This isn't you!"

But Chloe's face was a frozen mask. Scarlet droplets seeped from her ears as objects continued to rise around her. The barrage came like a storm—a hail of stones, twisted metal, and shattered wood, all flying toward them with deadly force.

"She can't hear you!" Tomas pulled Wally behind a market stall as the projectiles tore through the air where she'd stood. The shelter wouldn't last long—already the wooden planks were splintering under the impact.

Clay cried out as a stone caught his temple, sending him staggering into Brad's arms. Dark red matted his hair. Maya tried to reach them, but a twisted piece of metal slashed across her arm, tearing her sleeve and the skin beneath.

"Retreat!" Wally ordered, the animal instinct for survival screaming inside her. They wouldn't last long under Chloe's barrage. "Behind the bakery!"

They ran and crawled, using whatever cover they found. Fiona helped Clay, who was dazed and unsteady. Liam clutched his injured shoulder, his face pale with shock. Jordan and Zoey locked hands together as they fled. The assault pummeled the street, objects crashing around them and chasing their footsteps.

Finally, they reached the relative safety behind Tara's Hearth. The solid brick wall shielded them from the immediate danger. They huddled, gasping for breath, and assessing injuries. Wally's heart hammered against her ribs as she counted heads—all there, but all hurt.

Maya pressed her sleeve against the gash on her arm. "I can't take that again. Why is Chloe attacking us?"

"Kaine must have her brainwashed," Tomas explained, peering cautiously around the corner. "Something's wrong—Chloe looks sick. Really sick."

"Yeah. We're not much better." Brad winced as he touched a purple welt blooming across his cheek. "Is anyone else's head feeling like it's about to explode?"

A chorus of pained agreement followed. Clay's hands shook as he tried to wipe blood from his forehead. Liam sat with his back against the wall, his breathing shallow and rapid. Abby kept blinking rapidly, as if trying to clear her vision. Wally tried to ignore the pain shooting through her temples, but they were all deteriorating under the influence of the amplified signal.

"The device," Wally said. "Kaine's awakening our neural pathways, but it's hurting us like it's hurting Chloe."

"And if we don't stop her, we'll all end up like Chloe," Tomas added grimly. "Or worse."

"I need to get to Chloe. Talk to her," Wally said. "She's still in there somewhere. She wouldn't hurt us willingly."

"Are you crazy?" Maya said. "She just tried to kill us!"

Wally rubbed her aching left leg where a wooden board had slammed into her. "If Kaine wasn't controlling her, I could get through to her. I know it."

Tomas shook his head. "That device is too powerful. Kaine will use it to control you too."

"Then what do we do?" Fiona asked.

Wally surveyed her friends—each of them changing in ways they barely understood. She thought of what Block would do in her situation. He'd tell her to work together. Stick by each other.

"We use what we have," she said finally. "Our abilities can fight her."

"But we don't know how to control them," Jordan said.

"We have to try," Wally said. "Tomas, what can you see?"

Tomas stepped to the edge of the wall and focused his gaze on the hotel. "The device Kaine is holding is the central conductor for the signal. The energy patterns connect to nodes throughout town. And Chloe . . . the signal flows through her, gets stronger, then spreads outward."

"So, if we take out the device . . ." Liam said.

"The signal stops," Wally finished. "And we can reach Chloe."

"That's our target then," Tomas said.

"What abilities can you use under pressure?" Wally looked around the circle. "Now's not the time to hold back."

They exchanged uncertain glances until Abby spoke up. "I can mess with electrical stuff. Yesterday, my mom's tablet went crazy when I touched it. And the lights in our apartment flicker when I get upset."

"I can sense vibrations," Clay said. "Like, I feel people moving around, even when I can't see them. It's how I knew a SoldierBot was coming before it appeared."

"And I can create temperature changes," Liam added. "When I'm angry or scared, things get really cold around me. I think I froze my dad's coffee solid this morning without even touching it."

Each of them shared their emerging abilities—Maya could somehow accelerate plant growth; Brad mimicked any sound perfectly after hearing it once; Fiona discovered she could alter her skin, making it change color and texture when threatened.

"We each got different pieces of the puzzle," Tomas said. "All from the same neural implants but expressed differently."

Wally thought quickly, then sketched a rough plan on the brick wall with a white rock. It wasn't perfect, but it might work if they could surprise Dr. Kaine. Tomas would use his vision to guide them; Abby would disrupt nearby electronics to cause a distraction; Clay would track Dr. Kaine's movements; Liam would try to shock-freeze her hands to make her drop the device; and Maya's accelerated plant growth from nearby planters could create a barrier if they needed cover.

"What about you, Wally?" Fiona asked. "Your animal thing?"

"I'm not sure," she said. "The animals sense danger—they might help warn me if there's any danger we don't know about." She wondered where Block was amid all the chaos and said a quick prayer to keep him safe. If he knew what was happening at his hotel, he would certainly be there to stand by Wally. The fact he was missing alarmed her, but she shoved the thought to the back of her mind for now.

Each passing minute brought more destruction to Deer Valley, more danger to their families and homes. Blood still trickled from Brad's ear, and Clay's eyes didn't seem to focus properly. Whatever Dr. Kaine's signal was doing to them, it was getting worse.

Together, they emerged from behind the bakery, splitting into the formation they'd planned. Abby, Fiona, and Liam circled left, Maya and Brad right. Jordan and Zoey brought up the rear. Clay positioned himself to track Dr. Kaine's movements, while Tomas stayed beside Wally, guiding her with his enhanced vision.

A SoldierBot stood at the edge of the square, its green visor scanning. Before it could detect them, Tomas pulled Wally behind a toppled cart.

"Dr. Kaine's moved!" Tomas shouted loud enough for the others to hear. "They're inside the lobby." Then to Wally he said, "The device is still active—I can see the energy patterns pulsing through the windows."

Wally nodded, processing this change. The fight would happen in the hotel where she could use her knowledge of the layout and its many details against Kaine.

She took a deep breath, steadying her racing heart. "Let's finish this."

They ran across the square, dodging the abandoned stalls, splintered lumber, and upraised stones. The SoldierBot turned, its sensors detecting movement, but before it could respond, Abby approached and raised her hands in the shape of a V. The SoldierBot halted, and its armored frame twitched and shook. "Go on without me," Abby shouted. "I'll hold it."

Wally whispered another small prayer for her brave friend. She wasn't a religious person, but she needed some higher power to keep her going. *Please let us make it through this.*

Through the shattered lobby doors, Dr. Kaine stood near the reception desk, the Echo device glowing in her hands. Chloe sat rigid in a nearby chair, her gaze vacant. Soot and blood were smudged across her pallid features. Her body was present, but her mind lingered elsewhere, connected to the pulsing device that Dr. Kaine manipulated. Occasional tremors shook Chloe's shoulders, synchronized with the device's rhythmic glow.

Wally's throat tightened with rage. The device was killing Chloe.

"Now," she whispered.

Tomas raised his hand in signal. Immediately, the chandelier lights flickered violently as Jordan disrupted the electrical systems. Dr. Kaine looked up in surprise, the momentary distraction giving Wally and the others the opening they needed to enter the lobby. Liam's expression hardened as the temperature around Dr. Kaine plummeted. Frost formed on the device, spreading rapidly to her hands. She gasped, the sudden cold clearly painful, but her grip remained firm. Wally wondered if the device itself fought off the freezing attempt.

Maya reached out her hands toward the decorative planters flanking the hotel entrance. The dormant winter plants suddenly erupted with new growth, vines snaking across the floor toward Dr. Kaine, attempting to ensnare her feet.

But Dr. Kaine acted fast. With a twist of the device's controls, the signal intensified. The high-pitched tone pierced Wally's skull like a knife, dropping her to her knees. Around her, the others cried out, clutching their heads as blood began to trickle from their noses and gums.

Tomas staggered, his enhanced vision suddenly a liability as the signal overwhelmed him.

Dr. Kaine stepped forward, the device pulsing with its malevolent glow. "Did you really think your untrained abilities would match me?" she asked, her voice cutting through their pain. "You're nothing but children playing with forces you can't begin to understand."

Through tears, Wally saw Chloe stir in her chair, her

eyelids fluttering, then opening. Something passed between them—recognition, a silent plea. *Help us.*

"My sister didn't die so you could waste your potential." Dr. Kaine adjusted the device. The tone strengthened, and Brad collapsed completely. "You were meant for greatness—to reclaim this world from the machines. Instead, you've been pampered and protected while your true nature was hidden from you."

Wally fought to stay conscious as the signal bored into her brain. The owl flapped its great wings outside the window. *Danger-danger-flee.* But she couldn't. Dr. Kaine still held the device that was killing her and her friends.

"Your sad, little rebellion ends now," Dr. Kaine said. "It's time you understood your place in what's coming."

Wally tried to speak, to reach out to Chloe, but no words came. Around her, her friends lay sprawled across the lobby floor, some unconscious, others barely holding on. Their plan had failed completely. They were at Dr. Kaine's mercy.

As darkness crept into the edges of her vision, Wally thought of Block. She hoped he was safe, that he'd escaped the signal's effect. She'd failed him. And everyone.

THIRTY-TWO
MICROSCOPIC

BLOCK

Darkness unraveled itself slowly as Block's systems rebooted. His optical sensors calibrated, showing tiny pins of white light at first, then shades of blues, yellows, and reds. His surroundings came into focus—concrete walls, a metal bench bolted to the floor, steel bars across the entrance. One of the four jail cells in Deer Valley. How ironic the town council had locked him in the very holding area he'd helped design for bandits, troublemakers, drunks, and yes, on the slim chance a robot rebelled. It had never happened in the twelve years the cells had existed.

Until now.

Block was the first robot jailbird. What a disgrace.

But he had other urgent problems. The signal had been at its strongest, forcing him to shut down and resetting his internal chronometer. After running a system diagnostic, he reviewed the findings. Power reserves: 41 percent. Memory core: intact. Motor functions: operational but sluggish at 64 percent capacity. When he stood, his servo joints whined as if they too protested his jail stint.

Hello?" he called out, but his greeting was met with silence.

Through the bars, he could see Sheriff Green's empty desk. Papers and pens lay scattered across its surface. She must've left in a hurry. The holding cell sat at the rear of the modest police station, a repurposed hardware store from the pre-Uprising.

From somewhere outside, Block heard muffled screams. Then an energy weapon discharged. No, no, no. His most dreaded scenario had come true—the Soldier-Bots were attacking. People would be killed. Where was Wally?

An obtrusive archived memory bubbled up. In the early days of Deer Valley, he'd argued with Nova. Block wanted the Peacekeepers' weapons removed, but Nova had insisted their guns should stay. The compound needed security against rogue invaders. G9 had stayed neutral, insisting his units would do what was best for the settlement. Block reasoned they could keep a few guns locked away in case of any threat, but he'd been outvoted by the newly formed council, who wanted it known that the Peacekeepers that patrolled Deer Valley's walls would use deadly force, and they encouraged it to be spoken of widely. Well, it had been effective in keeping bandits and militias from hitting them.

They hadn't prepared for the scenario in which

someone hijacked the Peacekeepers and turned them against their own community.

Block pressed his chrome face to the bars, tuning his sensors to pick up any movement in the dimly lit office. A map on the far wall displayed Deer Valley's layout, red pins marking strategic points. His steel fingers gripped the metal bars. No way would it budge. He wasn't Oxford the Mech, after all. The cell lock was manual, not electronic—an intentional choice made during construction. No digital mechanism that could be hacked remotely.

He focused his sensors on the lock. Simple tumbler design. Given time and proper tools, he could probably pick it. But time was a resource he couldn't spare, not when Wally needed protecting.

He sat on the bench, processing scenarios of ways to break out. He tried to ping Maxwell, Shadow, Vacuubot, but it was no use. Every comm had been jammed by the signal. He was a CleanerBot, not an escape artist. An X4J6 was never supposed to be in jail!

He looked down at his left foot where he'd noted a tingle since yesterday. Robots didn't usually feel pain; it was an awareness. And then he recalled the narrow needle Maxwell had used a few days ago while injecting an experimental batch into Block's cleaning fluid system.

"Think of it as your microscopic maintenance crew," Maxwell had said. He explained they were nanobots designed to repair minor damage without external intervention. Block had filed them into the back burners of his processor in the chaos since Dr. Kaine's arrival.

By now the miniature machines would be

distributed throughout his architecture, doing their thing—cleaning his microbial systems, hydraulics, the weird empty spaces where gunk built up between wires. Block hoped that's what they were doing, anyway. He opened his forearm panel. The metal plate slid back with a soft click, revealing a tangle of coiled tubes and wiring. Could he see them? He didn't think it was possible. Maxwell had said they were so small, even the JunkBots couldn't detect them without microscopes.

"Excuse me, Nanobots?" he said, though he knew he sounded foolish. "Can you hear me? I'm trapped in a locked jail cell, and I need to get out. Any ideas?"

No answer came, of course.

They probably weren't attuned to Block's external environment; such a world would be too vast for tiny beings to deal with. Nanobots wouldn't understand spoken language either. No, that was too complex.

Was there some other way he could communicate with them? The nanobots were programmed to clean and maintain like he was. Block fished around in his CleanerBot code, searching for snippets that might make sense to other cleaner units.

He created a code packet with very basic instructions. The string of bits and bytes were more primitive, as if he was giving an order to a child who was learning English.

Emergency. Trapped. Open lock. Free. Help.

This was quite possibly one of his silliest ideas ever, but Block pushed the packet into his communication stream in the hopes the message might somehow cross over into the nanobots' frequency.

Then he waited, knowing he didn't have long before he'd have to abandon this course. He stood and banged on the lock. Could he rattle it hard enough to break it? It was attached to the front of the iron door in such a way that he couldn't make a solid hit against it.

He pinged his friends again, knowing it was fruitless, but he was out of ideas. Nothing but static. Outside, the blaring signal hammered the town. An explosion sounded, and his sensors detected smoke.

"Let me out!" he shouted into the empty office as he gripped the cell's bars. "Wally needs me!"

He shoved and tried to shake the bars which had no effect. A faint buzz emanated from his forearm, then a notification flashed across his internal display: *Maintenance Protocols Activated*.

The message was unusual; he hadn't initiated any protocols. He was about to cancel the activation when a stream of silvery liquid leaked from a tube in his leg, dripping onto the concrete floor like mercury. The puddle moved forward despite the even surface and split into smaller droplets that raced toward the cell door.

The nanobots had understood him! Block's optical sensors captured every detail as the silvery liquid swarmed up the bars. The metallic substance moved with a collective purpose as it converged on the lock.

"I don't know how you're doing this," he said to the strange substance.

Maybe Maxwell's "crazy idea" wasn't so absurd after all. Block had initially dismissed the nanobots as a frivolous experiment—cleaning technology too miniature to be practical. But now, watching them systematically disassemble the lock from the inside, he recalculated his assessment. They possessed an elegant efficiency, these microscopic maintenance workers. No specialized tools required, no elaborate hacking devices—just autonomous problem solvers doing what they were programmed to do on a microscopic scale.

The mechanism clicked as the machines infiltrated its inner workings. Tumblers shifted. Springs compressed.

The lock clicked open.

"You did it, tiny Nanobots!" Block pushed the cell door, and it swung outward. The nanobots retreated, flowing back toward his foot, climbing his leg like a silver stream seeking its source. They crawled up his plating and disappeared into the hydraulics at his knee.

"Thank you," Block said, though he knew the nanobots couldn't understand his words. He logged a future task to work with Maxwell on ways to communicate with the team of mini robots.

He walked toward Sheriff Green's empty desk, cautious in case any officers remained. They might want to capture him, though his logic processor told him the situation outside was so severe, Block's whereabouts would be low on the priority list.

A crash from outside sent Block ducking behind the desk, but only for five seconds. He stood, and there was only one directive—find Wally.

A robot approached. Its heavy feet thudded against the sidewalk that led into the police department. Block calculated his options. No rear exit. Windows barred.

Front door exposed. He squeezed himself between two tall filing cabinets.

The door swung open, and a SoldierBot stepped inside. It would scan the room, the empty cell. The robot had heat-seeking tech and would detect him at any moment. Block remained motionless and turned his power core as low as possible to cool himself down.

The SoldierBot walked past the desk. Its armored foot crushed a pencil, the snap loud in the quiet room. One more step would bring it alongside Block.

Block's cleaning protocols activated automatically in response to the stress consuming his threat indicator. His vacuum tube extended silently from his back compartment—useless against seven feet of military-grade armor. But then he noticed the silvery stream of liquid amassed at the end of the tube.

As the SoldierBot passed his hiding spot, Block extended the vacuum tube, letting it brush against the SoldierBot's neck joint, where the armor was thinnest. The shimmery nanobot liquid landed and instantly melted into the seam between helmet and body.

The SoldierBot turned to face Block. "CleanerBot," it said. The number 17 was emblazoned on its armor. Block and 17 had worked to build parts of Deer Valley's walls together. But there was no sign of recognition as it raised its gun arm and pointed at Block's chest where his CPU was housed. A direct hit there meant no return.

"17, it's me, Block." The SoldierBot paused, tilting its head. "You and I go way back, friend. Hey, I notice your armor could use a polish."

The SoldierBot looked down at its feet where the armor was caked in mud up to its knees. Its weapon arm lowered. "You . . . clean . . . dirt?" The words were stilted, as if the SoldierBot had reverted to a more basic language model.

"I'm a CleanerBot XJ46. I clean dirt, dust, grime, oil, spills, hazards," Block continued. He was stalling, hoping the nanobots would affect Number 17, but so far, Block was still close to being shot. "I specialize in hard-to-reach joints and fine detailing. Let me get to work on your muddy feet."

The visor flickered again, and Block knelt, quickly bringing forth his spray cleaning apparatus and dousing 17's feet. Mud washed off and splashed the floor and Block's feet.

Come on, Nanobots. Do your thing.

17's left leg twitched. "Anomaly . . . detected," it said, in a droning, staticky voice. "Foreign . . . objects . . . in primary . . ."

"That's my premium cleaning solution." Block stood slowly, watching to be sure 17 was no longer a threat. "Very effective for removing hacked code."

17's visor shifted from the contaminated green back to red. It straightened, lowering its weapon arm completely. "Unit G17 returning to standard protocols," it said. "Signal interference neutralized."

"Good job, Nanobots!" Block said. "G17, the town is under attack. Dr. Valerie Kaine has a device that's reactivated old SoldierBot programming in the Peacekeepers. We need to find G9 and coordinate a defense."

17's head tilted, processing this information. "G9 was last seen near the council building."

Someone shouted outside, followed by the crash of breaking glass. Block ran to the window. Three Soldier-Bots marched down the street, herding a group of terrified humans toward the square. Among them, Block recognized Maggie Crenshaw's silver hair and Ralph Folk's stooped posture.

"We need to help those people," Block said.

17 stepped beside him. "Direct confrontation inadvisable. Seven active SoldierBot units detected in the immediate vicinity."

Block's memory banks flickered with images of Wally, of his promise to keep her safe. He would find her, but he had to handle one problem at a time.

"I have a plan," Block said. "But I'll need your help, 17."

"Affirmative," 17 said.

"It's good to have you back to normal, my friend." Block assembled another code string.

Bad robots. Disable. Help people. Spray?

He second-guessed the message. Would the Nanobots understand? But he didn't have time to perfect the code. The SoldierBots were herding people away. It was now or never.

He released the code and scanned his leg for evidence of the Nanobots. Within a few seconds, they pooled into a glob of liquid that bubbled from his knee joint. Good. They learned fast. Block hoped this experience was somehow fun or interesting for them.

He pointed to a narrow container he kept for cleaning solutions.

"Get in," Block instructed, though he realized the

Nanobots wouldn't understand his language. "Target the neck." He pointed at his own. "It's where the armor is thinnest."

The liquid bubble morphed and slid into the container. Block hooked his high-powered spray washer to the end. His processor churned out 635 scenarios, half of which ended with him being shot on the street. Not good odds, but he didn't have a choice.

"Let's do this," Block said.

"Ready." 17 didn't extend his gun arm.

"Are you going to use that?" Block asked.

"I keep the peace," 17 said. "No guns. Never any guns."

If they got out of this, and that was a big *if*, Block would introduce a resolution to remove the guns from the Peacekeeper units. Let the town council chew on his "I told you so."

They slipped out the door and into the street, following the SoldierBots. Block's metal feet clanked against the pavement as he held his spray nozzle like it was as dangerous as an automatic rifle.

The market square lay three blocks east, and the council building stood at its northern edge. Block mapped the most efficient route, factoring in likely SoldierBot patrol patterns.

Movement at the opening of a side alley caught his notice. A SoldierBot rounded the corner and spotted them immediately.

"Hostile detected," it announced, raising its gun. "Surrender."

G17 moved with military precision, tackling the

advancing SoldierBot before it could raise its arm all the way. They crashed into a stack of chopped wood. Block rushed forward as they grappled, G17 struggling to maintain hold of the thrashing robot.

"I need to get at the neck joint," Block said.

As G17 pinned the SoldierBot against the wall, Block aimed the spray nozzle and squirted a dose of nanobots into the armor's seam. The SoldierBot convulsed, its limbs spasming as the microscopic machines infiltrated its systems.

"Five units approaching," G17 warned. "Approximately twenty seconds until visual contact."

Block looked around. No viable escape routes. No cover. Their only option was to go up on the roof.

Block pointed to a drainpipe that ran up the side of the building. "Can you boost me?"

G17 interlocked his fingers to create a platform for Block's foot. With a push, Block pivoted upward, his fingers catching the edge of the roof. He pulled himself onto the roof seconds before the five SoldierBots appeared at the alley entrance with raised guns.

G17 faced them, weapon lowered, visor glowing red in the darkness. "You are malfunctioning," he told them. "Your directive is to keep the peace, not hurt people."

The SoldierBots paused, visors flickering as they processed this revelation. G17 approached them slowly. "Let me help you."

Block crossed the slanted roof with care, his metal feet finding purchase on the shingles. He crouched at the edge, watching the scene unfold. One SoldierBot raised its weapon, targeting G17's processor.

"Hey!" Block shouted.

The SoldierBots craned their heads up to where Block waited. "Hostile on roof," one of them said.

Block aimed the sprayer, rapidly calculating trajectory and wind resistance. The SoldierBots were clustered together, their neck joints exposed as they looked up. One blast, five targets. The odds were slim, but possible.

He squeezed the trigger.

The nanobot solution arced through the air. The SoldierBots detected the incoming spray too late, as the liquid splashed across their faces and neck joints. The seams of their armor were exposed.

For several seconds, they scanned each other with their pulsating visors and knocked against each other's armor in confusion. Then, one by one, their visors flickered from green to red. Their weapon arms lowered.

"Protocol violation detected," the lead unit announced. "Emergency override engaged."

Block slid down the drainpipe, landing beside G17. "Status?"

"Nanobots successful," G17 reported. "All units returning to peacekeeping protocols."

The robots straightened, their postures shifting from aggressive to alert. Block recognized their designations—G3, G8, G11, G22, and G24. Helpful citizens of Deer Valley, all of them.

"We saw SoldierBots taking people toward the council building," Block said. "They need our help."

G3 stepped forward. "We'll secure the perimeter."

"Good," Block said. "We need to spread the nanobot

solution to as many compromised units as possible. Find Maxwell."

G3's visor flashed acknowledgment. "Understood."

As the five SoldierBots departed, Block led G17 down a side street toward the council building. The sounds of chaos intensified—energy weapons discharging, screams, the crash of breaking windows. Smoke billowed from multiple structures, and an eerie haze had settled in the streets.

"Block!"

The voice came from a shop front. Block turned to find Maxwell emerging from the dark hardware store. His four arms clutched various tools and devices, and his frame showed signs of damage—dents in his chassis, scorch marks on one arm, his head component askew.

"Maxwell," Block said. "You're damaged."

"Minor inconveniences." Maxwell's third arm pushed his head back into proper alignment. "I've been trying to find you. The communication systems are completely jammed."

"It's the signal," Block said. "I found a solution! At least for the SoldierBots." He explained about the nanobots, how they disrupted the signal and restored them to their peaceful programming.

Maxwell's optical sensors whirred. "My experimental batch. Of course!" His arms waved with excitement. "The microscopic maintenance protocols would identify the foreign signal as system corruption and neutralize it."

"Brilliant," Block said. "We need more."

Maxwell dropped the tools he held. "My workshop has three more batches in cold storage."

"Get them," Block said. "I sent five units your way. They're all good now. They'll help you disperse the Nanobots. I used a spray gun."

"Gotcha, my friend." Maxwell spun to leave. "I'm on it." He turned. "Wait, where are you two going?"

"There are hostages in the council building. I'll help them, and then I need to find Wally."

"I saw her with her friends about fifteen minutes ago, heading to the hotel," Maxwell said.

Block's processor surged with worrisome scenarios. "Dr. Kaine must be there."

"Once I get the nanobot solution, I'll head to the hotel." Maxwell said. "Maybe I can help."

"Be careful," Block said. "The SoldierBots aren't messing around."

"I've survived worse." Maxwell set off.

Block and G17 hurried toward the council building. Its windows were dark except for a room on the second floor.

G17 scanned the area. "Six SoldierBots guarding the perimeter. Four more likely inside with the hostages."

Block assessed his remaining nanobot supply. He didn't know enough to calculate how much remained, or how many robots they could disable. He looked at the council building, recalling its design from when he'd helped renovate it years ago. Blueprints flashed through his processor. The sprinkler system connected to a central water tank in the basement.

"I need to get into the maintenance room," Block said. "Can you create a distraction?"

G17 nodded. "Affirmative."

They kept low, ducking behind scattered debris, until they reached the side of the building. G17 spotted a drainage grate—access to the basement level. After pulling it open, Block descended a ladder that led into a narrow shaft.

"Give me five minutes," he said.

"Copy that."

Block lowered himself into a dark tunnel, where his optical sensors adjusted to the low light. The tunnel emerged into the damp and dusty basement. He had to dial down his cleaning protocol, ignoring the shelves of old paper records and maintenance equipment.

He navigated through the maze of shelves toward the back wall where the water system controls were located. His internal chronometer counted down the minutes as he worked, opening access panels and studying the pipes that fed the sprinkler apparatus.

Inside the main control valve, Block released the remains of his nanobot solution into the water reservoir, watching as the silvery liquid disappeared into the system. He turned the pressure gauge to maximum.

Four minutes and thirty seconds had passed.

He made his way to the basement stairs, ascending quietly to the first level. Through a crack in the door, he could see the main entryway. Two SoldierBots stood guard. Beyond them, the staircase led to the council chamber on the second floor.

Four minutes, fifty-eight seconds.

On cue, glass shattered at the main entrance. The SoldierBots turned toward the noise, raising their guns.

"Hostile detected," one announced. "Investigating."

They ran toward the front, leaving the stairway momentarily unguarded. Block seized his chance, racing across the lobby and up the steps.

At the top of the stairs, he paused. Voices drifted from the main chamber—mechanical and human. He peered around the corner to see the council common area. Humans huddled together on one side, their faces pale with terror. Maggie Crenshaw sat at the center, her arm around a weeping young woman. Ralph Folk stood near the window, his face tight with anger. There were twenty people, including children.

Four SoldierBots stood guard. G9 lay deactivated in the corner.

There was one problem with Block's plan. A big one. The sprinkler controls were on the far wall. He needed to reach them without being detected. Impossible, with four SoldierBots scanning the room.

A crash of metal tearing against metal erupted outside. *Thank you, G17.* Two of the SoldierBots moved to the window.

Block walked forward, staying close to the wall where no lights shone. One more meter to the sprinkler control. He reached out, fingers brushing the switch.

A SoldierBot turned. "Intruder."

Block froze as all four SoldierBots swiveled toward him. A hiss arose as they charged their pulse weapons. "Hello, there." He raised his hands. "I'm here for routine sprinkler maintenance. Council regulations require monthly testing."

The SoldierBots advanced. Block backed away, buying time.

"Hostile unit," the lead SoldierBot declared. "Neutralize."

Block lunged for the sprinkler control, pulling the emergency activation lever. Water burst from the ceiling nozzles, drenching the room—and delivering the nanobot solution on top of the SoldierBots, soaking everyone.

The SoldierBots staggered, and their visors flickered between green and red as the nanobots infiltrated their systems. They turned in circles and retracted their guns.

Finally, the lead unit's visor settled back to red. "Resuming peacekeeping functions."

Block moved quickly to G9. The nanobot fluid had reached him, and his systems came back online. His red visor meant success. G9 sat up and Block hugged him.

G9's voice modulator recalibrated. "The signal was too powerful."

"I know," Block said. "Maxwell made nanobots, and they can fix all of you back to Peacekeepers."

Maggie Crenshaw approached, water dripping from her silver hair. "Block," she said. "I don't know how you disarmed them, but I'm amazed." Her arms and legs shook from adrenaline, fear, and exhaustion.

Ralph Folk joined them, his thin frame shivering from the water. "We thought they were going to execute us."

Block stood. "We need to move everyone to safety. The signal is still active, and I have to get to the hotel. Wally's there with Dr. Kaine. It's dangerous."

"I'll go with you," G9 said.

Ralph spoke up. “The rest of us can go to the basement.”

“Good. Do it,” Block said. “G9, have the other units get these people to safety.”

As the recovered SoldierBots began organizing the evacuation, Maggie pulled Block aside. “I was wrong about you,” she said quietly. “About all the robots.”

Block’s processor registered the irony. “Fear makes us all do things we regret later.”

“If we survive this,” Maggie said, “I’ll make it right.”

Block barely registered her promise. The nanobots had given them a chance against the SoldierBots, but Dr. Kaine’s device was active and still controlling the minds of eleven teenagers with dormant neural implants.

He had to reach Wally before it was too late.

THIRTY-THREE
CLONES

VALERIE

Valerie slammed the hotel's heavy oak door shut and secured its bolt. The solid barrier would keep the growing mob at bay—for now. The glass windows were a risk, but at least the barricade bought her time. Never had she expected a useless CleanerBot and a few teenagers to put up such a fight. But she was in too deep. No retreat. No surrender.

She pressed her forehead against the wood, allowing herself a breath before turning to face the chaos she'd wrought. The hotel's elegant lobby, which Block had painstakingly restored to a pre-Uprising opulence with its chandelier and polished floorboards, now resembled a slumber party gone massively wrong. Overturned lounge chairs. Shattered coffee tables. The cloned teenagers scattered across the floor in various states of pain and unconsciousness.

She couldn't have predicted how seeing Olivia's face reflected in Chloe would affect her. The way Chloe's eyes widened in pain with each signal pulse. She had her mother's strength, and every frequency emission was chewing up her niece's life force.

The Echo device thrummed at full power, nestled in her palm like a living thing. The warmth of it pulsed in rhythm with her own quickened heartbeat. She guessed that only one more amplification was needed to fully activate the pathways in all eleven subjects. The many years of work, the searching, the planning, all culminated in this last stand.

If only Chloe would cooperate.

"Keep going," Valerie said, her voice sharper than intended as she crossed the lobby. Fatigue was getting to her, making her edgy. Forty-eight hours without proper sleep, living on stale protein bars and adrenaline would do that. "Maintain the signal strength."

Chloe knelt in the center of the lobby, a broken doll barely upright. Her fingernails had left bloody crescents in her palms. The serum would heal her eventually—Valerie was nearly certain of it—but for now, the side effects were troubling. Dark circles shadowed Chloe's sunken eyes. Blood crusted her nostrils and upper lip. Her gums bled and her shoulders trembled.

"I'm trying," Chloe whispered. Each word seemed to cost her. "It hurts . . . Everything feels like it's on fire."

Guilt twisted in Valerie's stomach, but she tamped it down. People said the same thing about chemotherapy —it hurts. That didn't mean it wasn't necessary. What was temporary pain compared to fulfilling the destiny Olivia had died for?

"Push through it. I know you can." She nudged the device settings, increasing the pulse rate. The small display showed power levels holding steady but signal dispersal wavering. Not good enough.

Through the lobby's windows, Valerie took in the scene. Her beautiful chaos. Far across the square, smoke billowed from the council building's eastern wing. Abandoned market stalls lay splintered. Outside on the steps, the robot dog Shadow remained crumpled and inert, exactly where she'd fallen when Chloe's amplified signal had overwhelmed her systems. The SoldierBots she'd activated through the amplification should be rounding up the townspeople, neutralizing any resistance, beginning the transition to her new order.

But something was wrong.

Several SoldierBots that had been advancing toward the southern gate now stood motionless, visors flickering from Echo green back to the neutral red. One by one, they were lowering their weapons. Turning away.

"Concentrate!" Valerie ordered, her control slipping. "You're losing them."

Chloe's entire body convulsed. A choked cry escaped her lips as she strained to reconnect with the signal. "I can't . . . hold them anymore. They won't . . . connect." Fresh blood leaked from her nostrils, dripping down her chin.

"Try harder." Valerie's grip tightened on the device, her knuckles whitening.

What was happening? Who was interfering with her

signal? Block. It had to be. That ridiculous robot janitor had somehow figured out how to disrupt her control over the SoldierBots. The knowledge burned like acid in her chest, but rage wouldn't help her now. If Plan A was compromised, she'd adapt.

Besides, she still had what mattered most.

She had Chloe. And through her, access to the others.

"On your feet." Valerie crossed to Chloe and hauled her up by the arm. The girl felt impossibly light, as if her substance was being consumed by the power flowing through her. For a moment, Olivia's face superimposed itself over Chloe's features. What would Olivia think of what Valerie was doing to her daughter? No. Daughter was the wrong word. *Clone.* Not truly Olivia's child—yet the most direct connection Valerie had to her lost sister.

A blow rocked the front door. Shouting voices came from outside, but the bolt held. She was running out of time.

Valerie moved to the nearest teen—Brad—and delivered a kick to his ribs. "Get up."

He groaned, folding in on himself before his eyes fluttered open. Confusion gave way to recognition, then fear.

"All of you," Valerie called out. "Wake up. We don't have time for theatrics. You have jobs to do."

Slowly, they stirred like sleepwalkers trapped in a shared nightmare. Tomas pushed himself upright, his hands shaking uncontrollably. Clay helped Maya to her feet, both swaying, perhaps from concussions. Fiona remained curled against the wall, tears tracking silently down her pale face. Liam staggered to his feet, blood darkening the collar of his plaid shirt.

Wally was the last to rise, her movements deliberate and cautious. Her eyes seemed to measure, analyze, search for weakness. Maybe the girl had been around robots for far too long. Well, that would soon change.

"You don't have to do this," Wally said. Her voice was steadier than it had any right to be after the neural assault Valerie had subjected her to. "Dr. Kaine, you can stop this all. Before more people get hurt."

A laugh bubbled from Valerie's throat—hollow and sharp-edged. "Deer Valley is the beginning. Next will be Chicago, then east. New York."

Another blow struck the hotel door, but it held. The voices beyond were louder, more frenzied. Townspeople gathered in front of the windows.

"My dad will make sure the town gives you a fair hearing." Wally took a tentative step forward, palms raised in a gesture of peace. "There are courts in Chicago. My friend Nova will see that there's justice—a jury who doesn't know you."

"Justice?" The word tasted vile on Valerie's tongue. How naive they all were, these children raised in artificial safety behind high walls. "Where was justice when the SoldierBots took my sister? When Mach X's experiments killed women to create you? When robots decided they knew better than humans how to run the world?" Her arm swept toward the destruction visible through the windows. "This isn't vengeance. It's a *correction*."

Wally exchanged nervous glances with Tomas and

Brad. Good. If Valerie was going to salvage this, she needed them to listen.

"You were created from the sacrifice of women who died to make you." Valerie softened her tone. She'd always been gifted at finding the chinks in the armor, the raw wounds that twisted things her way.

The device pulsed in her hand, like it was burning to be used. "You think this backwater settlement is your destiny? Playing at a normal life with robot guardians and fake families? You were created for something greater."

This would go her way. The clones were malleable, such young minds. "Each of you possesses abilities beyond your imagination. I'm the only one who will help you master your new powers."

A flicker passed through the group—a dose of curiosity beneath fear. The desperate need to understand themselves and where they came from. That same hunger had sustained Valerie after Olivia's murder, through the long years of searching and planning.

"I'm doing this for Olivia." She met Chloe's unfocused gaze. "For your mother, Chloe." Her eyes swept the circle of teens. "And for all the mothers whose lives were stolen to create each of you. I can help you find your real families. Track down your biological fathers. They could still be out there. Alive."

Maya's sharp intake of breath told Valerie she'd struck a nerve. Brad shifted uncomfortably. Liam's eyes widened with painful hope.

"No way. She can't promise that." Wally shook her head in dismissal. "She doesn't know where our biological fathers are. She's manipulating us to get what she wants."

More pounding at the door. Four or five people gathered and banged their fists against the glass windows.

"And what exactly do you think I want?" Valerie asked, curious about naïve little Wally's take.

"Revenge." Wally balled her fists, recovering some of her strength. She was an interesting subject; Valerie would need to spend more time understanding her once she had control. "You're nothing but a manipulator," Wally continued. "Using us for some warped idea of payback."

"Hmm. Revenge is such a limited concept." Valerie modified the device settings again, buying time as she formulated her response. "I want an Uprising against the Uprising. I want the natural order restored."

"You don't care about Chloe at all," Wally pressed. "Look at her! You'll kill her to get what you want. Where's the sense in that?"

Valerie's gaze flicked to Chloe. The girl's knees had buckled again, leaving her half-slumped against an overturned chair. Her breathing had grown shallow and fast —hyperventilation. Small objects around her vibrated in random patterns: a pen slid across the floor, a vase hovered inches off its stand, and glass shards skittered in tight circles.

"Temporary side effects," Valerie said, but doubt gnawed at her certainty. The serum hadn't been tested at these power levels. What if the strain was too much? What if Olivia's daughter got hurt . . . ?

No. Not daughter. *Clone.* And one of many. A necessary sacrifice for the greater purpose.

"My dad has more heart than you ever will," Wally said. "He'd never sacrifice me. He loves me as a person, not as some tool for revenge."

"Your *dad*?" Valerie's tone mocked, and she meant it. "A CleanerBot programmed to dust shelves and scrub floors? Is that the father figure you aspire to?" She stepped closer to Wally, ignoring the fight in the girl's stance. "No wonder you're so limited in your thinking."

"He values life," Wally shot back. "All life. Block would sacrifice himself if it meant protecting us. He would die for Chloe. Would you?"

The words struck deep. She heard Olivia's voice overlaying Wally's: *"We can't become monsters to fight monsters, Val. That's how we lose ourselves."* The memory surfaced from the last night they'd spent in the encampment, arguing about whether to join the resistance fighters who were planning to storm the tower.

Olivia had wanted to stay with her patients. *"Someone has to remember what we're fighting for."* Twenty-four hours later, she was gone.

Valerie tamped down the memory. She'd come too far to fail now. Her thumb fingered the device, tuning it to full power.

"You think you know what's best?" Valerie aimed the device at Wally's head. "You don't know the pain I went through for all of this. The sacrifices I made."

She pressed the activation button. The copper surface glowed hot, and the device emitted a focused pulse at Wally. The girl's body went rigid, and her back arched as the signal assaulted her. Her muscles contracted under the strain, and her teeth gritted against the pain. Her legs buckled beneath her, but somehow, she remained standing through sheer force of will.

"Stop it!" Maya screamed, but she stopped when Valerie pulled her gun.

Valerie kept her thumb on the device. Wally shuddered, her limbs spasming as neurons fired in chaotic patterns. If Chloe amplified this targeted signal, it would cause Wally's neural pathways to hemorrhage. Fatal brain damage within seconds. The ultimate demonstration of who held the power.

Satisfaction and revulsion warred within Valerie. This wasn't what she'd wanted—the needless death of one of the clones. But Wally's obstinance had forced her hand. It would be an example to the others, the consequences of stepping out of line.

Olivia's voice was in the back of her head. *You know who you sound like?* Stop it. Valerie wanted to carve out the part of her mind that replicated her sister's voice in its exact pitch. *You sound like Mach X.*

No. Valerie bit her lip so hard she tasted blood. "Chloe," she said. "Amplify the signal to Wally. Now."

Chloe's glassy eyes shifted between Valerie and Wally. Her lips parted, dry and cracked. "I . . . I can't."

"You can and you will." Valerie's display flashed a warning: *87% power—neural damage imminent.* "Show them what happens to those who defy me."

Wally's legs gave out, and she sank to her knees. Still, her eyes remained lucid, locked on Chloe. "Don't," she gasped. "Chloe, please. You're . . . my friend . . . my sister."

A crash sounded as something heavy struck the hotel's window. Valerie turned her head toward the sound. Through the fractured glass, angry faces pressed close. Townspeople with makeshift weapons—bats, axes, pipes. They'd gathered into a mob.

A brick sailed through an already-cracked window, shattering it completely. Glass rained down, narrowly missing Brad's head. Another followed. The door wouldn't hold much longer.

"Now, Chloe!" Valerie demanded, panic edging her voice. "Amplify the signal!"

Chloe staggered forward. Her vacant stare was gone. "No."

The single word hung in the air between them, simple and devastating.

"What did you say?" Valerie whispered.

"I . . . said no." Chloe took another step, this one toward Wally. "Enough."

Before Valerie could react, the deafening crack of a gunshot split the air. Chloe's body jerked, her momentum carrying her forward three more steps before she collapsed in a crumpled heap beside Wally.

Blood spread across Chloe's shirt with terrible speed.

THIRTY-FOUR
DISARM

WALLY

Time collapsed into a single, confused moment when the gun fired.

The sound reverberated off the hotel walls—a lone crack like thunder in wintertime. Chloe jerked and the forward momentum carried her three more steps before she crumpled beside Wally, sprawling across the floor that Block polished every Sunday morning.

"No!" The word tore from Wally's throat as she scrambled toward Chloe.

Blood stained Chloe's shirt. Wally pressed her fingers against the wound. She knew to do that from watching old movies and TV shows. Her mind struggled to process what her body already knew—Chloe had taken a bullet meant for someone else. Maybe for her.

She sensed a mouse lingering in the lobby's corner. Its tiny heart thundered. *Danger-blood-hide*. The creature's fear washed through her in sharp bursts, tangling with her own panic. The creature skittered away, breaking the connection.

Outside the broken hotel windows, the angry shouts ceased and were replaced by shocked murmurs. The gunman stood with his rifle halfway raised, his face a mask of dawning horror. "I didn't mean to . . . It was a warning shot," he said.

"Go home!" Maggie Crenshaw's commanding voice cut through the stunned silence. "All of you—leave now!" She pushed through the crowd.

Next to Wally, Chloe's eyelids fluttered. Her lips formed shapes with no sound. Blood bubbled at the corners of her mouth, and Wally wasn't sure if that was from the device or the gunshot.

"Stay with me," Wally whispered, leaning close. "Please, Chloe. Focus on my voice."

Heavy footsteps thudded across the lobby. Block appeared in Wally's peripheral vision, escorting Emery through the front entrance. The doctor's medical bag bumped against her hip as she ran toward them. Relief washed through Wally. Her dad was okay. He'd survived.

Block knelt beside Wally. "Are you alright?"

"I'm fine, Dad." Wally's voice was choked. "Chloe saved my life."

Block's metal fingers made a soft whirring sound as they brushed a strand of hair from her face. The familiar gesture sent a crack through her forced composure. Tears rolled down her cheeks.

Across the lobby, Valerie Kaine stood motionless, still clutching the Echo device. Her face had drained of color, and her lips parted in dismay. She switched off the device with trembling hands. Instantly, the tight tension in Wally's head eased. She hoped the others would feel relief too.

"Chloe," Valerie whispered. The name seemed to break whatever paralysis had gripped her. She hurried forward, dropping to her knees near Chloe. "I'm so sorry, so sorry . . ."

Emery knelt across from Wally, ready to tend to Chloe. Her professional calm masked whatever emotions churned beneath as she ignored Valerie. "Move your hands, Wally. Let me see."

Wally lifted her blood-soaked palms. Emery's face tightened as she examined the wound.

"Olivia wouldn't have wanted this," Valerie said, rocking slightly. "This isn't how I should honor her memory."

"Bullet entered below the left scapula and exited the front," Emery said, her voice clinical. She pressed a stack of gauze against the exit wound to stem the bleeding while checking Chloe's vitals. "Blood loss. Pulse is thready and weak."

Fear coiled in Wally's stomach. Emery worked with practiced efficiency, applying pressure to control the hemorrhaging while periodically checking Chloe's carotid pulse. "Her blood pressure's dropping. I need to stabilize her immediately."

Block stood behind Wally, shielding her from Valerie, who sat with her hands fluttering uselessly. "Will she survive? Please tell me she'll make it," Valerie said.

No one answered. Wally couldn't tear her eyes from

Chloe's unnaturally pale face. The freckles across her nose stood out like flecks of copper. Blood dried on Wally's hands.

A minute passed that felt like an hour. Sweat beaded on Emery's forehead as she monitored Chloe's rapidly deteriorating condition. The other teens huddled together against the far wall, shock rendering them silent observers in the eerie stillness that followed the signal.

Block was a solid presence at Wally's back. He placed a hand on her shoulder, and she leaned into the touch, drawing whatever comfort she could from the familiar weight of his metal fingers.

"I'm sorry," Valerie said, turning toward Wally. Her voice cracked. "I never meant for you to be hurt."

A fury rose in Wally. "You tried to *kill* me." Her words were heavy as boulders.

"I didn't realize . . . the signal got so strong. I got carried away."

"You knew exactly what you were doing." Wally gestured toward where the other teens huddled. "You were willing to sacrifice us for your revenge."

"I thought I was helping you," Valerie said. "Awakening your potential."

"You pointed a device at my head and told Chloe to amplify until my brain exploded." The memory sent a shudder through Wally's body. "I felt bad for what happened to your sister. How unfair it all was, and that you had a right to be mad until you tried to end my life."

Valerie flinched, and her gaze dropped to the floor where blood had pooled beneath Chloe. Shame twisted her features, aging her a decade in minutes.

Block moved between them. "Dr. Kaine," he said, his voice firm. "Give me the device."

Valerie's eyes darted to the device on the floor next to where she knelt. For a moment, Wally thought she might try to use it, but then Valerie's shoulders sagged.

"Take it," she said. "I wanted to honor Olivia, not become a monster."

Block took the device with careful movements, as if handling an explosive. He stored it inside the compartment in his upper leg.

The hotel door opened. Sheriff Green entered, followed by Maggie Crenshaw. Green's practiced gaze took in the scene—the blood, the injured teens, Emery performing chest compressions on Chloe's motionless form.

Emery looked up, her hands still applying pressure to the wound. "Her pulse is stabilizing, but it's dangerously weak. She needs blood and fluids immediately."

A collective breath released. Wally's entire body went weak with relief.

"We need to move her," Emery said. "Block?"

Block scooped Chloe into his arms with the gentle precision his programming allowed. Blood smeared across his chest plate as he cradled her against his chest.

"To the clinic," Emery said. "I need to get her into surgery immediately."

"Jenny," Maggie said to the sheriff. "The shooter?"

"In custody," Green said. "Half the town witnessed it. He'll face charges."

"And her?" Maggie nodded toward Valerie.

Green unclipped the handcuffs from her belt.

"Valerie Kaine, you're under arrest for assault, endangerment, destruction of property, and attempted murder."

Valerie offered no resistance as Green secured the cuffs around her wrists. Her gaze remained fixed on Chloe, cradled in Block's arms.

"I'm sorry," she said as Green led her toward the door. "I never meant for anyone to get hurt, least of all Chloe."

Wally wanted to scream at the absurdity of those words. Of course people got hurt. That was the inevitable result of the woman's hate, of her ceaseless desire for revenge, of using children as weapons. But exhaustion swallowed her fury, leaving only a hollow ache where anger should have been.

As Block turned to leave, Chloe's arm slipped from where it had been folded across her chest. Her hand dangled, fingers parted as if reaching for something. Wally caught it, squeezing gently.

The touch triggered a memory—Wally and Chloe at seven years old, standing on opposite sides of Mrs. Webb's bakery counter. Chloe's hair had been tied in braids, and her face was smudged with flour as she'd pushed a misshapen cookie across the counter.

"I made it for you," Chloe had said, not quite meeting Wally's eyes. It was an olive branch after weeks of teasing and small cruelties that had left Wally eating lunch alone.

"Why?" Wally had asked, suspicious but curious.

"Because . . ." Chloe had hesitated, her small fingers fidgeting with her apron. "Because Mom says everyone deserves kindness. Even if they're different."

Wally had taken the cookie—burnt around the edges, misshapen in the middle—and broken it in half. She'd handed one piece back to Chloe. "We're both different," she'd said. And they'd savored the treat together, the sweetness dissolving on their tongues, an understanding passing between them that needed no words.

Now, Wally squeezed Chloe's limp hand, recognizing their connection—an invisible thread of friendship. Of sisterhood.

Outside, the last angry voices had faded, leaving an uncanny silence in the square. The fires had been extinguished, leaving a hazy darkness. Wally's world seemed impossibly big and terrifyingly small at the same time.

As she followed Block and Emery toward the clinic, Tomas appeared at her side, his voice barely above a whisper. "Will Chloe be okay?"

"She has to be," Wally said. Any other possibility was unthinkable.

The night air carried the scent of smoke from the day's destruction. Buildings could be rebuilt. Broken windows replaced. Blood washed from floors. But trust—that was harder to restore. Valerie had sparked a bitter divide in Deer Valley. Never in Wally's life had she seen such animosity toward the robot citizens.

A fox slipped between buildings, pausing when it sensed Wally's attention. Unlike the panicked responses of past days, this encounter felt different. The fox conveyed a strange alertness, an awareness beyond any immediate danger. *Change-coming-prepare.* Not a warning exactly, but a recognition. Whatever was happening to Wally and the others—their abilities awakening—the natural world was making room for them. Before she could even fully process it, the fox slipped into the darkness.

Ahead, Block moved with care, calculating each step precisely to minimize jostling his precious cargo. Wally had watched those same steel arms stack dishes, fold laundry, brush her hair when she was small. Now they carried her friend's life.

Tomas offered his hand, and Wally took it, grateful for him. Behind them, the others followed—Maya, Clay, Liam, Brad, Abby, Fiona, Jordan, and Zoey—all silent, all changed by the day's events in ways they were only beginning to understand.

"What happens now?" Tomas asked.

The question hung between them. Wally thought of all they'd discovered—about themselves, their origins, and the dormant abilities that had awakened within each of them. Abilities that they would need to learn to control.

"We start over, I guess," she said. "We help each other figure out what we are."

As they approached the clinic, Wally saw Emery preparing the surgical suite, her movements quick and precise. Wally prayed she could work a miracle.

A crow landed on a nearby lamppost, its feathers ruffled against the evening chill. When it caught Wally's eye, no foreign thoughts invaded her mind. No warnings or urgent messages. Just the ordinary presence of a bird watching the strange procession below.

But as Wally stared longer, something subtle shifted.

The crow tilted its head, obsidian eyes reflecting the clinic's lights. Not communicating, but . . . waiting. The silence in her mind where the animal's thoughts should be felt deliberate, as if the crow was consciously holding back, choosing to witness rather than speak. Animals had been warning her for days. Now they were watching. What would she and the others do with their newfound abilities?

The crow spread its wings and lifted into the night sky, a shadow against the dark.

Maybe that was a good sign. Maybe the worst was over.

THIRTY-FIVE
WIN

BLOCK

The clinic's antiseptic scent registered in Block's olfactory sensors as precisely 3.7 times stronger than the cleaner he used in the hotel. Emery had doubled her sanitizing protocols since Chloe's surgery—an excess that Block privately appreciated. His vacuum attachment twitched inside its housing, as if itching to be of use.

"Ready?" he asked Wally.

She nodded, her fingertips pressed against the gift bag she clutched—a small collection of chocolates and a handmade card the other teens had signed. Block's sensors picked up the slight elevation in her heart rate, the tiny tremor in her fingers. Three days had passed since the shooting, yet the trauma lingered in her system like static electricity.

They walked the corridor toward the recovery room. Block matched his pace to Wally's, keeping his servos at their quietest setting. Through the window of Chloe's room, he saw Mrs. Webb asleep in a chair, her head tilted at an angle that his ergonomic protocols calculated would cause significant neck discomfort upon waking.

She stirred after Wally shuffled her feet outside the open door. After a yawn and quick stretch, she stood. "Block, Wally! It's so nice to see you." She turned. "Chloe, honey, you have visitors."

Wally and Block slowly entered the room. Chloe lay propped against white pillows, her skin still pale but markedly improved from the deathly pallor of three nights ago. She was connected to several monitors that emitted soft electronic beeps.

"Hey." Chloe's voice was thin but steady.

"Hey, yourself," Wally said.

Block hung back with Mrs. Webb, allowing the reunion its proper space. His visual processors captured everything—the careful way Wally approached the bed, the tentative smile that passed between the girls, the invisible thread of shared experience that connected them.

"We brought contraband." Wally set the gift bag on the bedside table. "Don't tell Dr. Emery about the chocolate."

"My ethics module forces me to report nutritional violations," Block said, then cycled his optical sensors in what Wally had taught him was a decent approximation of a wink. "But they're temporarily malfunctioning."

Chloe laughed. "Thanks for coming. Both of you."

"How's the recovery going?" Wally asked.

"Emery says I'm healing faster than expected. Something about our enhanced capabilities." Chloe shifted, moving the I.V. line that ran from her arm. "At least one useful side effect of being a clone, I guess."

Block watched Wally's face for signs of distress at the casual reference to their origins. Finding none, he registered a small marker of progress in his parental assessment subroutines.

"There's news," Wally said. "About Valerie Kaine."

Chloe's monitors registered a momentary spike in heart rate. "What happened to her?"

"She's gone," Block said, and Mrs. Webb sighed in relief. "The council voted unanimously to send her to Chicago for trial. G9 and two other Peacekeepers left to escort her yesterday."

"Was she . . . did she say anything?" Chloe asked.

Block replayed the memory file from the town square—Valerie being led to the transport E.V., her shoulders squared despite the handcuffs, her eyes scanning the crowd until they found him. "She asked about you and your recovery."

What Block didn't relay was Valerie's final words to him at the transport: "This isn't over, CleanerBot. What's awakened in those children can't be put back to sleep." The statement had registered as a credible threat in his probability assessments.

"She really thought she was helping us," Chloe said, her fingers twisting the edge of her blanket. "In her weird, messed-up way."

"Even those with good intentions can do terrible things," Block said. "It's up to us to make it right." His words were a truth applicable to humans, clones, and robots alike.

"What's going on with the others? Are they okay? What do people know about us?" Chloe asked, her voice dropping to a near whisper.

Wally glanced at Block, who gave a quick nod. "All the parents know everything now," she said. "Emery called a meeting. There were charts and lots of detail."

Mrs. Webb came forward and squeezed Chloe's foot through the blanket. "I learned a lot, and I understand. I love you, Chloe-bear."

Tears ran down Chloe's face, and the monitor beeped slightly faster. "Love you too, Mom."

"The parents took it better than expected," Wally said. "Mrs. Jenkins cried. Mr. Landry asked forty-seven questions about neural pathways."

Chloe frowned. "I'm not moving stuff anymore. At least I don't think I can."

"Not since the Echo device was disabled," Block said. "Emery believes the signal was needed to keep the abilities active. Without it, they've gone dormant again."

"For now," Wally added. "Maxwell and Emery are studying the device and the old Project Echo files and computer that was discovered in that empty warehouse."

Block's analysis showed a 73.4 percent probability that the abilities would resurface in time, with or without external stimulation. But today was for healing, not for troubling predictions.

"We should let you rest," Block said, noting the fatigue markers in Chloe's posture.

"One more thing." Wally reached into her pocket

and pulled out a smooth black and red stone, polished to a shine. "From all of us. A symbol of survival, and of being stronger than we thought."

Chloe closed her fingers around the stone, a smile breaking through her exhaustion. "Tell everyone thanks. And that I'll be back for movie night as soon as Emery springs me from medical prison."

Outside in the corridor, Wally exhaled a long breath. "That went well."

"Yes," Block agreed. "Her recovery trajectory is on track."

"Not just her injuries." Wally pushed her hands into her pockets. "She had the most direct contact with Valerie. The most manipulation."

Block considered this as they moved through the clinic's lobby. Several patients waited, minor injuries and winter colds that seemed refreshingly mundane after recent events. Normality was returning to Deer Valley—or rather, a new version of normality that acknowledged the robots could malfunction and that eleven teenagers had uncommon origins that bonded them forever.

"Our next stop is Maxwell's workshop," Block said. "If you're up for it."

"How are they?" Wally asked.

"Recovering. Complaining. The usual."

Maxwell's workshop was more organized than its typical state. Tools hung in precise rows and parts were cataloged in transparent bins. Even the perpetual layer of metal dust seemed diminished.

Shadow lay on a charging platform, her armor freshly polished. Vacuubot hovered nearby, conservational protocols still in effect as their systems rebuilt. They both turned at Block and Wally's entrance.

"Greetings," Vacuubot said, landing on top of a cabinet. "I hope you're here to rescue us."

"How are the repairs coming along?" Block asked.

"We're fully functional," Shadow said, rising from the pad to demonstrate. Her movements were fluid, though Block's sensors detected a minor delay in her right hind leg hydraulics. "Maxwell's work is to be commended."

"Don't encourage him," Vacuubot said. "He's been practicing his comedy routine on us for sixty-seven consecutive minutes, and that's not the first time today."

Maxwell emerged from a storage alcove, all four arms carrying different components. "My captive audience seems unreceptive to my new material on the differences between CleanerBots and ToasterBots."

"Both emit smoke when malfunctioning," Vacuubot offered.

"Both make humans happy in the morning," Wally added with a grin.

Block's processing units considered the joke's construction. "I fail to see the humor in comparing my sophisticated programming to a single-function kitchen bot. ToasterBots can't vacuum the tall corners of the hotel lobby. What are they good for?"

"Toast! Without which we wouldn't have toasted PBJs, my favorite." Wally's laughter filled the workshop —a sound so welcome that Block immediately archived the recording in his primary memory core.

"The nanobots saved the day," Maxwell said, setting

down his components. "They completely neutralized the signal's effects on the SoldierBots' programming. I'm studying them to see what other benefits they might provide."

"You're sure we can trust them?" Shadow said. "The thought of microscopic beings flooding my system is disturbing."

"I'm running lots of tests," Maxwell said. "And Block can verify that they saved his tin can butt."

"Affirmative," Block said, ignoring Maxwell's jab. "I believe we can trust them, but it's logical that we let Maxwell run his tests and give us a final report before we inject them into more robots."

"How many Echo Nodes did you find in total?" Wally asked.

"Nine," Maxwell said. "All deactivated and disassembled. I've been analyzing their components."

"Any danger of someone rebuilding them?" Block asked.

Maxwell's four arms made a simultaneous dismissive gesture. "The central control unit is unique—military-grade technology from before the Uprising. Without it, they're just fancy antennas."

The conversation turned to repairs around town—the bakery's wall, Fathom's cart, the fire damage in the council building and library. Block found comfort in the practical details of reconstruction. The community would heal its physical wounds.

The emotional ones would take longer.

"We should head out," Block said to Wally. "Emery will be starting soon."

They said their goodbyes, with promises to return the following day. Outside, Block's temperature sensors registered 28.4 degrees Fahrenheit—cold, but not unbearable for humans properly dressed. Wally had bundled appropriately in her puffy jacket and wool hat that she pulled low over her ears.

"Do you think the support group will help?" she asked as they walked.

Block considered the question. "Humans benefit from communal processing of shared trauma. The statistical improvement in recovery rates is significant."

"That sounds like a robot answer," she said. "What's a dad answer?"

Block slowed to match her stride. "I believe it will help, yes. Not just you and the other teens, but the parents too. Understanding can turn fear into knowledge."

"I still have questions nobody can answer," Wally said.

"About your biological origins?"

She nodded, her breath forming small clouds in the cold air. "Emery says she'll help us search for connections. DNA matches in old databases, that sort of thing. But most of the records were destroyed in the Uprising."

"We will find what information we can." Block's statistical analysis suggested a 31.7 percent chance of locating definitive biological parentage for the teens—not encouraging odds, but better than zero. He kept this calculation to himself.

The library's meeting room was already half full when they arrived. Chairs arranged in a circle contained familiar faces—parents sitting close to their teenagers, Emery at what might be called the head position, though the circle had no true beginning or end.

Mrs. Webb had left Chloe's bedside to attend, her exhaustion obvious in the shadows beneath her eyes. Tomas sat with his parents, their hands resting supportively on his shoulders. Clay's father glanced up as Block and Wally entered, offering a nod.

"Welcome, everyone," Emery said once they were seated. "This is the first of what I hope will be regular meetings to process the recent events."

Block was no expert in emotion, but these humans —the parents who had raised laboratory-created children as their own—showed no signs of rejection. Their protective postures spoke volumes.

"I've prepared some resources about neural implants and the cloning technology used in Mach X's program," Emery continued. "But first, I'd like to open the floor for questions. Nothing is off-limits."

"Will the abilities come back?" Mrs. Grace asked, her hand tight around Maya's. "The telekinesis, the plant growing, all of it?"

Emery's gaze met Block's for an instant; they'd reviewed hundreds of scenarios, but there was no way of knowing how the abilities would behave. "We don't know for certain. The neural pathways exist, but without external stimulation like Dr. Kaine's device, they might remain dormant."

"Or they might not," Wally said. "I still feel . . . different. Like something inside me has changed permanently."

Murmurs rippled through the circle as other teens nodded in agreement.

"If the abilities return," Emery said, "we'll face it together. Learn to understand them."

"What about biological family?" Tomas's father asked. "Is there any way to know where . . . who . . . ?"

"I've begun compiling a pre-Uprising genetic database," Emery said. "Many records were lost, but not all. With your permission, I'd like to take DNA samples from each teen and begin a systematic search. It might take years to track them down, but there's some hope."

Block watched the facial reactions throughout the room—hope, apprehension, curiosity. His own emotional subroutines registered concern for Wally. Finding her biological origins would provide answers and perhaps comfort to her, but would it lead her to forget about him? About his role as her dad?

As the meeting went on, questions flowed more freely as the initial tension eased. Block contributed technical clarifications when needed but mostly observed. These humans were adapting to a new reality with remarkable flexibility—a trait he'd always admired.

After the session wrapped, Emery sat with Block and Wally. "You've been quiet," she said to Block.

"Processing," he said. "Humans need time to integrate new information. So do I."

"We've received a message from Oxford and Cybel," Emery said. "They've asked for Wally's help."

"Is it the marine life anomalies?" Block asked, recalling the radio conversation from a week ago.

"What anomalies?" Wally asked.

"Unexpected migration patterns and strange behavior off the Oregon coast," Block said. "Similar to what you experienced with the land animals here."

Wally's interest was piqued. "They want my help? Even though my animal communication thing isn't working right now?"

"Oxford believes your neural pathways might reactivate in proximity to the affected wildlife," Emery said. "It's a theory, but . . ."

"When do we leave?" Wally asked, already calculating the adventure.

Block's parental protocols generated immediate risk assessments—travel dangers, distance from medical facilities, potential recurrence of signal interference. But he'd kept Wally sheltered in Deer Valley for so long. She needed this chance to explore. Perhaps he did too.

"We'll depart once the weather breaks," he said. "May, most likely. The coastal weather will be more hospitable then."

"A road trip." Wally's smile returned, and the weight of recent events lifted. "I can't wait to see Oxford and Cybel!"

"Assuming the town can survive without its only hotel manager for a few months," Block said.

"I'm sure we'll manage," Emery said with a smile. "Maxwell has volunteered to run standup comedy nights in your absence."

"All the more reason to return quickly," Block said.

Later, as they walked back to the hotel beneath a sky turning purple with evening, Block calculated a different kind of scenario—one of possibilities. The quiet wintry street, the restored Peacekeepers resuming their patrols, the pattern of footsteps from humans headed home for the day—all of it represented a resilience he'd only ever found in Deer Valley.

"Do you think we'll find answers out west?" Wally asked.

"About the marine anomalies? Perhaps."

"No. About who I am."

Block placed a gentle hand on her shoulder. "You already know who you are, Wally. The question is who you will choose to become."

She considered this as snow crunched beneath her boots. "I want to help people. And robots. And animals. I want to understand what's happening to all of us."

"That seems reasonable," Block said, as his internal chronometer marked the exact time of her statement—cataloged with the precision that differentiated his programming from human memory.

The hotel stood across the square, plywood covering broken windows—battle scars from Valerie's assault. Repairs would take weeks, but the lights shining through the intact panes still signaled sanctuary. Tomorrow would bring new challenges: repairs to oversee, council meetings to attend, preparations for their road trip. But tonight was for rest, for processing, and for spending time with his daughter.

"Race you to the hotel," Wally said suddenly, breaking into a run.

Block calculated the appropriate response—allow her to win by exactly 2.3 seconds, maintaining both her confidence and the appearance of genuine competition.

Instead, he sped up his servos to maximum efficiency, so his metallic limbs propelled him forward with precise balance.

"That's cheating!" Wally called, falling behind him.

"I'm simply operating at peak performance." Block slowed, noting her laugh—a sound his audio processors had been calibrated to prioritize above all other inputs.

She grabbed the door handle a half-second before he reached it. "Still won."

He would always let her win. It was part of being a dad.

He recorded the moment alongside thousands of others—data points mapping their shared history. This memory—Wally's flushed cheeks, her bright eyes, and excitement—was filed away in his memory archive. It was his to cherish. Never to be forgotten.

Robots and Ruins will continue...

Dear Reader,

Thanks for reading *Echoes of Steel*! More episodes are coming. There are many stories within this book universe, waiting to be told.

The best way to stay updated on my writing is to sign up for my email newsletter where I send personal and writing updates about once a month. CameronCoral.-com/sign-up

Have you read the Rusted Wasteland series? You can download *STEEL APOCALYPSE (A Robot's Journal)* for free by visiting: CameronCoral.com/BlockJournal

Cameron Coral

P.S. - Did you enjoy this book? I'd love a review wherever you purchased this book if you have a few minutes. Reviews mean a lot to me. They show me you want me to keep writing, and they help other readers discover my books.

ALSO BY CAMERON CORAL

Robots and Ruins Series:

VAULT'S PROMISE

ECHOES OF STEEL

Rusted Wasteland Series:

STEEL GUARDIAN

STEEL DEFENDER

STEEL PROTECTOR

STEEL SIEGE

STEEL SOLDIER

STEEL LEGACY

STEEL APOCALYPSE (A Robot's Journal) - free on cameroncoral.com/blockjournal

Cyborg Guardian Chronicles:

STOLEN FUTURE

CODED RED

ORIGIN LOOP

Rogue Spark Series:

ALTERED

BRINK

DORMANT

SALVAGE

Short Stories:

CROSSING THE VOID: A Space Opera Science-Fiction Short Story

ACKNOWLEDGMENTS

Dear Reader,

As I write this letter, the world is highly uncertain with geopolitical turmoil. My empathy trait is high, making me feel deeply connected to the world around me. The news and strife affects me deeply.

Since I was a kid, reading books has been my escape. The library was a favorite spot for me to head and walk out with eight or more books at a time. Libraries are how I discovered Stephen King, Ray Bradbury, Isaac Asimov, Margaret Atwood, and so many other authors.

It's been ten years since I started my author journey—when I got serious about writing and publishing. Now, putting words on the page is my escape. *Echoes of Steel* is my fifteenth novel! Writing about Block and the characters from his world is an incredible honor. Their stories of resilience in the face of chaos has become more relevant than I ever anticipated.

Without you reading my books, none of this would be possible. For that, I am grateful. Please reach out to me anytime over email or on social to say hello and let me know how you're doing. info@cameroncoral.com (Yes, that will reach me).

Looking at our world today, I never imagined the real world would approach the dystopian chaos in my fictional worlds. But it has, and that's something that worries me.

I'll keep on writing because it's what I know best—more books about heroic robots who do the right thing. The bad guys lose, and the good guys win at the end.

It's my hope that this will be the case in our real world too. That heroes will win, the good in humanity will rise to the top, and that our futures are hopeful.

With warm gratitude,

Cameron Coral
April 2025

ABOUT THE AUTHOR

Cameron Coral is an award-finalist science fiction author. Her book *Steel Guardian* about a post-apocalyptic CleanerBot placed second in the Self-Published Science Fiction Competition (SPSFC).

Growing up with a NASA engineer in the family instilled a deep respect for science and for asking lots of questions. Watching tons of Star Trek episodes helped, too. Her imagination is fueled by breakthroughs in robotics, space travel, and psychology.

After moving around a lot (Canada, Arizona, Maryland, Australia), she now lives in northern Illinois with her husband and a "shorty" Jack Russell terrier who runs the house.

Want a free novel, advance copies of books, and occasional rants about why robots are awesome? Visit her website:

CameronCoral.com

facebook.com/cameroncoralauthor

instagram.com/cameroncoralauthor

tiktok.com/@cameroncoral

PRAISE FOR STEEL GUARDIAN (RUSTED WASTELAND BOOK 1)

"Block, in short, is one of the finest and most noble characters - finest and most noble *people* - I have ever encountered in literature. Sure, Coral may have inadvertently tapped into a long-overgrown pocket of traumatic empathy in my psyche that was last torn open and punched repeatedly when I watched Johnny 5 getting disassembled in Short Circuit 2, but (not to spoil) he comes through it just fine and I consider this anguish well worth revisiting ... A simple story with a huge heart and a lot to think about. Can't ask for more than that."

-The Book in Hand

"The lovable CleanerBot was a joy to follow through the story as it learned to care for its newfound charge and find it a person it deemed worthy to be its guardian. The world was well made, the other characters unique, and the plot interesting. A must read if you enjoy stories about lovable robots facing mortal danger!"

-FANTASY-FACTION

"It's very rare when my connection with a character is instant, but I adored Block from the very start. He has such a clear distinct voice that hooked on my heartstrings. The plot is just breakneck speed. This isn't a long book and the entire time the main characters are on the run and trying to reach a place called New Denver where AI and humans live together in relative peace, and I love the friendship that develops. I absolutely adored this book."

-Weather Wax Report

"With clean prose and unparalleled cliffhangers at the end of each chapter, this novel is a joy to read and nearly impossible to put down."

-Matthew Cushing, SPSFC judge

"Set in an essentially post-apocalyptic world the main aim here is to get the baby to safety and to give them to a family, or person, who is worthy. It's such a simple premise but it makes for such a wonderful story. Despite the fact Block is a robot you start to see him have emotions and he develops such an attachment to the baby. For me, I think that emotional journey is the highlight of the book."

-FanFiAddict

"Block is a delight ... A fun road trip with a robot questioning his place in a world where humans are almost extinct."

-Willam C. Tracy, author of *The Seeds of Dissolution*

"A very enjoyable protagonist, an underdog not just because he's a cleaning robot, but because he's an old, outdated cleaning robot, and a cleaning robot who still has affection for humans ... A great fun romp with some twists on old tropes."

-At Boundary's Edge

"*Steel Guardian* is a good robot-centered read. Fans of AIs, robots, and post-apocalyptic settings should check it out."

-Eclectic Theist

"*Steel Guardian* drew me in immediately ... The author cleverly uses Block's ponderings about his loyalties and past experiences to slowly reveal his background and current world circumstances. This book may encourage readers to question their own behaviors/beliefs and what it means to be human."

-L.V. Ditchkus, SPSFC judge

"Great story. Block, the Cleanerbot, is engaging from the very beginning and the story immediately caught my attention with its strong voice and confident storyline."

-Veronica Strachan, SPSFC judge

Made in the USA
Columbia, SC
02 April 2025

2cf0a0e0-508b-4e57-bc9d-1016f52e6997R01